Readers love
BA TORTUGA

WITHDRAWN

Long Black Cadillac

"It's a wildly adventurous and very, very hot exploration of vampire lore and the kinds of shenanigans that 'bloodsuckers' and those who hunt them can get up to."

—Rainbow Book Reviews

Two of a Kind

"Full of joy, drama, laughter, and so much love it just spills over the pages…."

—Scattered Thoughts and Rogue Words

"This one isn't too sweet and not over the top, it's just the perfect cowboy love story…."

—The Blogger Girls

Rainbow Rodeo

"…this was a wonderful, fast paced book that I really enjoyed and couldn't set down. If you are into gay cowboys and the rodeo circuit that's this book will bring a smile to you face."

—Love Bytes

By BA TORTUGA

Published by DREAMSPINNER PRESS
www.dreamspinnerpress.com

SOFT PLACE TO FALL

BA TORTUGA

DREAMSPINNER
PRESS

Published by
DREAMSPINNER PRESS

5032 Capital Circle SW, Suite 2, PMB# 279, Tallahassee, FL 32305-7886 USA
www.dreamspinnerpress.com

Soft Place to Fall
© 2019 BA Tortuga.

Cover Art
© 2019 Tiferet Design.
http://www.tiferetdesign.com/
Cover content is for illustrative purposes only and any person depicted on the cover is a model.

Trade Paperback ISBN: 978-1-64080-768-6
Digital ISBN: 978-1-64080-767-9
Mass Market Paperback ISBN: 978-1-64108-111-5
Library of Congress Control Number: 2018938133
Trade Paperback published April 2019
v. 1.0

Printed in the United States of America
(∞)
This paper meets the requirements of
ANSI/NISO Z39.48-1992 (Permanence of Paper).

To my girl for bringing me home.

ACKNOWLEDGMENTS

THANK YOU so much to my agent, Sartiza Hernandez, for her faith in this project, and to both my Js, for their honesty. This book wouldn't have happened without y'all.

CHAPTER ONE

PLEASE, GOD, Stetson prayed. *Please let him answer the phone. Just this one time, let him put me first and answer the motherfucking phone.* He looked up at the bright blue of the Santa Fe sky, praying into it as he had for years. *Pardon my French, God. I'm a little stressed out, but I need this. I need this more than I've ever needed anything.*

Stetson doubted that would be true, if he thought about it for any length of time, but he didn't intend to think on it. Hell, he just wanted to live through this phone call.

He lit his Marlboro, took a deep, deep drag as he listened to the phone ring, watching the nurses and the people come and go from the big adobe building that was just like all the other big adobe buildings that housed doctors and nurses and sick people all over the city.

You'd never imagine how many nurses smoked, but a lot of them did. He'd smoked with everyone in this building.

"Hello?" The smooth, drawly Texas voice always surprised Stetson. Rodeo cowboys should sound like uneducated hicks. Hell, they were gorgeous and irresistible; they ought to open their mouths and be stupid.

It took him a second to speak because he couldn't believe Curtis answered.

"Hello?"

"Uh. Sorry. Sorry, it's Stetson. Stetson Major." *You remember me? The guy you walked away from eight years ago?*

"No shit?" The raw surprise almost made him smile. "You got a new number, but I saw five-oh-five and worried something had happened."

"Yeah. It's been a long time." *Forever.* "How are you doing?"

Stetson knew the answer to that. He followed Curtis Traynor in the news and in the rodeo magazines and watched every event on TV. It was like poking at a sore tooth with your tongue. Still, he asked. It was polite, and it kept him from looking like a giant dickwad.

"Pretty good, man. What's up? Has to be serious for you to call my happy ass." Curtis just didn't have patience for bullshit, never had.

"I have a favor to ask. I wouldn't if it wasn't important." Hell, how many times had he wanted to pick up the phone just to have a booty call? Just to beg for a half hour of contact?

He hadn't. Not once. This was different.

"Shoot. I'll see what I can do, whatever it is." He heard the unspoken thought that "whatever" might be nothing.

"It's my mom." Suddenly he couldn't talk; the words stuck in his throat like day-old grits.

"What's wrong?" Curtis's voice changed completely, his concern immediate and gratifying as fuck. Curtis had always loved Momma, and Lord knew Momma loved Curtis like breathing.

"It's Alzheimer's." Three years ago, he'd found her in the barn, scared and crying. Now she was in a facility, and.... *God. You have to focus, man. Talk to Curtis before he hangs up.*

"Oh fuck, Stetson. I'm so sorry. How—how bad is it?"

"It's bad. She doesn't have... I mean, shit. Look, man. She wants to see you. She wants to know why you aren't coming to see her."

"Oh Lord." Curtis stopped for a second, and Stetson had a terrifying worry that he'd lost the connection and he'd not be able to get it back. "You mean she don't remember we split up?"

"No. No, she... well, you know she always cared for you." Sometimes he thought she'd liked Curtis and his wild ways so much more than she'd liked him. Shit, thought. He knew. Stetson was too much like his granddaddy, just an old cowboy bound to the land. Momma longed for the road, and she'd lost the chance of that when she'd lost Dad.

"She was always good to me, for sure." Curtis paused for a long moment. "What do you need?"

"Every day she asks for you. Every day she cries. Can you please come see her, just once? Just one day?" Just so he could not listen to her cry for one goddamn day?

"Oh fuck, Stetson. Of course I can." He heard the sounds of people talking, a lot of them, all of a sudden. "Look, I was on my way out to Dallas for the Stampede, but I'm in Denver at the airport right now. I can be there in about eight hours."

"I hate to ask, but—" *But not enough not to do it, right?* "—thank you. We're in Santa Fe." Eight hours would be late for Momma, but if Curtis could just stay for a visit in the morning, then he could pay to fly the man to Dallas a few hours later.

"Oh hell, if you're not up in Taos, it will be faster for me to fly into Albuquerque and rent me a truck. I'll text you when I have a flight and all."

"I appreciate it. I'll... I'll pay you back." He'd sell off the last couple of cutting horses if he had to.

"Bullshit you will. This is for your momma." Curtis snorted. "I love her more than my ostrich Luccheses. This your number now? The good one to text?"

"Yeah. Yes. I'll be here. Thanks again. I owe you."

"Text me the address, huh? Are you at a hotel?" He could hear more people talking, could hear Curtis murmuring to someone who sounded very polite. Counter worker?

"I have a trailer here. I'll get you a hotel room, though. Something decent."

"I can do that, man. Just hang in there." Curtis sounded like he always did—capable and in charge. It set up a hurt, deep in the pit of his belly, and didn't that just piss him off?

"See you soon." He hung up the phone before he could snarl, because God knew Curtis was doing him a favor. He stood there, staring at his cigarette, which was burned down to the filter. Goddamn.

He went to sit on one of the benches outside the main doors, shivering against the wind. God, his head hurt. He could go back in there soon, though, and tell her Curtis was coming.

"Hey, Stetson." Mariposa sat down next to him, handed him a cup of coffee. Her scrubs featured Scooby-Doo today, and she had to be freezing, but she didn't seem to be cold at all.

"Hey, lady. How are you today?"

"Good. Tired. My littlest has a head cold. How're you? Holding up?"

"I'll make it." Though really, he thought he might just die. "I got ahold of my ex. He's coming in tonight."

"That the one Momma Major is so worried about?" At his nod, Mariposa reached over and patted his hand. "Good for you. You're a good son."

A good son wouldn't leave her in this place to die, but he hadn't figured another answer. She was setting fires, ending up curled into corners of stalls with the horses, stark naked and raving. He'd had to do something. The ranch was dangerous.

"I try. I hate this, lady." He just wanted his mom back. She wasn't that damned old. Early onset, late middle stage when she was diagnosed. Now she was barreling into the final stage and declining fast.

It wasn't fair. She was the strongest woman he'd ever known.

And all she wanted was to see the son of a bitch who had broken his fucking heart and left him to run a three-hundred-acre ranch on his own.

"I know, and I'd tell you it will get better, but it won't. It will be over soon, though."

"Thanks, honey." His heart hurt, and his butt was cold. "I guess I ought to go tell her, huh?"

"Sure. She'll be tickled. Drink your coffee before it gets cold. I brought you some of the good stuff."

"Oh. Hazelnut syrup?" She was good to his mom too. Mari was just a good woman.

"You know it." She leaned against him, gave him a grin. "You're gonna make it, cowboy."

"I sure hope so. I love her so much."

"Good. Moms deserve that, huh?"

"They do." He grinned at that, because his momma would say that. "Remember who pees when she sneezes because of you, right?"

"You know it, cowboy." She winked over at him, dark eyes warm, gentle.

"Okay, lady." He knew he couldn't have another smoke. Momma would smell it. "I'll see you later."

"I'll be around in about twenty."

He headed inside, nodding to… shit, everybody. He fucking knew every single person who worked here. He hated this. The best place he could afford still had that sour smell of urine and despair, and an aura of sadness among all the families he saw coming and going.

He opened the door, finding Momma was sitting there, tears on her cheeks. "Hey, lady. What's up?"

"You haven't been to see me in days."

"I helped you eat, not half an hour ago."

She shook her head. "I know better. I missed you."

"I called Curtis. He's on his way." He hoped she'd be pleased. He hadn't gone hat in hand in a long, long time, and it burned him that it was Curtis that he had to start with.

She brightened immediately, clapping her hands. "I should get my hair done."

"I can call Miss Sophia to come do it." She'd done Momma's hair a bunch since she'd been moved here.

"Thank you." She gave him a smile, and it only wobbled the tiniest bit. "I like Curtis."

"I know. He loves you dearly. He can't wait to see you."

"Is he doing well this year?" She looked brighter, more engaged.

"He is. He's favorite to go all-around." That he didn't have to make up. Curtis was the best in the world—bareback, saddle, and bulls. One, two, three. High-riding cowboy in the hunt for title number three.

Now that he wasn't a butt-hurt kid, Stetson got it. There was no way he could compete with the money and the sponsors and the lights. He was just a broke-dick cowboy eking out a living in the high desert sand. Back then, though, he'd thought he was hot shit and worth giving all that up for.

Now, all that knowing didn't matter one damn bit.

"Good for him!" Her face crumpled a little, and for an awful moment, he thought she was remembering what was really what. Then she perked right up, smiling at him. "Can I get my hair done, son? And can there be enchiladas for supper?"

"Anything you want, Momma."

"Will you eat with me? I get so confused sometimes, but it's better when you're here."

He was going to scream. Cry. Fall over. Stetson felt that way at least fifteen times a day. Instead, he smiled. He was a cowboy, dammit. He owed her this. He owed her his life. "Only if you don't mind me having tacos."

"My goofy taco-loving baby boy."

"Handheld goodness." God, her moods swung like a rusty gate.

"But no garden."

"God no. Leave that to the Texans." Some things didn't belong on tacos. Maybe on a tostada, but yeah. Tacos, not so much.

She laughed, sounding young all of a sudden, like he remembered her being when he was a little boy and she was just magic. He smiled along, grabbing her hand when she reached for him.

"Oh, I miss those days," she said, as if she knew what he was thinking. "You had this terrible cowlick...."

"I prob'ly still do. That's what the hat is for, right?"

"Yes. Your dad always said that." Her face creased, but she never forgot about Dad, thank God.

"He did, and he'd do this." He ruffled his hair, messing it up.

She hooted. "Oh, yes. You look so like him."

"Poor me." Momma had always been the striking one. She and Daddy had both been dark-haired like him, but she had dark skin—exotic they called it for a girl. Swarthy for a guy. He had Daddy's looks—less round, more angular, less Pueblo, more random cowboy. Momma showed up in his eyes, which were black as a bird's.

"Oh, hush. Your daddy was the most beautiful thing I ever did see."

"Well, I look like him, full stop." Momma'd always said that. He was Daddy's boy, head to tail.

"You have my nose." She squinted at him. "Is there Jell-O?"

"I can grab you some. Hold up." Two things she wanted that he could get. Go him.

"Thank you, love." She sounded tired now, and Stetson knew when he got back she'd be asleep.

Still, maybe she'd remember Curtis was coming. Maybe she wouldn't cry no more. Maybe this would make things better.

He stopped right outside her door, sucking in air like a stoner at a Grateful Dead concert, because it was that or lean his head back and howl.

Every time he thought he'd reached the edge of what he could do, he proved himself wrong. Every single time. He'd done all this. He could handle seeing the love of his life again.

He could for Momma.

CHAPTER TWO

SANTA FE always gave Curtis a happy. The city had a vibe going, all colorful and almost foreign, like it didn't belong to the States at all. He loved the rodeo there too. It was tiny, with an arena maybe a quarter of the size of the big shows, but the purse paid out almost a million dollars all told, and every damn cowboy on earth wanted to win it. Truly amazing.

Coming to see Miz Betty because she was so sick? Not so wonderful.

Knowing that Stetson Major only deigned to call him after so long because he needed Curtis to make believe, pretend the reality wasn't they hadn't laid eyes on each other in damn near a decade? Man, that fucking sucked.

The drive up from Albuquerque had a stark beauty to it with snow on the ground, and that was early, he thought. Snow usually hit at Thanksgiving.

It was dark by the time he found the hospital and a parking spot. He sucked in the air, the cold hitting his lungs and making him cough for a second. Lord, he'd thought Denver was dry. This was threatening to kill his nose hairs altogether.

He hunched his shoulders, preparing for the antiseptic smell and general sadness of the place. He'd do anything for Miz Betty, though. He really would. That was why he'd come a'runnin' when Stetson called.

Just outside the doors, there was a cowboy hat attached to long legs and a pair of work boots with a hole in the bottom big enough to ride through. The face wasn't visible, but it didn't matter. He would know Stetson Major from across a football field without a JumboTron. That laconic bastard had the finest belly in the known universe, and Curtis worked with men who did a thousand crunches a day.

Someone was having smoke breaks when they'd quit maybe nine years back.

Curtis walked over and tapped one boot toe.

The hat brim lifted, and there he was, face-to-face with the one that got away, those dark brown eyes looking... well, about as exhausted and unhappy as he'd ever seen them. "You came. She'll be pleased," Stetson murmured.

"I sure as shit hope so." Curtis studied the lines on Stetson's face like they were a map that would lead him to understand how they'd fucked up so damn bad. "You look like hell."

"I try." Stetson looked at the cigarette that was burned down to the filter, then fieldstripped it and threw it away. "You ready to see her? She got her hair done for you."

"I am. If she's still awake. I'm here for whatever you need me to do."

"Thank you. She thinks we're still an item. If she asks for Daddy, just ignore it. Arguing ain't a thing with this."

Stetson led him into the hospital, which was nicer than he'd expected, really, and took him into the warren of hallways.

"I'm sorry, man. She's always been such a pistol." He didn't want to see her sick, frail.

Stetson looked at him, gave him a nod and an expression that was all about regrets.

Curtis wanted to reach for Stetson's hand, but he didn't have the right to do that now. Hadn't had that for a long damn time. This wasn't about them, and there was no fucking them, was there?

There hadn't been.

What there was didn't have even embers left. They weren't even friends. Stetson had wanted a househusband to move cattle through the high desert scrub, and Curtis had wanted a traveling partner. Neither one of them had gotten what they wanted.

Fuck, neither of them had wanted a single thing they might have had with anyone, in reality. Neither of them had been ready to compromise.

He took a deep breath when they paused outside a room with the label written in black Sharpie. *Major*. This was real, then.

"It's all right." Stetson opened the door and stuck his head in. "Momma? Momma, Curtis came to visit you."

"Curtis? Get your ass in here!"

She sounded so normal, but shock slapped him in the face when Curtis saw her. She couldn't have weighed more than a bird, and her face held deep lines carved into it.

"Curtis! Why haven't you come to see me? I know Stetson's been missing you like a lost tooth. Silly rodeo man, always on the road. You remind me of my husband, forever running after something. Did you meet him yet?"

"Yes, ma'am." He hoped that would work as an answer for anything. Curtis walked over to the bed so he could kiss her cheek. "I sure did miss you too."

"Bless you, sweet boy. It's so good to see you."

He smiled for her, even if it strained his cheeks. You didn't go to hell for this type of lying, right? "That sure is a pretty nightgown."

"Thank you. I hate that you have to see me in bed. I'm going home soon. Stetson promises I'll only be here a bit longer. I have to get my strength up, you know?"

"That's it. They'll have you lifting weights and running laps soon." God, her cheeks had hollowed out, her little touches of blush and lipstick bright as hell against her pale skin. Where was the sunbaked lady he'd known so well, hale and hearty and giving a whole ranch full of men and critters hell?

He kept looking at Stetson, but the man might as well have been a pillar of salt, he stood so still and silent. That face seemed carved out of a block of granite. Expressionless. *Jesus.*

He sat next to Betty and took her hand. "Should I tell you all about my season?"

"Please. I want to hear everything. Everything about your life. I knew that Stetson would end up with a rodeo man. It was inevitable. He was born to it. The only thing he got from me."

Curtis glanced at Stetson again. Once upon a time they would have laughed at her saying something like that. Now it didn't seem funny at all. "You know it. We're irresistible, us circuit guys."

"Yes. Yes, free and easy and the best friends you'll ever have." She was beginning to blink slowly, maybe getting sleepy. "Tell me about it, Curtis."

He started telling stories, hoping she wouldn't remember what season he'd been on when she last saw him. He thought maybe she simply wanted to hear his voice.

In ten minutes she was sound asleep, and Stetson came over to lower the head of the bed before dimming the lights, then kissing her cheek. "Night, Momma."

Curtis gently let go of Betty's hand. He waited for Stetson, not sure what to say, what to do. He couldn't think of a worse thing to happen to someone like Miz Betty, and she was the cornerstone of Stetson's life.

Stetson went to the door and waited for him, then closed it. "Thank you for coming out. She's been asking for you for eons."

"Not a problem. I can stay for a few days. I just need to know her schedule, maybe know what to look for if I'm upsetting her." He ached to touch Stetson, to comfort the man he'd spent so much time with, had once known so well. It wasn't his place, though. This wasn't real, except for the fact that a good woman was dying too young.

"Yeah? She's in and out a lot, but she'd welcome you being there." Stetson nodded to a nurse, who offered him a smile.

"See you tomorrow, Stetson."

"Yes, ma'am." Stetson tilted his hat to a petite Hispanic nurse. "Have a good night."

They walked outside together, and Stetson pulled out a pack of smokes.

"Thought you quit," Curtis murmured.

"I did." Stetson lit up, drawing deep. The man had a mustache now, a scruff that was more a day or two without shaving than a beard. "Let me get you a hotel room, and then I'll feed you."

"Sounds good. I looked into a couple three places, but I got my flight so fast I didn't have time to reserve a thing."

"There's a nice one with kitchenettes and stuff right close." Stetson got on his phone and bing, bam, boom, Curtis had a room. "You got it for as long as you need it. I texted you the confirmation."

"Thanks." He chuckled. "Food and sleep are important."

"Come on. There's a diner right down the way. You want to follow me?"

"Sure thing." He wanted to shake Stetson, tell him to smile, but Curtis just waved him on, heading for the rental. That wasn't his place, and it wasn't a bit fair to want something for his sake and not Stetson's.

Stetson climbed into a dark pickup, and Curtis shook his head. Stetson moved like an old man. He wasn't. He was fixin' to be twenty-nine, but Curtis guessed that didn't matter. Shit like this with Betty, it aged a man.

Curtis got the truck started, waiting for Stetson to lead before sliding out into the light traffic. Small for a capital city, was Santa Fe.

The diner was tiny—just a hole-in-the-wall that he'd never go to on his own—but Stetson pulled in and headed for the door like the way was built into his muscles.

The place did smell like heaven. Red meat and bacon, chile and bread. Okay, Curtis could get behind anything this yummy no matter what it looked like on the outside. He settled into the booth across from Stetson and took off his hat.

"Stetson, honey. How's Mama?" The waitress was as round as she was tall, her long black braid shining in the artificial light.

"She has her good days and bad days. Coffee and whatever this yahoo wants."

Curtis smiled at the lady, whose name tag read *Minnie*. "Coffee please, ma'am."

"You got it." She reached out and squeezed Stetson's shoulder.

Stetson sat there, looking at him, staring at him like he was a mirage or something. The silence stretched until he thought it would snap, Stetson barely even blinking.

"Hey," Curtis finally said. "I'm glad you called me."

"Liar. I appreciate you coming. Momma needed to see you. She was tickled."

What about you, Stetson? Did you need to see me too? If she hadn't asked for me, would you have ever once unbent enough to call?

Curtis grabbed the coffee Minnie set in front of him, sipped to keep from saying it out loud. It was a crazy, stupid thought and would only lead to madness. "She's in a bad way, huh?"

"Apparently it gets worse, but yeah. She ain't never going home."

"Lord." He had no idea what to say. None. "I—who's working the ranch?"

"I got Mr. Butler feeding for me three days a week and José Garzas doing it the rest. I get home once every three nights or so."

"Uh-huh." He studied that lined face carefully. "When was the last time you slept?"

"Oh, I get rest." Ah, Stetson, the master of the nonanswer answer.

"That ain't what I asked." The "baby" almost slipped out, and he hadn't called anyone that in damned near eight years. No one. Hell, he could count on one hand the men he'd spent the night with....

"I don't know. I drove out to the ranch last night, and they called me at six saying she was needing me."

"That's what? Two hours each way?" Shit. He was taking the couch and making Stetson sleep on the bed.

"Yeah. Don't worry. I got the horse trailer here."

"The horse—shit no. You come stay at my hotel room."

No way his Stetson was staying in a goddamn horse trailer. What the ever-loving fuck? It was cold, even for Santa Fe, and a man could chill his bones clear to breaking. Wait. Stop that shit. This wasn't his anything. He was here for Betty. Still, Curtis wouldn't leave a dog out in the cold, would he? No, sir.

"You already put yourself out, Curtis. Coming out."

"Uh-huh. It's one of them kitchenette places? Then it will have a sofa. I may not share a room much anymore, but God knows I'm still used to a bunch of snoring guys." That was that.

More coffee came, and Stetson drank deep, not even doctoring it. The man usually took cream and two sugars. Damn.

"So, what's good here?" Curtis asked.

"The enchiladas. The mole bowl."

"Hmm." He glanced at the menu. "Ever try the green chile cheeseburger with the fried egg?"

"I have. The green chile rocks right now."

"I'll go with that, then." He was starving. He'd missed out on a couple of meals somewhere along the line. He usually flew first class these days, but trading in his ticket, he'd had to go coach on this short hop, and then he'd hit Albuquerque at a crap time to stop.

"I'm going to have a burger, I think."

"Sounds good." They ordered, and Curtis went ahead and got the appetizer basket too. Onion rings, fried cheese, more fries. Stetson needed to eat.

Hell, Stetson needed to talk. The hard-assed son of a bitch was wound so tight he was fixin' to explode.

Curtis waited until Minnie left them again before leaning his elbows on the table. "How long has she been down here?"

"Uh… it's been almost three years since I couldn't let her be alone. A tad less than two since she's been… in a place like this." Stetson wouldn't meet his eyes. "She wants to stay home, but I couldn't keep her safe at the ranch. I tried to, but I couldn't."

"Of course you couldn't." He wondered if other folks had blamed him or if Stetson just blamed himself. No one was harder on Stetson than Stetson Major.

"You been riding good this year."

It sent a little jolt through him, just to know that Stetson had been following him. "I've been working hard. Thank God Finals are almost here." He was ready for a break. He wasn't old, but he was getting long in the tooth for all-around cowboying. Even if he only rode two events at some places now, it was still a hell of a beating his body was taking every week.

"Yeah. Yeah, it's late in the season."

"Yep. The Stampede was my last one going in to NFR, but I don't need the points."

"I'm sorry for calling, but I didn't have a choice. She don't remember."

"No, I can see that." There'd been a shitton of times for Stetson to drop him a line, and it had taken a sick old woman crying to get him to pick up the phone. *Sorry for calling. Fucker.* "You know I love your mom." Thing was, love had never been the problem.

"I do. She loves you dearly. She always did. Didn't talk to me for six months after we split up."

"Wow." Considering Stetson and his mom lived together on the ranch, that was saying something. Miz Betty sure could be stubborn. "I'm sorry." He kept saying it.

"Eh." Stetson waved one gnarled, tanned-to-leather hand. "Happens. No big thing."

Uh-huh. Except he knew better.

Stetson hadn't been calm and cool before it was all over. Neither of them had been. Lord, what a knock-down, drag-out that had turned out to be. They'd called each other everything but lover. Hell, he'd driven off with a shotgun shell hole in the tailgate of his pickup.

Curtis grinned a little. "I was bruised for a week after that one fight."

"Yeah. I ain't sorry for that." He got a slow wink.

"I bet not. You had a hell of a right cross." He'd put Stetson up against anyone in a brawl. Man could throw, and take, a punch.

"Still do."

Jesus Christ on a Popsicle stick. That was a smile.

The expression gave him a warm glow in his lower body, and he had a stern, totally mental talking-to with his privates.

He wanted to just.... Hell, he wanted to take Stetson, beat the living fuck out of the son of a bitch, then swoop him away and hold the man until everything was better. He knew that Stetson wouldn't thank him for it, that was for sure. Hell, he wasn't sure he'd thank himself for it. Fact was, he was still a rodeo man and always would be, and Lord knew Stetson had precious little respect for that kind of life. Still, there had always been something about Stetson, some deep calling that made him want to grab on tight.

Their food came before he could start making grand gestures, though, and damn, that cheeseburger tasted like heaven on a plate. The app basket came out with the food, but they dug into it anyway.

Stetson ate like he was starving, like there was a hole in him that needed to be filled.

Curtis reckoned there was. If he could give Stetson a real meal and a good night's sleep, then he'd accomplished something no one else had in what looked like months.

Stetson's phone rang, and the man jumped, expression going all worried. He grabbed it, looked at it, then sighed. "Just a telemarketer."

How bad did your life have to suck that you dreaded a phone call? Curtis held out his hand, and Stetson handed over the phone, seeming a little surprised that he had. Curtis tucked it into his pocket. "I'll pull call duty tonight."

"What? I—I didn't mean for you to—I'm just—" Stetson appeared damn near panicked, but Curtis knew how to deal with an emergency situation, if nothing else. He'd spent a good amount of his life in one dumbass emergency after another. He was a Texan and a cowboy, after all. They only came in dumbass.

"Shh. Easy. Please, cowboy. Just be easy for a second," Curtis said.

"I don't remember how," Stetson confessed, looking hangdog as all get-out.

"I'll try to help." Curtis waved a french fry. "You want dessert? That pie might be calling my name." A case stood up front with three kinds of pie, all perfect and creamy.

"The pie here is stellar, but I'll have the sopapillas."

"Oh." Oh God, how long had it been since he'd had fried dough with honey? "Yes, please."

Stetson chuckled softly. "Been too long since that was a standard, huh?"

Lord, yes. What passed as home for him nowadays was the Western Slope, where it was way more Midwestern than Southwesty. Meat and potatoes and plenty of pie. Sopapillas were Stetson. New Mexico and good memories. "I forgot how good they are here."

"We know chiles and fry bread if we don't know anything else."

"No shit." Denver could claim green chile all they wanted. Curtis knew better. "Two orders of sopapillas, please," he asked Minnie.

"You got it." She took the plates and refreshed their coffees.

"Better?" Curtis asked. He knew from stress, and sometimes powering through a big meal could blunt the panic, the terrible ache inside.

"Yeah. I haven't been on regular mealtimes, you know. Running."

"I bet." How weird was this? Awkward mainly because it felt like old times, as if he'd never been gone. Yet this was a different man across from him.

Stetson's eyes had gone old. There were little lines at the corners, a scar splitting one eyebrow that hadn't been there before. There wasn't a hint of gray—Stetson wasn't even thirty yet, why would there be?—but if he saw Stetson in the stands at an event, he would have pegged the man at fifty, maybe fifty-five.

They lapsed into silence for a few moments, both of them thinking too hard for this time of night. The sopapillas came out and saved them, piping hot pockets of fried golden perfection.

The honey was thick and smooth, and he groaned as he bit into the sweet. So good.

When he glanced at Stetson again, the man watched him like he was Christmas morning presents under the tree on Christmas Eve.

"They're good," he said, licking his lips clean.

"They are."

"You haven't even had one yet."

Stetson glanced down at the basket of bread and flushed. "Right."

He didn't even feel ashamed of the jolt of pleasure that gave him. He wanted Stetson to see him, to miss him, dammit. To want him. Even if it was a lie.

They'd burned brighter than a bonfire on New Year's together. Good to know a spark still existed, because as many other guys as he'd tried on for size, none burned him to the ground like Stetson had.

Stetson was his one true thing, and Curtis knew it. Too bad they just… hadn't worked. He munched another sopapilla to keep from saying something, anything, stupid.

"I don't know what to say to you. I just want to keep thanking you. Momma's been excited all day. She even got her hair done."

"Well, I'll hang around and see her some more. Just spend a little time. Is there anything else I don't mention besides your dad and us breaking up?" Curtis wanted to keep missteps to a dull roar.

"There's no way to know. Some days she's clearer than others, but sometimes I'll mention one of the dogs and she won't remember. Sometimes there's nothing that calms her down."

"Okay." The weight of that had to be huge on Stetson. Curtis could help him carry it for a few days, at least. "Well, I got your back for as long as I can stay."

"I'll pay for the hotel and to get you wherever too. I just…. Even just one more visit would be amazing."

He reached out with his sticky hand and covered one of Stetson's. "I don't hate you, Stetson, and your mom is the best lady I've ever known. I'll do anything I can. You ready to go put your feet up?"

Stetson nodded. "I guess I'd better, yeah."

"You know where this hotel is? I can follow again."

"I do. Yeah. Come on, cowboy."

Stetson rose, but Curtis grabbed the bill before Stetson could touch it. Medical bills sucked, and Miz Betty couldn't be on Medicare yet. Medicaid, maybe, but neither of those covered everything.

"I…."

"Shut up, Stetson. Come on."

Time to put this exhausted man to bed and let him lay his head down. Maybe pray a little for Miz Betty.

Stetson followed him like a ghost, then led him to the Old Santa Fe Inn, the sound of the river burbling away. Nice. That would make sleeping easy. The place was a remodeled motor court too, so he could park in front of his room.

Now, the bed didn't look anything like an old motor court. Curtis approved.

"I'm gonna let you get some sleep, cowboy. You rest and holler at me…. Oh, you got my phone."

"Yep. Sit your ass down and take off your boots." He had sweats in his bag that would fit Stetson's skinny ass.

"Huh?"

He just pushed Stetson down. "Sit your ass down, man."

Stetson popped back up like a jack-in-the-box, eyes rolling like a fractious horse. "I can't stay here."

"Bullshit you can't. You want to tie it up, we can. I ain't forgot how. I swear to God, though, after I wipe the fucking floor with you, I'm gon' strip your heinie down and pour your butt in this bed and you're gonna sleep. You want to have to explain to your momma why you're all tore up?"

They stared into each other for a good long time, and Curtis thought for a second Stetson was either fixin' to nut him or kiss him, and he was weirdly disappointed when Stetson dropped his eyes.

Stetson plopped down on the bed, and Curtis bent so he could grab one boot and tug at it until it popped off. Stetson's sock had a big hole at the toe, which said more about the man's state of mind than anything else. The guy was a freak about his clothes.

Holes in his socks, holes in his boots—someone's head was in the clouds, and those sons of bitches were dark and fixin' to storm.

Curtis didn't say a thing, though. He just started on Stetson's shirt, slapping Stetson's hands away when he tried to help.

Stetson stared at him like a goat looking at a new fence, pretty eyes dull and red, all the fight sucked out of him.

This wasn't fair. Not a bit of it.

He wanted Stetson to have called him because Stetson couldn't bear not to hear his fucking voice, because the wanting between them was too big to ignore. That hadn't happened, though, not in all the years apart, and if wishes were horses, well, he'd have a lot of horses.

Curtis backed off, then grabbed his bag. "Here's some sweats, and I got you a toothbrush when I checked in." He handed over both the pants and the baggie from the hotel. "Go wash up, okay?"

"I don't...." Stetson stood up and headed away, hat still on his head.

"Oh, Roper." He chuckled softly and eased the felt hat off. "There. Loosen your brains a little, huh?"

"Sure." Stetson gave him a ghost of a smile before slipping into the bathroom and closing the door behind him.

He changed into a pair of pajama pants and a T-shirt, then dug out his kit bag before sitting on the bed and grabbing the TV remote.

Stetson's phone was blowing up—texts from folks, some he knew and lots he didn't, asking after Miz Betty, then phone calls from all over the country. Telemarketers, he guessed. He didn't reckon Stetson knew a lot of folks in Chicago and Portland.

He turned off the sound for now, knowing the buzz would be enough if the hospital called. That number was in Stetson's contacts, as was "Night Nurse," so those he would answer. Curtis was just fine with doing night duty.

Stetson meandered back in, looking like a wandering ghost. "I can sleep in the chair." He stumbled over the rug on the floor, almost going down but landing half on the bed instead.

"I got you." Curtis helped Stetson stretch out, propping his head up with a pillow. "No worries, okay? I'm not going to attack you in this state. I'm gonna hit the shower. I have your phone, so don't you try to run off."

Stetson nodded. "I ain't going nowhere. Swear."

"Good deal." Curtis ducked into the bathroom and turned on the water, cranking it up as hot as he could stand. Cold showers had never done dick for him.

Besides that, he wasn't even turned on. Shit, he wanted to wrap around Stetson and lie to the man, tell him everything was gonna be okay. He knew it wouldn't be, not for a long time. Losing a parent, well, they were both too young for that, yet.

Not that Curtis hadn't basically lost his dad when he took up with Stetson. His mom still called him once a week.

He soaped up and got himself all clean, avoiding going into the hotel room for as long as he could. He still couldn't wrap his mind around this. He didn't know how.

It was supposed to be that Stetson was pining for him but was healthy and happy except for the broken heart part. That things were great, barring the fact that Stetson needed Curtis like his next fucking breath. This was supposed to be different, goddamn it. This was his fantasy, to have Stetson call, need him.

Not to have to call because Betty was dying and half out of her mind at way too fucking young.

He hit the wall, letting the vibrations rocket up his free arm, jostle his shoulder. *This wasn't what I prayed for, Lord. This wasn't it. I swear, if you could make her better for him, I'd go and never pray to have him back. Not ever again.*

Not that praying had ever gotten him anywhere where Stetson was concerned. Damned fool stubbornly resisted anyone's will but his own.

Finally Curtis was feeling beet red and loose-limbed, and he dried off, got himself decent and his teeth sparkly, and headed in. Stetson was there, raven wing hair a mess, tears staining the man's cheeks even in his sleep.

"Oh, Roper. You shoulda called sooner." He didn't give any breath to the words, just crawled up into the bed and pulled Stetson into his arms.

It told him what he needed to know, that Stetson came, cuddled in and let him hold on. The man had no one to lean on, no one to vent to.

Curtis could do that for Stetson. At least for a little while. It would never be enough, but he'd take what he could get. This wasn't about him.

This was about… well, family, he guessed. Family would work.

CHAPTER THREE

"OH, CURTIS. I can't believe you have to see me like this. I should be cooking you boys something good to eat, not laying in the bed like a laze...."

"Now, Miz Betty, you know it's enough to just have a chat with you."

Stetson listened to Momma talk to Curtis like the cowboy was her best friend, and tried not to feel jealous. What good would it do, really?

Curtis didn't have to make her take her meds. Curtis didn't have to sign the orders to restrain her when she lost her mind. Curtis didn't have to be the bad guy.

Of course, that didn't stop the little voice in Stetson's head that insisted that Momma'd always wished Curtis was her son, that she'd given birth to the famous all-around cowboy instead of the staid, boring one.

It had been like that from the get-go. Curtis was pretty, was vibrant and hot.

When is your cowboy coming home? Do you think he'd like tamales? Are you going to go with him? You rope well enough.

Christ. Like he didn't have to stay home, do his job, feed and pay bills and exercise horses. Like he hadn't known that once Curtis had gotten back in the swing of things, he would find what he needed.

Eh. What did it matter now?

She was happy. That was what was important.

Happy and laughing and making jokes and knowing who Curtis was. That was a damned improvement by anyone's standards.

"Well, it's getting on to suppertime, Miz Betty. I ought to get on out of here and let you have some food."

Curtis was patting Momma's hand, and his mom was nodding, but mainly he thought she was nodding off.

"I have to run to the ranch tonight, Momma, but I'll be back in the morning to see you." He uncurled his fingers from the fists they'd become and bent to kiss her forehead.

She smiled up at him. "Are you bringing Curtis with you?"

"Now, Momma...." He couldn't make those kinds of promises.

"I'll come by one way or the other," Curtis said. "I'll stick around a couple days, at least." How many magazine covers and news articles had seen that exact smile? Quite a few, if the stack in Stetson's back room was any indication.

A couple of days. God, at three hundred a night, that was going to be the end of him. Were there cheaper places? Sure, but Curtis was used to better, not sleeping in an Army cot on the floor of the horse trailer. Christ, he didn't know how—how was he supposed to survive this? The longer Momma was sick, the more his whole life was built on eggshells and clouds that couldn't hold.

"Stetson, you should take Curtis out for a nice supper. It's the least you could do, with Curtis coming home to visit, just on my account."

"Sure, Momma." A steak dinner. Right. Maybe if he sold his plasma.

"Silly boys, sneaking out to the barn all the time. You know, you could build a casita. Or you could go on the road with him. I always wanted to go on the road, but I got stuck at home. Where's your daddy, Stetson? Is he going to bring me daisies?"

"Sure, Momma." There was no use in arguing. He was too tired. "I'll make sure and let him know."

Curtis looked at him, all wide-eyed, and he stared right back. What the hell was he supposed to do? Let her lose her husband over and over? No fucking way.

Took them another half an hour to get out of the hospital, but Stetson didn't wait much after that, lighting up as soon as they walked outside and drawing Curtis aside. "Look, I appreciate you wanting to stay, but I get it that you have to get back to work."

"I can stay a bit."

No. No, you really can't, asshole. I'm fucking broke-dick, and I don't know what to do next. I'm scared and tired, and you're still beautiful, and I'm... lost. "I appreciate it, but—"

"No buts, Roper. Miz Betty asked me to stay. She seems way better today."

"It's not real." He knew that. This whole thing wasn't real. He was in a fucking nightmare that just kept battering at him, and there wasn't any waking up in the morning happening for him.

"I know. I was just trying to make it better." Oh, Curtis wasn't allowed to do that, to be all long faced and hangdog. Not right now. Not when the only happiness he'd heard from his own momma in weeks had come from the man who had told him he'd never be buried to his balls in the dust like Stetson was. "You don't have to be all pissy because she likes me, you know. You've always been a little bitch about that."

He didn't stop to think, not for a single second. His fist shot out, connecting with the son of a bitch's jaw, and Curtis's head popped back, then rocked forward.

"Okay, then." Curtis landed a blow to his gut that almost doubled him over, then got him with a jab right in the nose.

Fuck, that stung like a bitch, and he landed a wild haymaker, damn near going ass over teakettle as Curtis answered with a couple of half-hearted rabbit punches to his kidneys in thanks. Stetson twisted and got his hands around Curtis's hips and shoved, needing to put some space between them. They broke apart, both of them panting a bit, although he knew Curtis's was more altitude than exertion.

"Your turn, Roper."

"What?" He snuffled and snorted.

"We're beating on each other, right? More in that working-out than a fixin'-to-kill-each-other way, sure, but still, we're having a fight in public. Don't embarrass me." Curtis was a pure-D asshole, but the quirk of his lips made Stetson roll his eyes.

"Come on, fucker."

"What? That's all I get?"

"Yeah, you bastard. That's all you get." That's all he had. Still, he could breathe, couldn't he? Deep breaths that didn't hurt so bad.

"You feel better, Roper?"

He didn't bother to answer. Instead he simply shrugged, intending to tell Curtis to fuck right off. What came out was "I can't afford the hotel more than maybe one more night."

His cheeks burned at the words, and his pride took another blow, this one sharper than any fist. Curtis needed to know, though. Might as well start out like he could hold out.

Curtis pursed his lips. "I could stay at the ranch, if that won't be a huge problem."

"Yeah? If you don't mind." He had the trailer here to sleep in, and Curtis wouldn't have to hold the hours he did, or baby his truck along. "I'm real sorry. I know it's an inconvenience."

"It's fine, baby." Curtis didn't even acknowledge using the nickname. Asshole. "Shit, you know that drive is dick all to me."

"Yeah. Yeah, you got all that highway mileage." He managed to dig up a grin, and it came easier than he'd expected. "Come on. I'll pick up a pizza on the way. You remember how to get there still?"

"I do." Curtis nodded, reaching out to touch his arm. "You okay to drive? You were out like a light last night."

"Yeah. I was…. It was a long day." And to be honest, he didn't remember even getting to the hotel. He'd been on autopilot. "I got to run and get my dirty clothes out of the trailer so I can do a load of laundry tonight."

"Sure. If I get there before you, no one will shoot me, right?"

"Nope. The gate's unlocked. The house key's right where it always was. You want sausage and pepperoni on your pizza or are you being healthy right now?" Roughstock boys had to watch their weight, and Curtis was in fighting trim despite the green chile cheeseburger last night.

Curtis chuckled. "I'll go with peppers and green olives." After pulling out his wallet, Curtis handed over a twenty, his expression brooking no arguments.

He hated that he knew that it would help too. He was going to owe Curtis for the rest of his life.

Maybe longer.

That was okay. He sorta owed everyone on earth, from his neighbors to random people at the hospital.

The ones he had to worry about right now were the creditors. He was balls deep in owing and without a fucking thing to show for it. God, what a mess. "Veggies. Gotcha" was all he said, trying for a grin and probably failing. "See you at home."

"I'll be there."

Stetson walked away, heading to the little horse trailer parked in the back of the hospital parking lot, trying to remember how to breathe. He gathered up his trash and his dirty clothes, leaving just his book and the cot and his blankets for tomorrow night.

Okay. He'd get on the road, order a couple of pizzas once he got about halfway there, and then head home to check the horses and pay a couple three bills.

Thank God he had a bed in his office at the house under a shitload of boxes. He cleaned that out, he could sleep there, and he wouldn't have to share with Curtis. He'd passed out last night, but if he had to know

Curtis was right there, well, Stetson wouldn't be able to bear it. Part of him hated Momma for this, for making him have to deal with this.

A worse part of him was thankful for a second to pretend.

This whole thing was just…. Shit marthy, he needed to do something that wasn't wrong for a while. The animals did that for him, calmed him down, made him serve someone else's needs for a bit.

He checked the oil in his truck before starting her up and heading north.

Home.

God, it was time to go home for a night.

CHAPTER FOUR

THE GATE appeared just the same when Curtis opened it so he could bump onto the ranch road. The J Bar M sign still sat on top, not a bit of rust on it.

The road could use a good grading, but Curtis knew there'd been some flooding last year. He'd heard about it in Santa Fe.

When he pulled up on the house, he just sat there, teeth in his mouth, trying to remember how to breathe. It needed some work, sure, but it was the same house that Stetson had brought him to ten years ago when he was recovering from a broken pelvis. The same simple, normal ranch house.

He almost doubled over with the pain that punched him in the gut then. Fuck, this felt like home.

Of course, he'd wanted to leave. He'd needed to. He'd had a life that wasn't this hardscrabble existence in this beautiful place. How the fuck could a land so pretty be worth so little for feeding critters? Everything here bit, scratched, or snowed on a man.

"Okay, come on." Curtis got out of the truck, looking around for Aimee the border collie.

A trio of dogs—all three collies, but none he knew—came tearing around the house, barking and wagging in time. Curtis knelt, figuring it was best not to try to go in until he made friends. Aimee had to be gone by now. Lord, he'd never even thought about it, but she'd been almost nine the last time he turned his back to this place.

They all had collars, and they came to him easily, pushing into his hands like they were old friends. Not guard dogs, then. Working dogs, sure, but not trained to keep people away.

"You guys need a brushing." He scrubbed ruffs. "Are you allowed in the house?" Curtis dusted off his jeans.

They all followed him, right up into the covered porch, and there were three dog beds next to a pair of rockers.

"Ah, well, sorry, guys. You stay out here." Curtis dug the key out of the pot of dead geraniums next to the front door. Miz Betty had always cared for the plants. Curtis would have to see about getting Stetson something hearty and all-weather for his key hideout.

He opened up the front door, the scent of Stetson like a fucking ghost in this place. A pair of even more worn boots than the ones Stetson wore sat by the door, and a neat line of hats marched across the wall, the gimme caps on hooks, the cowboy hats upside down in U-shaped hangers. Curtis placed his hat in one of the empties and dragged his bag over to lie by the couch.

The place hadn't changed, and that wasn't really an exaggeration. The furniture hadn't moved, had just gotten that much older. The TV was still the big old console thing that had always been sitting there. Could those even get a signal now?

He turned it on, just to see. Okay, no. Fuzziness. Maybe Stetson watched TV in the bedroom. He knew Miz Betty's bedroom was on one side of the front room, Stetson's on the other. He honestly couldn't remember if there was a guest room. God knew he'd never had to use it.

The kitchen told a story of a man who wasn't here and was running his ass off. There were piles of bills and paperwork on the table, along with an ashtray and a dried-out coffee cup with the handle broken off at the bottom. One fruit bowl had a sad, desiccated apple, and the mousetrap on the floor by the sink proved why the pups weren't allowed in.

"Lord." The dishes in the sink were all cereal bowls and forks. The trash held a metric ton of frozen-dinner shells. Curtis shook his head and began to clean up some, washing dishes and wiping out the fruit bowl. He needed something to do, some way to keep his hands and mind busy. He could drive himself nuts worrying about Stetson.

He cracked a couple of windows, even though the air up here was frigid, just to freshen things up. Then Curtis turned in a big circle, trying to decide what to do next. Someone had to be doing the feeding, so there was no sense in going to the barns, though he would feel more at home there, probably.

He ended up heading out to the covered back porch, finding what had to be Stetson's place to watch the world. This vantage point exposed the mountains, the sunset, the barns, and what had been the ranch hands' home, back in the day. The huge chair was surrounded with more dog beds, a huge fire pit in front of it and a standing beer cooler close by.

Well, that made him smile.

"Now, this I can get behind." He settled in one of the comfy chairs, and sure enough the dogs came trotting up, wanting more ear rubs and loving.

The horses came to the fence, a half dozen following the lead mare out to see what was what, to see if someone was bringing more food.

They looked good, fuzzy for winter, fat and sassy and needing riding.

"Exercise, you guys. You all want it." Curtis could hang out a few days, do a little riding. Sounded good.

He heard the sound of truck tires on gravel, then boot steps echoing through the house before the back door opened. "Reckoned I'd find you out here."

"It's a good spot. You get that pizza or do I need to dig in your freezer?"

"I got pizza and a six-pack. They're on the counter." He got a half grin and a dip of the brim of that hat before Stetson headed out toward the fence. "Sugarbaby!"

The lead mare lifted her head, ears twisting and turning, and then she came running. She stuck her nose over the fence once she reached Stetson, blowing gently. Someone was spoiled.

Stetson leaned in and reached for her, resting their cheeks together. Spoiled and possibly Stetson's best friend.

God, he wanted to be the one Stetson still reached for when the stubborn bastard needed to be touched.

Curtis shook himself a little. Jealous of a horse, for Christ's sake. "I'll get plates and all, babe."

Babe. Listen to him, acting like he was ready to just fold himself back into Stetson's life. Christ. He was the worst kind of fool.

"There's paper ones in the kitchen." Stetson's voice was husky, rough, and a little raw, but the man patted Sugarbaby's neck, rubbed her ears. "I'll be back in a bit, sweet girl."

"I'm on it." If Stetson needed a moment, Curtis was smart enough to give it. He walked into the kitchen, and his mouth watered right away. Oh, that pizza smelled good, all garlic and tomato and fresh bread scent.

He wasn't sure whether to clean off a spot on the kitchen table or just fix a plate and take it back outside. Stetson answered the question by joining him inside.

"Nippy out there if you want to keep the pizza hot."

"But it would keep the beer cold." Curtis winked, trying for a hint of a smile, at least.

"True that. Come on. We'll sit in the front room. I keep intending to move all that shit on the table to the office, but I ain't done it yet."

"I see you still got that old TV," he teased. Curtis loaded up a plate.

"Momma had hysteria when you moved anything, so I stopped trying. Now, I just can't. It'll probably just stay like this forever."

"Why can't you?" He knew he was being mean, but Miz Betty wasn't ever coming home.

"Well, I mean, I'm capable, just…. I'm not…. I got enough shit to worry on."

"Oh." Curtis nodded. Now he saw what Stetson meant. "I was just teasing."

"Right. Sorry. I guess… I don't know. I spent a few years making sure everything was just like the day before. She'd sit in front of this TV and stare at it and laugh like she was watching something."

That sounded like hell on earth, and Curtis set his plate aside for a moment, walking over to wrap his arms around Stetson's middle. "I'm sorry."

"Me too." Stetson looked at him, stared at him with these wounded fucking eyes for the longest time, and then Stetson wrapped those arms around him and held on tight. Curtis swore his heart stopped long enough to make him dizzy, and when it started back up, it took up the same rhythm as Stetson's.

They stood there for a long while, breathing together, until Stetson's stiff muscles relaxed some. Yeah. That was it. Give and take. Warmth and care.

"You still smell good. Still." Stetson looked over at him, and for a long, breathless second, Curtis thought the man was going to kiss him, but then Stetson stepped back. "Pizza. It's too good to forget."

"It smells amazing." Curtis's hands shook a little when he reached for his plate. "I'll come back for the beers."

"Good deal." Stetson touched his wrist, then grabbed a couple slices for himself.

They took their food out to the front room before Curtis went back for the beer, then settled in to eat as if they did this every day. Crazy.

He pulled the cheese off his pie, only leaving enough to taste. He hated this bullshit, but it made a difference between seven point six and eight seconds.

Stetson chuckled. "Still eating for a bird, huh?"

"Yeah. Someday I'll retire and get round as an Italian granny."

"I'd like to see that. You ain't got an ounce of fat on you."

Like Stetson had room to talk. The man had never been soft, but now he was downright spare, his clothes hanging on him. Curtis would have to feed him real food for a few days. Grocery store tomorrow so he could stock the empty fridge and pantry enough for Stetson to have a few weeks' worth of meals.

Stetson finished his beer, eyes watching him like he would disappear in a puff of green smoke like the Wizard from Oz.

Curtis got it; the unreality of the situation wasn't lost on him. "That was damned good pizza."

"I know, right? It's my favorite place here in town. How's the altitude treating you, Tex?"

Curtis snorted. "I been up in Colorado and Wyoming so much this year, I'm all acclimatized."

"You did good in Cheyenne."

"You been keeping up, Roper?" He remembered Stetson saying something that first night, but it still amazed him. Seriously, the idea that Stetson knew his stats made him super warm.

Stetson shrugged. "Ain't every rancher can say he knows an all-round champ. I'm proud to have known you."

"You still know me, dork." His gut ached at the thought of being someone Stetson used to hang with.

"I do. I can't tell you how much I appreciate this, you coming. It means the world."

"I'm glad to have done it to help your momma, you know it."

"No. No, I mean, yes, of course. But I ain't thanking you for Momma. It means the world to me."

"Oh." His cheeks warmed. "Well, then I'm extra glad, Roper. I miss you." He said the words and realized he meant them. Curtis would have told anyone he hadn't thought of Stetson in years. Now he knew better.

"Yeah. I know all about that." Stetson stood up, stretched. "I got to get out and check the horses, the barns. The good TV's in my room, if you want to watch. I'll switch the sheets and let you have the bed in there. The little room off mine's an office now, and Momma's side of the house is...."

"Hey, I can take the couch. God knows I've slept on enough of them." He didn't want to put Stetson out when he could very well have paid for his own hotel.

"Yeah, but... I thought about it some on the drive up. I ain't gonna, I mean.... Shit, we're grown and I got a big bed. I mean, for tonight."

They'd slept together last night, hadn't they?

"Sure." His heartbeat kicked up. "You need help out there?"

"I hope not, but you're welcome one way or the other. I miss being here."

"I bet." Curtis tugged on his jacket, breathing deep of the mountain air outside.

Stetson grabbed a handful of baby carrots, then led him out toward the barns, but the horses came swarming long before that, begging for attention.

Someone spent a long time out in the pasture and not in the house.

"Hey, lady." There was Sugarbaby again, demanding a treat. She tossed her head when Curtis got too close, but then nosed at him curiously.

Stetson passed him some carrots, the man still jabbering away at the others, touching and leaning, utterly unafraid of teeth or hooves. Curtis had a fine respect for what a bronc could do, but these babies were tame.

"Are those goats?" *Good Lord.*

"Uh-huh. Goats. Alpacas. Donkeys. Three ostriches, a good-sized herd of elk, and there's a momma bear that keeps breaking down the fence on the near side to the river."

"Elk?" Curtis blinked.

"Yeah. If I keep 'em fenced, they don't get hunted so much. I have to cull the herd maybe once every two or three years."

"Wow. Can I see them?"

"Sure. Tomorrow we'll ride out. I don't handle them. I want them to be scared of people, but you can watch them. I called the big bull elk Frank, after the bullfighter. The llamas and all are just over here behind the barn along with the donkeys and ostriches."

He shook his head, following as Stetson moved through the herd, heading to turn the lights on in the barn. The place was spotless—either Stetson was working his ass off or the man had the best neighbors on earth. Maybe both. People loved Stetson easily; Curtis knew because he'd fallen for the man in minutes.

Curtis could see the years falling off Stetson like the man was taking off a coat, checking feed and water, whistling away. The other critters obviously knew that sound, because everyone started chittering and braying and hollering for attention. The donkeys came to the fence separating them from the horses, those long old ears twitching, and Curtis took them the last of his carrots, loving their smart brown eyes and soft noses.

Stetson laughed, Sugarbaby nudging him in the butt and almost sending him ass over teakettle. "You evil old bitch. I will send you to the factory and have your happy ass made into glue."

Right. As if.

"I can just see you being mean to her." Curtis winked when Stetson glanced at him. "So, you have to tell me about the three-legged goat."

"I wish there was a big story," Stetson said. "Someone left her here. Folks are having tough times, and so… I get lots of bonus critters. It's okay. I don't mind so much."

"I guess a few more mouths to feed are easier for you since you run so many horses." Just cattle up here ran pretty cheap, but Stetson was paying for a lot of feed anyway.

"I guess. I mean, I don't know. I'll worry on that later."

That sounded kinda ominous. He hoped Stetson wasn't thinking of anything drastic. People sold land off too fast sometimes in order to pay bills when there was usually help available.

Stetson wandered through the next set of barns, feeding away. Lord have mercy, this was where Stetson belonged, up here in the mountains, easy in his skin, feeding beasts. Not in some hospital. Seeing the improvements Stetson had made out here totally explained why the house was shabbier.

This was Stetson's home. That house was Miz Betty. Someday soon, she would be gone, he knew, and Stetson might start over in there. A lump lodged in his throat at the idea, but that was how it happened. Old folks passed on, and younger ones took up the mantle. He'd hated this place when he'd driven away, cursed this ranch for being more important than him, but seeing Stetson here, now, Curtis got it. This was what every rodeo cowboy longed for, somewhere in his genes. Land and critters and space to breathe that was his.

Stetson began to laugh, the sound ringing out as he watched a pair of goats goof off, playing together.

Curtis wanted to take everything but this and handle it, let Stetson do what he loved and only that. He wanted to protect this man with everything in him.

Too fucking bad that wasn't how the world worked. Shit, loving each other hadn't been an issue. Loving each other. Wanting each other. Even liking each other. Pride had been their downfall, and that wasn't gonna change. He couldn't be less than who he was, and neither could Stetson.

Still, that didn't change what his heart wanted, did it? No, sir.

Curtis sighed, then yelled and jumped three feet sideways when an ostrich leaned over the fence and tried to bite off his nipple. "Holy shit!"

"Watch them. They bite."

"No shit? I end up missing parts, you won't think it's so funny, Roper."

"No missing parts. I like all your parts right where they are, thanks." Stetson smiled at him then, eyes as warm as could be. Damn.

Curtis told his body very sternly not to get all happy. Anything started sticking out, that ostrich might go after it. "Yeah? Me too."

"I bet. She's coming after you again."

"Birds. You have giant birds, man." He moved out of range.

"They're more like dinosaurs than birds, really. Alice, for fuck's sake. Leave the man alone."

"It has a name?"

"What am I supposed to do, call her Mrs. Ostrich? How do I know whether she's married or just in a civil union with Butch?"

"There's another one named Butch?" Okay, Stetson clearly spent too much time alone.

"And Edie. Edie's the little one. Butch is evil. Don't mess with him. Alice is just mean."

"Lord." He detached the goat from his jeans. "Gimme cows any day."

"You just aren't nearly as adventurous as me, that's all...."

"Nope. I just get on two-thousand-pound animals for a living." He winked over, the refrain old and familiar.

"Adventure. Sheer stupidity. Sheer stupidity. Adventure."

"Hey, now!" He laughed out loud, which startled all manner of weird creatures. One of the little goats head-butted him, and when he jumped, the donkey stole his hat.

When he glanced over at Stetson, the man was howling with laughter, clinging to the top rail of the fence and wheezing with it. Curtis had to grin. He'd done that, made Stetson laugh. Well, him and a bunch of freaks from the animal kingdom.

"Dear God, I've missed you, cowboy. I swear you're still something else."

"Come on, Roper. Let's finish up the chores and go watch a movie, huh?" They could snuggle in the bed and pretend they weren't broken up for a little while. Even if Miz Betty wasn't there to see it.

CHAPTER FIVE

STETSON GOT up at four, bundled up, and headed out to feed. There was snow on the air, and the wind felt like an old enemy, slapping at his face. This time of year in Taos could be bleak when a man wasn't already down.

It was okay, though. Curtis could stay sleeping for a few hours, then come down to Santa Fe and see Momma. Then maybe Stetson would just suck it up and drive back out here again tonight.

A little voice in the back of his head said, *And then what? Sleep next to him for another night before he goes back to a life that doesn't have a broke-dick cowboy in it?*

And yeah, that was it. That was sorta it, balls to bones.

There was nothing left. He was gonna lose the horses, the menagerie, the land, the house. His truck was paid off, the trailer, so he was gonna hold out 'til spring, then take the horse trailer up deep into the mountains and stay there until....

Hell, he didn't have an until.

He had right now, tomorrow, when Curtis left to go back to real life, and then until Momma passed.

That was it.

"So if I want to lay next to Curtis for another night, you can go fuck yourself." He didn't know if his little voice was listening, but he reckoned it didn't have a choice.

He got himself into the barn, latched the door, and slapped his hands together to warm them. "Hey, y'all."

Smokey nosed over the top of the stall, the gelding not liking being trapped in there. He was laid up, though, one hoof cracked all to hell. Had to keep the old boy contained. "Hey, buddy. Who the hell am I going to get to take you on, huh?"

He gave scritches, then sighed and opened the stall door, pushing Smokey back. "I need to give you a look, now. Be nice."

Smokey would stand for him but hated to have his feet touched on a good day. The farrier always had to duck around this old man. He turned to press his butt against Smokey's side, then slid his hands down that long leg, giving plenty of warning.

"You kick me and I'm gonna be pissed, old man, you hear me? I need to make sure your hoof is better." That and make sure there wasn't any stench coming from it. He'd been babying Smokey along.

Head bobbing up and down, Smokey let him have a look. Not bad. Better than he'd feared, but he really needed to get out there every day. The guys he had feeding were great, but Smokey was a fricking challenge.

"You're healing. I approve. And for not stomping my brains into oatmeal? You get sweet feed." He hummed, letting everything else slide away for a while. The animals didn't care nothin' about money or ex-lovers or anything else. They needed what they needed, which was food, water, and care.

Simple shit.

Good shit.

He stopped by Barney's stall, the poor old guy too old to be out in the cold now, and damn near blind, to boot. Stetson scratched his nose, watching those fuzzy ears swivel back and forth. "Hey, shortie. How you doing today? Maybe I should clip you to a lead and take you for a walk, huh?"

Barney whinnied at him, coming right to him, head pushing into his hands. His hands knew just where to scratch, just how to soothe. What was he going to do? Send Barney to be dog food? Shoot him and let him rot? He rested his forehead on Barney's. "I don't know how to fix this. I'm so fucking scared, guys."

Barney lipped at his hand, demanding his treat. Spoiled rotten beast. He gave Barney a scant handful of feed. "There you go, huh? I swear, if I could find you another home, I would, but no one around here is any better off."

And no one would thank him for an old pony that hadn't been any good for anything since Daddy had brought him home for his fifth birthday.

Well, that wasn't true. That ornery pie-eyed paint had taught Stetson what being thrown felt like. Every single time he'd tried to get Barney to cross the cattle guard out on their ranch road, Barney tossed his ass to the dirt and trotted back to the barn.

Still, every time it had happened, Momma and Daddy had shaken their collective heads and told him to cowboy up and get back on.

Every single time he'd saddled up again, ridden, then brushed and fed and watered and checked hooves, because that was the cowboy way. God gave them critters; they took care of them.

"You want that walk, Barney?" He grabbed a lead to clip to Barney's halter. Sure enough, that tail swished and Barney backed up, waiting for him to open the stall door. "I got you, buddy. I won't steer you wrong."

One way or the other, he would figure this out. He would. He had to.

They headed out to the pasture. "Cowboy up or get in the truck, right, Barn?"

Barney's whinny cut through the morning like an air horn. Stetson actually smiled. Right. Ponies didn't give a shit about taxes or losing the land your mom's family had owned for four generations and your daddy expanded to something amazing.

They cared about fresh air and carrots and sweet feed. And other horses.

They sure as shit didn't care about the old cowboy that showed up with said sweet feed, who was losing his momma and his mind. Oh, that was funny, except not.

They took two turns around the fenced-off pasture, Barney eager, not even stumbling once. What a good boy. Stetson turned him back toward the barn, but he didn't balk, just followed Stetson right on back to where it was warm.

Good, Stetson wasn't sure he was up to a fight this morning.

What he was in the mood for now was going to check in on Curtis…. Yeah. He stabled Barney and rubbed him down before checking in on a few more of the older horses. Then he wanted home.

By the time he headed back to the house, he was feeling like himself, and he held on to the thought, knowing it wouldn't last farther than his driveway. The moment he went inside and saw his mom's empty kitchen and Curtis's go bag on the floor… well, he'd be pissing off those voices again.

That was okay. He'd take what he could get.

Stetson laughed, a low, raw sound, when he saw Curtis still in his bed, wrapped around his pillow. Christ, the man was beautiful. Dark brown hair curled a little long over forehead and nape, and those bright blue eyes were closed, hidden by dark lashes most women called unfair.

He was going to go to his grave loving this man.

Okay. He needed to get headed down to Santa Fe. Shower. Cereal. Driving. That was his life, after all. These days.

He took one more long look, and then he got moving and got out of there. Momma was waiting on him.

CHAPTER SIX

CURTIS WISHED he'd been able to ride in with Stetson, but the damned fool had left him in bed, a note on the bathroom mirror.

"Cereal on the counter. Hot water heater works good now. Feel free to bring sausage biscuits."

He shook his head, grinned at the stubborn fool. Stetson made him absolutely crazy. As if he would rather sleep in than be there. He wasn't lazy, and Stetson knew it. Someone was running from him.

His phone rang, Miles Bend's name showing up.

"Yo! Buddy!"

"Where the fuck are you, CT? You okay?"

"Yeah. Had a friend having a family emergency, so I stopped in to help out."

"Anything we can do?" Oh, Miles was a damn good friend.

"Not right now. I'll let you know." He needed to get to the hospital, so he headed out to his rental, grabbing a protein bar out of his bag. Cereal was too much sugar. He needed nuts and a tiny touch of honey.

"Good deal. Stay in touch."

"I will. Hey, who won Dallas?" Curtis asked.

"Nate. He's on a wee hot streak. Asshole."

"Yeah." Curtis chuckled. "I'm going to kick his butt at the Finals."

"You know it. I expect you to take the whole shebang." Miles had his back.

"I'd better. I put too much time in this season not to." Curtis hopped in the truck and went hands-free with the phone.

"No shit on that. So where the hell are you? I mean, I know you said helping a friend, but where? Texas?"

"Santa Fe." He winced a little, waiting for Miles to question him.

"Santa Fe? Like as in the place where you look for Stetson every time you ride?"

"Yeah." He sighed, hating that the reason for him being here was so bad. "His momma is real sick."

There was a pause and then a sigh in return. "Man, that sucks. I'm sorry. Can we do anything?" Miles asked again.

"I don't think so, buddy. She's got Alzheimer's. I'd say she's going into the last stage soon. She don't remember that me and Stetson ain't seen each other in a while." The thought turned his stomach, made a lump lodge in Curtis's throat.

There was a long pause, then, "I'll say a prayer that it's easy as it can be. I know that's a hard row to hoe."

"It is. I hate to see her like this, but she was damned tickled to see me." Anything he could do to make it better.

"Well, you're a good guy, that's for sure." Miles's voice dropped. "How's he looking, your ex?"

"Skinny. Tired." Beautiful. Still the best thing Curtis had ever seen in his whole life.

"Ah. Well, that's a thing, I guess."

What the hell did that even mean? Maybe it was just one of those things folks said when they didn't know what to say. Curtis chuckled. "Yeah. I'll holler at you if I need you, buddy, I promise."

"Keep your chin up and remember us. Don't get lost in the desert."

"I won't. Later." He hit the button to hang up and hunted the satellite radio for something to wake him up some more. He hated to admit it, but now that he was older he could see staying on longer, letting the desert sink into his bones and nail his boots to the ground.

Letting Stetson sink into him, into his fucking soul.

That way lay madness. They'd never been able to make it work. They wanted different things, and neither one of them wanted to change. Hell, it wasn't healthy to do that, right? To try and change for someone? Better to just drop it.

Curtis chuckled, the sound raw as hell. Drive. No thinking. He'd stop in Santa Fe and grab breakfast burritos and sausage biscuits. It was way easier to get egg whites in Santa Fe than in Española or something.

He sure wanted to dive into some green chile chicken stew, though. Maybe he could get the shit to make it tonight. He had a feeling Stetson would want to go home again, recharge with the horses and all. They could have a fire in the fire pit, drink a beer.

He grabbed food and good coffee, then headed to the home. Time to visit Miz Betty and spend a little time with his Mr. Wrong.

A whole new crew of nurses greeted him this morning, and he wished he'd gotten doughnuts or some such for them. This had to be the suckiest job ever, dealing with dying folks and their hysterical families. Saints, the lot of them.

Stetson was heading out as he was walking in, face like a thundercloud. "I need a cigarette."

"What's up, babe?" Uh-oh. That didn't look good at all. "I brought food."

"Thanks. She's just in a temper. I just need a few minutes, okay?"

"Sure. Why don't you go sit and eat in the truck? I got Miz Betty a couple of hash brown thingies."

"She'll love that. Thanks, cowboy. I appreciate you."

I appreciate you.

God, when had those words become something he ached to hear? "You holler if you need me to come back out with you for a few."

He headed in before he could say anything else, because he would just want to go sit with Stetson, and he was meant to be here for Betty.

Betty was sitting up in the bed, her cheeks as red as her son's. "Curtis."

"Hey, Miz Betty. How are you doing today? I brought you fried potatoes."

"I… I'm embarrassed, to be honest. Stetson let me think…. You must think I'm a doddery old woman, and aren't you dear to come out and…. Fried potatoes, huh?"

He raised a brow. "Yes, ma'am. I know you like them."

"Thank you. You aren't his lover anymore. He made you leave, ran you off. I remember now."

Curtis pulled a face, wishing Stetson had warned him that "in a temper" meant lucid and pissed off about it. Besides, it had been more he'd left in a fit of fury and Stetson hadn't ever run after him. "We both screwed up, Miz Betty."

"Yes, well. It was the dumbest move he ever made, letting you get away."

"Oh, I doubt it." He winked. "Men are fools, aren't we?"

"Yes." She shook her head. "He looks like shit, and if he doesn't stop smoking, I'm going to beat his butt."

"I'll tell him." Curtis settled on the chair Stetson had vacated and pulled out the food. "I'm sure sorry you're not feeling well, Betty."

"I'm dying and we both know it. Are you here for me or for Stetson?"

He met her direct gaze with his, a smile quirking his mouth. Now this was the Betty he knew and loved. "I'm here because he asked me to come."

"Nice." She ate part of the hash brown and then put it down. "I'm tired. I wanted Stetson to be happy, I guess. That was you. He was happy with you."

"We had some good times, for sure." What else could he say? "I still love him. We just had different ideas, is all."

"Yeah. He's a homebody. He didn't get that from his daddy, no way."

Curtis didn't know about that. Parker Major had left his family regularly for the circuit when Stetson was a baby and had died in the arena when the man was a teenager. Curtis reckoned the need for a stable base had come from his daddy, about a hundred percent.

"Did you want some tea or something?" he asked, sidestepping that discussion.

"No. No, I don't think so." She offered him a half grin. "I'm sorry you had to see this. Stetson shouldn't have called just because I was silly."

"He's a good son, Betty, a good man."

"I know that." She sighed. "I worry what he'll do when I'm gone, is all. That ranch is hocked to the sky."

"Shut up, Momma." Stetson's voice snapped out, sharp enough to sting. "I'm fine."

She set her mouth in a mutinous line. "Sure, son. Fine and dandy."

Lord, he did hate to be in the middle of a family thing.

"Thanks for breakfast, cowboy. I appreciate it. You get you some hash browns, Momma?" Stetson stood near the bed, shutting down the conversation with an iron fist. It would have been more impressive if it hadn't been sad.

"I did." She picked up another piece and nibbled. "Thank you, Curtis."

"You're both very welcome." Curtis went for a smile, trying to smooth feathers.

Stetson was all stony-faced, but the man kept his mouth shut, and soon Miz Betty was jabbering about something that he didn't know about at all, something from some time in her memory. Her sharp gaze had gone cloudy again, and Curtis wondered if that was a strategic retreat or a real loss of self.

From the sad resignation on Stetson's face, he was betting on the latter.

It fucking sucked. This was no fair, no fair at all. He would rather see a snappish Miz Betty than this blank, almost girlish and confused lady.

"Hola, Señora Betty. Time for your bath." A cheerful, round nurse walked in, smiling at him, then Stetson. "Sophia is here to set your hair too."

"Do I like Sophia, son?" She looked to Stetson, then him, and Stetson nodded.

"You do, Momma. She's real nice. Come on, cowboy. Let's go."

"See you later, Miz Betty." Curtis bent to kiss her cheek, seeing the tear there but not mentioning it. That would be rude.

"We'll be right downstairs, Momma," Stetson murmured. "You enjoy your hairdo, huh? Sophia is a nice lady. She painted your toes for you, remember?"

Her entire face lightened up at Stetson's words. "Yes! I do like the pretty colors."

"There you go."

Curtis grabbed the bag of food and followed Stetson out of the room, listening to the nurse jabber at Betty. Man, had it only been a half hour in there? It had seemed like the clock had stopped.

"Sorry about that. She comes and goes."

"I guess. She's pretty sharp in there sometimes, huh?"

"Yeah. That's almost worse. Then she's pissed off."

"I guess then she knows that something is wrong." That would sure piss Curtis off. He feared head injuries for just that reason. No one wanted to be trapped inside a burning building of a body. Worse to be trapped in a functioning one and not be you no more.

Stetson nodded to him and led him to this quiet little lounge with big old couches and some tables and an ancient TV blaring some ladies' talk show. "You sleep okay?"

"I did. I would've run in with you, Roper."

"I left early, but thank you. I try and spend a couple nights in the horse trailer, just to save."

Gas. Tires. Oil. That was all left unsaid, but Curtis got it. "Shit, you can leave your truck here, and we'll take the rental home tonight. You got a four-wheeler if you need something on the ranch, right?"

"I do. It's better than a work truck, you know?"

"Yep. Gets in way tighter spots, even with a trailer." Bam. Go him. He'd gotten him a passenger on the way back tonight.

He could think of precious little better than time alone with Stetson in the dark, music playing, miles flashing by. Well, unless it was fucking Stetson until neither of them could see, but that wasn't what his mountain cowboy needed right now, was it?

Not that he hated the idea conceptually. In theory it sounded heavenly. He just knew he needed to tell his dick to stay down and give Stetson breathing room. For now.

Stetson opened his coffee and drank deep, leaning back into the cushions.

"I still got two burritos." He'd had one with egg whites, but the rest were normal in case someone else wanted one.

"I'll take one, if you don't want it." Stetson nodded. "Although I had a bowl of cereal this morning."

"Hey, if you have one, so will I." He'd always been able to con Stetson into eating by having something himself.

"Yeah? Thank you. I appreciate it. I keep saying that, but it's true."

"Oh, Roper, I just give a shit, is all. Always have."

"Yeah. Yeah, that wasn't ever our deal."

"I know." He was starting to wonder why their deal had been such a big thing that he left.

Hell, he wanted to know why the fuck they couldn't have a new deal that didn't involve misery. Well, part of that was Stetson's momma, he guessed, at least right now.

Stetson ate his burrito without a word, head down, so fucking quiet.

Curtis wanted to crawl over on the sofa with him and cuddle him. He had this terrible urge to hold Stetson all the time, which was kinda counterproductive, because he couldn't shield Stetson from any of this.

"Is there anything else I can do? I can stay for about a week, so I might as well help out."

"That long?" Stetson grinned at him, the look a mixture of amusement and longing. "I'll have to buy chicken breasts and egg whites to feed you."

"You have a lot of cereal," Curtis agreed. "I can get groceries. Y'all have a Whole Foods."

"I eat cereal and whatever frozen suppers are on sale."

"Well, like I said, I'll buy the groceries. I know I'm a prima donna." He had to be even more careful now. Back in the day, he'd eaten light so he could drink beer. Now he put on five pounds by looking at a cheeseburger like he'd had at the diner the other night.

"No, you have a career to protect, huh?"

"I do. Least for a while longer." He chuckled, thinking how his shoulder probably wouldn't last too many more seasons. The bulls and broncs were getting stronger every fucking year. And him? Well, he wasn't.

"You're the best, cowboy. You have a lot to be proud of." That dark gaze caught his, holding it, making him flush.

"Thanks. I figure on backing off some next year. This needs to be my year."

"You'll do it. I have faith in you. You rode Appleseed, after all."

"Yeah, and everyone predicted that one would kill me."

"I made good money betting on your skinny ass."

"No shit? Well, bet on me in the all-around. I'm gonna do it." Curtis knew the warm glow of pleasure he felt was silly, but it spread through his belly anyway.

"You got it." Stetson nodded like that was that, grabbed his coffee cup, and drank.

"You want to get out of here for a few, Roper? Just drive a little or something?"

"God, yes. I hate it here. That antiseptic smell...."

He could only imagine. Curtis had been in the frickin' hospital once for an entire week, and that had made him crazy.

This had to be the worst kind of hell.

"Well, let's check in with the nurse's station so they know and head out." Curtis stood, waiting for Stetson to join him.

Stetson took his hand, levered himself up, and surprised him with a quick, hard hug. "I know it ain't real, cowboy, but...."

Curtis took it, the scent of Old Spice and Irish Spring soap strong. He loved touching this man. They fit together like hand in glove. Always had.

"Shut up." He patted Stetson's back. "I got you."

"I.... Come on. We got to get moving, huh? We can just drive." Stetson all but charged to the nurse's station.

"We'll take the rental." That way Stetson couldn't smoke, and they'd be less likely to break down.

"Works for me." Stetson could hide behind the brim of his hat better than anyone he'd ever met. "You can drive."

"Sure, babe." Curtis loved driving around Santa Fe, with its weird warren of roads and crazy buildings. Maybe they could even head down to Madrid and back.

Wherever, so long as Stetson relaxed. He was so tense he was gonna explode, and that did no one any good.

Maybe Curtis could feed the man again too.

Something decadent so he could watch Stetson eat. He lived for those little sex noises Stetson made when he ate barbecue or cheesecake or something.

Maybe cannoli. Watching that gave him a happy that wouldn't quit.

"What are you grinning so hard for?" Stetson asked after he'd left a note with the nurses to call if anything happened.

"Thinking about watching you eat." Might as well hang for a sheep as well as a lamb. The statement was honest, at least.

Stetson blinked at him, and then he got a warm, pleased grin.

Yeah. Woo. He led the way out to the truck, a little bounce in his step. Okay, so the situation sucked. Didn't mean they couldn't make the best of it.

He had the one he wanted for a couple of days. He might as well be hip-deep in it.

CHAPTER SEVEN

STETSON HAD called the nurses, and they said Momma was sleeping hard, the bath and hairdo wearing her out, so they headed out to the ranch while there was still daylight.

That was when he remembered why he lived here, why he stayed. His soul was in this land, buried in the dirt like the pueblos. The sky was huge and blue, the sun sinking into his bones and making the cold seem like it wasn't even there.

Curtis whistled, shoveling manure like a man possessed. Silly man, happy with something to do for him.

He found himself aching to get Bell and Vixen saddled up, run them down along the river. They needed the exercise, and it wasn't like it was hot or anything…. He stared off at the horizon, the longing huge.

"You wanting to ride, Roper?" Curtis asked.

"How did you know?" He hadn't said a word.

"You keep looking at the clouds. I haven't had a pleasure ride since I went to visit Shelly in Montana a few years ago."

"No shit? That's a long time, cowboy. We could go now."

"We so could." Curtis moved close, bumping hips with him. "Let's play."

"I'll grab the saddles. You get the horses."

"Point me and shoot me." Curtis slapped one hand on his leg, so tickled it was palpable.

Curtis didn't know his stock anymore, did he? He whistled up the horses, and Bell and Vixen came right up, eager as all get-out.

"Oh, look at you two." Curtis clipped leads to harnesses and led the horses into the yard for him to saddle up.

Blanket. Saddle. Cinch strap. The motions were easy as pie, natural as breathing. Stetson found peace in the simple actions, in the warmth and the scent of the horses.

"You should ride every day, Roper." Curtis watched him like a hawk.

"I do when I have time." He tried not to get defensive. Curtis wanted the best for him. There was no accusation going on there. Just a desire for him to do something he loved.

"That's not what I meant, butthead. I meant you can tell it makes you damn happy."

"It does. I love the horses; you know that." His horses were his whole world. The goats and donkey and everything else were amazing, but the horses he needed like air. There were days, years even, where nothing else made sense.

"Yessir. More than anything." Curtis took the reins once he had Bell tacked out. Then he measured the stirrups against one arm. It gave Stetson a happy, seeing the easy motion, the way Curtis was made for this, sorta like he was.

Stetson got Vixen ready quick as a snap, the sweet girl stamping and tossing her head in excitement. "Don't make me put on a tie-down, you pain in the butt."

"She's ready to go, huh?" Curtis grinned, swinging up easily on Bell.

"She's a butthead, and she needs exercise." Stetson settled in the saddle, feeling like this was where he belonged, one hundred percent, balls to bones. "Let's head down to the water, see what we can see."

"Sounds good. Lead the way, huh? Been a long time." Curtis didn't look like he'd been out of the saddle at all.

"Doesn't look it."

"Thanks, Roper."

Curtis had called him by that nickname ever since they'd met. Stetson had curled his lip and said, "Roughstock riders. All hat and no cattle."

Curtis had laughed and said, "What are you, a roper?"

He was, but not professionally. Professionally he was a cowboy. Cattle. Horses. Land. Periodic woodwork on the side. Maybe more than periodic.

They headed out, the wind bracing, stealing his breath, and he loved it. He loved how the cold air really curled a man's nose hairs, how the sky was so frickin' clear and the land was so red and tan and vibrant.

For the first time in months, he felt himself relax, let himself feel like he was home. He grinned when Vixen tossed her head again, then gave her a lot of rein. "Go, girl."

They started running, Vixen taking off like shit through a goose, her hooves churning up the dirt. He heard Curtis whoop, and Bell was behind them suddenly, pushing them. No way would Bell outrun Vixen, though.

He leaned down, reducing the resistance and letting the speed wipe him clean. They hurtled toward the river, Vixen surefooted on the uneven ground, skirting rocks and brush.

God, please, he prayed. *Help me. Help me survive this. I need you.*

They pulled up in a lazy circle before they hit the riverbank. He didn't want Vixen too close to the loose soil there. If she wanted a drink, there was a cutout a few hundred yards downstream.

"God, baby." The heat in Curtis's voice surprised him, and he raised one eyebrow in question. "Look at you ride."

Stetson felt himself flush—from top to bottom, just flooding with heat. Those blue eyes took in every detail, and he couldn't escape them. Didn't want to.

"You were born for it, I swear to God." Curtis didn't hide his hunger, the way that he wanted to touch. Taste.

Oh God. Stetson remembered that.

Curtis had an amazing mouth and loved to use it. Kissing, sucking, licking…. His cock hardened, which amazed him a little. Still worked. Go him.

He shifted in the saddle, and Curtis grinned at him like he knew what he was thinking. Hell, it had to be obvious, even with him straddling leather.

"You be good now." He didn't want that. In fact, he was hoping for not good at all.

"Too late for that, Roper. I'm a bad boy."

"Flirt. I remember all too well how bad you could be."

"I'm not flirting. I'm stating intent. I'm gonna have you, Stetson." Curtis was so damned… sexual. He'd always loved that.

"Are you?" He didn't think he'd mind. In fact he might beg for it, just one more time.

"I am. I been thinking on it a lot, and I reckon it's what we both want, even if it's just while I'm here this time."

"It is." Why fight it, right? He wasn't going to get a lot more chances at this. Shit, his chances were rolling downhill straight to hell.

"That's it." Curtis chuckled, nudging Bell into a walk along the river.

They wandered, nice and easy, not talking, just being there. The horses seemed to feel the same way, tails and ears flicking. The wind was quiet down here, and the water was burbling along.

He liked that Curtis didn't need to babble, that they could be still. They stopped at a clearing where he could see straight down through to the mountains. This was his momma's favorite place in the world, this cut of land.

I was born right down there, son, in the same house your gran was born in right down there. He could hear her, clear as a bell, telling him the stories of his people, one after another, generations of love right here.

He almost doubled over with the pain of it just then. She would never see this view again, not in person, and if he showed her a picture, would she remember?

Vixen danced underneath him, and Curtis reached for him, quick as any safety man he'd ever seen in an arena. "Hold it together, Roper."

"I'm trying, Curtis. I can't fucking breathe."

"I know. I want to make it better for you."

But Curtis couldn't. No one could. Stetson grabbed Curtis's hand and held on. That was the best he had.

Curtis tugged him down off Vixen, then pulled him into a hug that damn near hurt, he needed it so much. His horses all ground tied, so he didn't worry about it, just held on.

He didn't cry, didn't kiss or think. He just held on tight.

The solid feel of Curtis holding him up, breathing with him, made it better. A lot better.

"I'm sorry, cowboy. In a perfect world...." Well, he'd be rich and stable and he'd be one of Curtis Traynor's sponsors, not a broke-dick dirt farmer.

"Shit, that's never gonna happen." Curtis kissed his cheek, purely platonic. "No one wants perfect, Roper."

"Handy, since no one gets it." He looked at the view, the gorgeous sight of bright blue bouncing off the red dirt of the desert.

"It's so quiet here." Curtis sounded pleased, not unhappy. Stetson reckoned the rodeo life was rarely silent. That had been one of the reasons he didn't want to go with Curtis. Not the biggest reason. Hell, not even in the top ten, but it was a reason.

"It's heaven." He believed that, with all his heart. This ranch, the land, it was the closest to the good Lord as he could hope to get.

"It's God's country, for sure. And I'm from Texas, so that means something." Curtis chuckled, a teeny puff of sound.

"I promise not to tell you were unfaithful, cowboy."

"Thanks." The chuckle turned to a full-out laugh. "I got to uphold the Lone Star, or they'll run my ass out on a rail."

He found himself smiling, and he leaned into Curtis's arms for a second longer before pulling away to stand on his own holey boots.

"You ready to do some more riding, babe? I want to see some of that ghost town."

"Let's go. You want some water? I grabbed a couple bottles."

"Sounds great." Curtis took a bottle from him, long, tanned throat working hard when he swallowed. Stetson wanted to touch, wanted to feel Curtis's Adam's apple bobbing under his fingers.

He took a deep breath. Ghost town. They'd gone there a lot when Curtis had stayed with him before.

There wasn't any cell service that far out either. No one could bother them. He wanted to just keep riding, to forget everything else for a long while.

Maybe it was shitty of him, but he could live with that fact.

"Hey." When he looked over, Curtis smiled. "I put some granola bars in my pocket."

"Did you? I'd share one with you." Curtis kept trying to feed him; he must be skinny.

"Cool. I'm starving." The cooler air and higher altitude meant Curtis needed more too. Man had not one spare ounce on him.

"That doesn't surprise me. You're at your fighting weight. You looking forward to heading back?"

"I want the season over, so kinda." Curtis shrugged before pulling out a bar for them to share. "I don't know. I'm thinking of skipping stock show season in January."

"Yeah? I've gone to Fort Worth a few times, but not in a while." Thinking of skipping the big shows? That didn't bode well.

"There's some high-dollar money there, but if I win the season this year, I can take off until Austin, maybe."

"That's in what? March? April?" He'd never been there. Austin was expensive, especially now.

"Yeah. Ish. Houston is close to the same time." Curtis sighed. "I got nowhere to stay if I'm not traveling, really, so maybe it's a pipe dream."

He opened his mouth to tell Curtis the man could stay with him, but that was a pipe dream too. Curtis came for Momma, and he had no way to know if Momma'd be here in the spring.

"You ought to buy you a place, huh?"

"That's your thing, Roper. I never thought I'd live long enough to ponder retirement."

Stetson wasn't sure what the fuck to say to that. His thing, like this place, this land, was just another weight around his neck when he would sell his soul to keep it.

"I didn't mean to piss you off, baby."

"I ain't your baby no more," he snapped. "Fuck, man, I appreciate you coming out, but you don't have to stay. You made Momma happy. That's why you came. I promise the grass isn't going to come up and wrap around your boots, hold you here. It's the wrong time of the year, and we don't have enough water for that anyway."

"Whoa. Whoa, now. What's got a bee in your bonnet?" Curtis looked confused as all get-out, and didn't that just piss Stetson off more?

"Why would I be bitchy? I got nothing to bitch about, man. You left, and we both know your happy ass never so much as looked back for me. Not once. You could have…. Anytime. Any fucking time you could have called up and said something, but you didn't." His fists clenched up and both horses started tossing their heads, whinnying at the tension in the air.

"Neither did you."

"What?"

Curtis shrugged, lip curling just enough to make Stetson want to beat the living fuck out of the bastard. "I didn't see you calling or coming to an event none. I didn't see you out there looking for me, any more than I looked for you, so quit being a titty-baby and walk it the fuck off." Curtis wheeled around so they were facing each other. Then one hand landed on the center of his chest, not quite a blow, totally not a caress. "You want to fight, Roper? Bring it on. I'll let you kick my ass, and you can pretend not to know I allowed it. We fucking broke up. I was a kid with big balls and dreams, and you were fucking scared to walk away from here in case it changed while you weren't here to watch it. Now you're a lonely old fuck with a dying momma, and I live in my fucking truck chasing the bright lights and broncs. Suck it up, buttercup, and get the fuck over yourself."

"Fuck you, Curtis." Shit, he hadn't heard Curtis say that many words in a row… ever.

"There are a metric fuckton of goat heads down here, Roper, and I'm too old for that shit."

God, that slow drawl made him want to smile. "I missed you. I was scared to call. What if you didn't remember me?" He felt a little as if the question scraped his soul like a wire brush.

Curtis hooted, the sound lonely and sad. "Like I wouldn't know you in my cups or in my grave. There ain't a handle made for the knife we sharpened between us."

No. No, that was true. They hurt each other in the deep places.

"I don't like to think of you living in your truck, Curtis."

He got this warm smile that threatened to plant a seed in him.

"And I don't like to think of you dealing with this all alone, Roper."

"You're welcome to stay here through the holidays, you know. I just... I mean, shit, never mind. Who wants to be here like this?" His cheeks burned with a mixture of rage and want and shame.

They looked at each other for a long, silent minute—hell, it might have been a month that he stood there, lost in Curtis's eyes, before either the cold or the weight of all their combined bullshit got to them and they turned as a man and got back in the saddle.

"I'd love to stay through Thanksgiving. I don't have to be anywhere until two days before the Finals."

"Would you?" The words were out of his mouth before he even thought to yank them back.

"Yeah." Curtis beamed at him. "Been staying in hotels the last few years. Hell, I'd rather eat at the Golden Corral with you than do that."

"We probably will. After Momma's meal there at the hospital."

"Sounds good." Curtis nudged Bell close, their legs brushing. "Anything with you does."

"Yeah. I hear that." He sighed softly. "It's getting colder. We got to get back and feed."

"We should." The old ghost town was just in sight, the off-kilter mining office roof still intact. Curtis nodded to it. "Remember that weekend we camped there?"

"I do. We damn near froze our balls off." They'd managed to keep warm, though. More than warm. They'd performed some amazing gymnastics.

"We also found a way to make heat," Curtis said, echoing his thoughts.

"We did. Although that family of coyotes were sure unhappy about us being there. You remember how they howled?" It had been eerie as fuck for him, and he'd grown up around the critters. Curtis had damn near swallowed his tongue.

"Oh God. I thought we were gonna get eaten." They'd laughed and laughed the next day.

"You did. Lord, they were so loud."

They turned back toward the ranch, both chuckling. Lord have mercy, he could remember Curtis running to the door, all naked, chucking firewood at the coyotes, howling like a monkey.

Stetson laughed harder, making Vixen snort and toss her head.

"Don't you get bucked off, Roper."

"No. No, it's been too good a day for that. Thank you for this."

"You're welcome." Curtis grinned at him like this whole thing was perfect. It would be too, if it wasn't about his mom dying.

Still, it was what it was, and he was going to take it.

CHAPTER EIGHT

"HEY, MIZ Betty. Looks like they got a big old feast set up in the dining room." Curtis had come on inside while Stetson parked the truck. They were still in his rental, but Curtis tried not to drive in the snow, and God knew, it was coming down out there.

Betty had started slipping bad after that morning where she'd been so aware and present. She'd stopped talking much and had looked at her beloved iced tea like it was foreign to her. It was as if she'd had that moment of amazing clarity because she was about to lose what little she had left. He hoped today God would give them a little miracle, just a day where she could enjoy herself.

Betty stared at him, blinking at him all slow, like a sun-dazed lizard.

Damn. Curtis pulled up a chair. "Stetson is on his way. Are you looking forward to pumpkin pie?"

"Are you a nurse?" she asked. "My nurse is a girl."

"No, ma'am. My name is Curtis, and I'm a friend of your son's." He kept his tone cheerful. Showing he was upset would push her into panic.

"Stetson. My son's name is Stetson. He's working horses today." She did smile then, as if the thought of Stetson was a ray of light.

"Is he? Maybe he'll come see you. It's Thanksgiving."

"Did my momma come and bring her pie? She always makes the pie, and I make the turkey and tamales."

Stetson walked in. "Hey, Momma. Having a good day today?"

"Where's your Grandma Flora, Stetson?" Betty was ramping up. Curtis knew his nearness might be setting her off, so he eased out of the chair and faded to the back of the room.

"Are you craving her pie, Momma?" Stetson came to her, smiled, but it wasn't happy. It was so sad.

"She always makes the pie, baby." Miz Betty smiled at Stetson, holding out a hand.

"She does."

Her frown deepened. "Parker, I meant to tell you that I couldn't make fudge this year."

"Daddy won't care, Momma."

"I just didn't have time." Betty patted Stetson's hand. "I got my hair done, though."

"It looks great. Did you want to get in the chair and go see the dining area?"

"No. No, I don't want to go anywhere right now. I want to watch the parade."

"I think the parade is over, Momma."

"I want to watch the motherfucking parade!" Her scream was loud and sudden and had him jerking out of his chair.

"Curtis, can you grab a nurse, please?"

"Yeah." He pelted down the hall, looking for anyone who might be able to help. "Mrs. Major needs a nurse," he told Anna at the duty desk.

He could hear her absolutely losing her shit, then the sound of flesh on flesh.

The nurses ran in, and Stetson stepped out of the room, a handprint on his face like it was painted there.

Fuck. Curtis walked over and put his hand on Stetson's hip. "You okay?"

"Yeah. Yeah, I'm… I'm going to smoke."

Betty was screaming her dead husband's name. God, this sucked so hard.

"No. Come sit in the truck with me a minute." No smoking, damn it. That was bad for a body.

"Just for a minute." Stetson was fixin' to lose his shit.

Curtis tugged him outside and took him to the truck. Lord, the snow muffled the whole world, making it seem like they were the only two people around.

He could feel Stetson trembling beneath his hand.

Curtis steered Stetson into the back seat of the king cab, where they could sit together, then grabbed him for a hug.

"I don't know how I can do this." The whisper was soft, scared as hell.

"Oh, babe, I'm sorry. I got you." He did. He'd come back after the Finals. He would stay as long as he could because Stetson needed him. Him.

"Because I'm such a prize. I couldn't even stay awake to screw around last night."

"Hey." Curtis stroked Stetson's cheek. "You need rest more than anything. I understand that, okay? Just breathe."

When had Stetson gotten old? The lines carved into that dear face owed way more to worry than to smiling. This wasn't even a middle-aged man. Stetson was still young, dammit.

He had this crazy urge to tie Stetson down and get in the driver's seat and go. Anywhere. Glenwood Springs. Jackson Hole.

Hell, Durango. Even Denver. He didn't care; he just wanted to escape. That wouldn't help, and it wouldn't be right, especially for Betty. Didn't stop the urge.

"Hell of a Thanksgiving, huh?"

"Shit happens." He said it against Stetson's neck.

"Yeah. Yeah, that it does."

"I'm just sorry she's having a tough day. What do we do now?"

"Wait to see if they have to sedate her. If they did, we'll just go and have supper together."

"Okay, sure. You want me to go check?"

"No. No, I'll just text Mari. She'll know. She's a really good lady."

"Cool." When Stetson pulled out his phone and took a few steps away, so did Curtis, hunting for someplace not the Golden Corral to have Thanksgiving dinner.

He picked the restaurant at the La Fonda first, calling one of the biggie wows at the restaurant, praying Roberto was still working there. They'd ridden together for a season and a half, until the skinny son of a bitch broke his pelvis.

"La Plazuela, how may I help you?"

"Hey, there. Can I speak to Roberto please?"

"Just a moment, sir." He got put on hold, which he thought was a good sign. Of course, it wasn't like Roberto was a rare name out here.

"Hello?"

Score. Curtis knew that voice. "Hey, vato. How's it hanging?"

"Who is this? I know that voice...."

"Curtis Traynor, man. How's domestic life treating your happy ass?"

"Well, I'll be goddamned. How you doing, ese? All good?"

"Well, I've been riding great, for sure."

"You in town? I'll buy you a beer."

"I'm staying with friends up near Taos, but I can buy you a beer this weekend if you can do me a solid." He held his breath, hoping Roberto didn't tell him to go fly a kite. They'd been buds back on tour.

"If I can, sure. What you need?"

"Thanksgiving dinner? I know you might not be able to get us in at the restaurant, but we'd eat in the bar or something. My—" Curtis glanced at Stetson, who was still on the phone. "My guy's momma is real sick, and I want to do something special for him."

"I have a two top for you at six. No problem. Anything for you, Curtis."

That gave them a few hours to sit at the bar and…. Oh, maybe they should just get a room. He loved the La Fonda.

"You're a rock star. I owe you huge." He'd see if Stetson could get his friends to feed back at the ranch, just one more time.

"I'll see you at six. You thinking about staying here? I can forward you to Janelle."

"That would rock, man. I appreciate you." He really did. "We'll get together over that beer."

"Sounds good. Hold up."

He held on while Roberto transferred him, and by the time he hung up, he had a room and a dinner and a champagne romance package.

It felt a little over-the-top, a little weird, but… dammit, he wanted to give Stetson something. Something really good for this holiday. He deserved it so much.

"She's down for the count. She lost it, I guess. You think I should go sit with her? You think it's bad if I don't?"

"No. I think if she's sleeping and stuff, you should let her rest. We need to get the desk ladies anything?"

Stetson shook his head. "They've got all the pumpkin pie they can eat."

"Well, come on, then." He crawled out of the truck and walked around to the driver's door. Stetson was the only one he'd drive in the snow for, as a rule.

"Where are we going?"

"La Fonda. I have a buddy who's saving us a place at La Plazuela, and I got us a room. Do you think someone can hop over and do the feeding?"

"I paid Nestor to do it. I wasn't sure how things were going to work out. If she wanted dinner, we would have stayed late."

"Woo." And hoo, even. That was the best news ever. "Good deal. You got a good shirt on. We'll have a few drinks, have a meal. Have a nice long shower."

"That sounds like heaven." Stetson stepped into the passenger side, and the man looked at him like he was a real hero.

"It will be. I swear, babe." He was going to give Stetson the best Thanksgiving he could. Things would only get worse with Betty now, and they both knew it.

"Okay. I believe you." Stetson reached over, took his hand.

"Of course you do. I got your back. Always." Curtis got them moving, heading in toward the Plaza.

"Why did we break up? Do you remember?" Stetson said it with a tiny edge of sarcasm, but the question was serious too.

"I was on the road all the time. You stayed home. Hard to be a *we* when you're never together." Was that oversimplifying? Probably. "Simple fact is I was young and stupid."

"You weren't the only one. Momma hates me a little bit for not going with you."

"I don't think so, babe." Betty hated the whole world when she was aware of it, he'd bet. "I think she hates that she's leaving you so soon and wishes we'd settled together so you had someone full-time." It was easy to have perspective from the distance he had.

"Yeah, well, what's done is done, right?"

"It is." And he didn't want to talk on it too much since very little had changed, really. Lord, the area around the Plaza was already starting to light up with Christmas decorations. Not luminarias. That would come later, but it was pretty.

Stetson turned his hat in his hands, spinning it slowly.

"No more thinking, babe. Not today. We'll get to that, but not now."

"No? We're just going to eat turkey and pie?"

"Yep. Bob in the hot tub."

"Like I was Tracy Lawrence's frozen turkeys."

"Oh God, I love that story."

Stetson's grin made the world seem almost sunny. That was a damned fine thing. Curtis would take it.

They pulled up to the La Fonda and parked in the garage, leaving the snow behind them. The lobby to the historic hotel was buzzing, people chatting and wandering, music playing.

"You want to get a stool at the bar, Roper?"

"We can do that or I can grab one of them sofas."

"Oh, I like that. I'll get us a beer if I can. If not I'll grab a Coke."

"Sounds good. I could use a beer."

"I bet." Curtis wandered up to the bar, which was hopping, but not so busy he couldn't get service. "If I grab a beer, can we have them on the couches over there?" he asked.

"Sure, honey." The bartender grinned at him, her eyes lit up. "Give me five, huh?"

"I'm on it." He watched Stetson settle on a big couch, pulling into himself, still and silent. Seeing that made Curtis's heart hurt. He wanted to see the goofy, sexual guy he'd known.

Maybe he could coax that man out to play for a day or so. That would be something, right? Was that selfish? Was it better to just let Stetson fade and get all dry?

No, even if this was the most self-serving thing Curtis ever did, he wanted to make Stetson happy for a bit. Just for a few hours.

A day or two. Hell, he wanted to share orgasms, like ten or twenty. Food. Sex. All the good things in life.

They'd already gotten to ride horses.

"Here you go, hon." The bartender handed over two longnecks. Not Coors, thank God. Bud. He'd take it. "Fourteen."

He handed her a twenty. "Keep the change."

She'd remember him and give him what he wanted while they were at the hotel.

"Thanks!"

He grabbed both beers and headed over to sit with Stetson. "Here, babe."

"Thank you, sir." They clinked bottles, both of them sipping, just sort of watching the people around them.

Everyone had their own thing going, from the high mountain cowboy types waiting for the band to set up in the bar to the tourists bundled up against the outside air, just passing through and taking pictures of the famous Inn at the End of the Trail.

"I love how the whole Santa Fe cliché lives here." Stetson chuckled, waving his beer at a couple wearing Pendleton blanket coats and high boots.

"I know. The jewelry alone would fund my tour for a year."

"At least. Maybe two. I'm not sure that couple over there dripping in Old Pawn wouldn't do it, all by themselves."

"We could mug them." Curtis winked when Stetson almost snorted beer.

"Yeah, I can just see it." Stetson rolled his eyes like thrown dice and started drawling. "Pardon me, ma'am. Stick 'em up, y'all."

"Yep. That would be me. The gentleman robber."

"The classy Texan. I like it." Stetson grinned at him, the smile honest, happy. "I can see you as a bandit on the Santa Fe Trail, following the drovers and sneaking in."

"Yeah? You like the idea of me in all black?" Curtis loved to listen to Stetson spin yarns.

"An oilcloth coat and a hat pulled all down, your six-shooter on your hip."

"Lord, if I could hit the side of a barn with a baseball bat, that might be a good image." Curtis was a terrible shot. His daddy had despaired, and told him when he came out that it just figured.

There was that laugh again, and Curtis felt his heart clench. *Yeah. Fuck yeah.* He wanted that—not even Stetson's hard little body, which okay, he could slurp up with a spoon—but the happy laugh.

Curtis almost suggested seeing if they could check in right now, but he knew Stetson needed to ease into the evening, needed to unwind. His self-serving intentions only went so far. He guessed he might just love the son of a bitch still.

Curtis sat there for a moment, not surprised at all, just a little... off-kilter. He'd always known he still loved Stetson. Now Curtis knew he was still *in love* with him.

Stetson's laughter faded into soft chuckles, then disappeared. "You cool, cowboy?"

"I'm great, babe." Curtis shrugged off his weirdo moment. "You know I like your stories."

"I remember that. I can't help it. I love my Westerns."

"We should have a John Wayne marathon." Stetson had a thing for the really old movies. *Red River* and *Stagecoach*, that sort of thing.

"I'd like that. You know how I feel about the old stuff. Although the remake of *3:10 to Yuma* didn't suck."

"How could Russell Crowe and Christian Bale suck?" Rowr. Sad ending, lots of pretty. He could handle that.

"You have a point. Although I'm really more of a Kurt Russell guy."

"Yeah, you always did like that *Tombstone* movie, huh?" Curtis had adored Val Kilmer as Doc Holliday.

"Lord yes. I wish it was still like that, sometimes. No bill collectors, no taxes. Just horses and fast-draw pistols and land." There was a hunger in Stetson's face that stunned him, made him lean back some.

Maybe he could understand the need for a simpler life, but Stetson was looking for an escape.

"I hear you," Curtis said easily, not wanting to get into anything deep.

Stetson chuckled. "Now you? You got the cameras and the lights, the fame, the selfies. I bet you got yourself a publicist."

"I have the sponsors. They all have publicists that work for them. I keep it simple." Some of the guys he knew who'd broken out into bull riding had coaches and publicists and shit. Whole teams of people to kiss their asses. That wasn't Western one bit.

"Good." The single word was all Stetson seemed to have to say on the subject too. Just *good*.

He clinked his beer bottle against Stetson's, winking when his man glanced at him. God, his man. He was gonna get his heart broke again.

Stetson smiled, the look slow and wicked, promising things that needed to happen for both their sakes.

He chucked his worry right out the mental window.

"So, the special is turkey, I think. All the trimmings, including green chile biscuits." Curtis was tossing the diet today too. It was Thanksgiving. Calories didn't count on holidays.

"Oh, man. That sounds like heaven on a plate."

"I thought so. There are two kinds of pie." They shared a knowing glance. They would have one at supper and get the other to feed each other in their room.

If he was lucky, they'd only get one fork.

They sat and chatted, and Curtis would swear he saw Stetson relax with every passing second. Two beers in and Stetson began to laugh freely, the sound real, not sad and desperate.

They were on their third when Roberto saw them and headed over. "We had a cancellation. You lucked out, hombre. You get in early."

"You rock." Not that he wouldn't have taken food out in the bar over staying at the nursing home. Anything was better for Stetson today, but this was extremely awesome. "I owe you one, buddy."

"You do." One hand was held out to Stetson. "Roberto. Pleased."

"Stetson. Thank you so much."

"You're welcome, man. Happy Thanksgiving." Roberto gave them a sunny grin, and the hostess took over, leading them to a table for two tucked away along the back wall, away from the glass windows. That made it quiet, a little darker, more intimate.

Stetson took his hat off, put it on one of the hooks on the wall, and he did the same.

"Hi, boys. Roberto says you need a Thanksgiving dinner, so I'm guessing you want the special?" The waiter looked like a doll baby.

"I'd like that, please. Curtis?"

"Me too. The whole shebang." Thanksgiving was his cheat meal every year.

Stetson looked around the restaurant, gaze a little stunned, he thought, like Stetson was confused about something.

"What's the matter, babe?" He took Stetson's hand once they ordered iced tea.

"I just… look at this crowd. It's Thanksgiving. I mean, I get that some folks don't have people or are out of town, but…."

"But you'd be home if you could." Curtis nodded. He got that. Stetson was a man of tradition, a parade and football and turkey-in-the-oven kind of guy.

"Yeah." He got a twisted smile. "I know, I'm an old fuddy-duddy still. Prob'ly worse now. I appreciate you finding us a table, and it smells great. I was just surprised, is all."

"Yeah. I've been on the road every year since my last at your house. And you can stop with the fuddy-duddy shit. I wouldn't love you if you weren't you." *So there.*

Stetson stared at him, eyes wide as saucers. Definitely time to switch to tea so he could finish up the festivities later.

"You know, you're a butthead," Stetson finally replied.

"Am I? For what? Telling the truth?" He leaned his elbows on the table, wanting to hear Stetson's answer to that one.

"For telling me you love me still. You know it ain't fair."

"I know." Curtis paused, trying to push his thoughts into some kind of order. "It's true, though. I do. I miss you. I'm not sure it would be any different if we tried again, but I do care."

Stetson reached out and touched a button on his shirt. "Even if we did, right now, my life is broke and yours isn't. I appreciate it, though, the… shit, I don't know. Sentiment sounds kinda bitchy."

"Lord." He grinned. They were both dorks.

"Here you go, gents." A second waiter brought them rolls and their tea. "Green chile cheese breads."

This was New Mexico, after all.

They toasted with the biscuits, laughing as they did, the tension between them dissipating with a pop. Curtis moaned when the biscuity roll melted in his mouth. There was cornbread in the basket too, but he knew it would be too sweet for his Texas mind.

They didn't chat much; they just ate and watched each other, the other diners. The silence was comfortable. Comforting. Not strained at all, and Curtis wanted to fist-pump and cheer.

This was what he wanted. To give Stetson what no one else did, a few minutes of peace. Well, and a hot meal and good company. He hoped he was providing those too.

He reckoned he was, on both accounts.

When dessert came, they ordered coffee, strong and hot and flavored with pinyon. Yum.

"Oh, that hits the spot. Nice and sweet. I can't say when I've liked a cup more."

"Mmm." Curtis grinned into his cup. Stetson and his sweet tooth. The pie, now, that had homemade whipped cream. Uhn. He did love that stuff.

Stetson watched him lick the cream off the spoon, gaze sharp, hungry. "I think I'm gonna have to ask for more whipped cream."

"Okay." Curtis could get behind that.

To his utter shock, Mr. Staid and Steady waved the waiter down and asked for more. Oh, hello. Curtis chuckled. Yum.

The bowl of extra cream came, and Stetson pushed it over to him. "Take what you want, cowboy. I ordered it for you."

"Spoiling me rotten." Curtis grinned wide.

"Yeah-yeah. I just want to watch you enjoy it. It makes me ache."

"In a good way." He hoped so, for damn sure. This might just be working.

"In the best way."

"That's a fine thing, Roper." He shifted in his seat, everything tight below the belt.

"It is. You wanting me as bad as I'm wanting you?" Stetson looked upon him like a starving man at a banquet.

"I am." He wasn't gonna lie. They might be in some sort of holiday bubble that would never repeat itself, but Curtis felt as if this was his chance... well, for something. It was too new to figure out what.

"Good." Simple as that. Just good. "Eat your pie, cowboy."

"Yessir." He scooped more cream onto his pie before taking a big bite. Uhn. The pumpkin part was a little sour, spiced with comforting winter flavors. The crust was flaky. The cream made it so much better.

Stetson chuckled, the sound husky and sexual, but when Curtis glanced up, Stetson was deep in his coffee.

Tease. That was so much more like his old lover that Curtis ached inside.

Stetson took a bite of his own pie, humming a little deep in his chest. "This is good pecan pie. You want a bite?"

"Please." He half expected Stetson to offer over his plate for Curtis to scoop up a bite. Instead, Stetson fed him a bit from his fork.

Okay. He was going to cream his jeans, right here and now. It had been so damned long. So long.

"You like it?"

"Rich. Smoky." Curtis licked his lips. "Good."

"Yeah. Yeah, like the smell of a good fire, huh?"

"Exactly like that, and maybe a glass of whiskey."

"Yeah. Something nice and smooth." Stetson winked at him. "Not that I know dick all about whiskey."

"Nope. You're a beer man." Wasn't that a song?

"I most definitely am. Cheap and easy."

"Hey, now. I don't think you're easy at all." He waited for the pinch he knew was coming.

It landed on his inner thigh, sharp and teasing.

He hooted, then looked around. No one was paying them any attention. He finished up his pie before licking the cream remaining out of the bowl.

"Look at you!" Stetson stared at him like he'd grown a second head. "Lord have mercy, cowboy. You're... something else."

"Am I? I told you, no limits for Thanksgiving. I'll need to work it off later, though."

"I might—" Stetson went ruby red but didn't drop his gaze. "I might could help with that."

"I just bet you could." Curtis wanted to go get their room. Now. Still, how often did Stetson get to linger over a meal? He wouldn't push. "You ready to head upstairs? I am. I'm ready for you."

Now his cheeks heated. "I am." He waved down their waiter, hoping he wasn't being too much of a dick. "Can we get the check, please, sir?"

"Absolutely. Are you charging it to your room?"

"We haven't checked in yet, so I'll go ahead and pay." He handed over his debit card.

"Thank you for supper, cowboy. I appreciate it."

"I loved sharing it with you." He really did. The last few years had been lonely, and he hadn't even twigged to it until this week.

"Maybe...." Stetson stopped, shook his head. "I did too, cowboy. More than you'll ever know."

"Good." The waiter brought back his card so Curtis could sign the check. He stood, then held out a hand for Stetson. Tonight wasn't for maybes. It was just for them. A secret getaway.

They'd deal with the real tomorrow.

When Stetson took his hand right there in public, a savage sort of joy filled him. They checked in without a word, then headed upstairs. New beds, the desk man said, and he hadn't blinked an eye when they asked for one king. Santa Gay for the win.

They went up, both of them putting their hats aside and sitting to take their boots off. He guessed they'd both done this before—together and separate—so there was no reason to act like virgins. He felt weirdly calm, even with the shivery goodness of knowing Stetson was right there.

Curtis reckoned he knew what he wanted. No wondering.

He reached up to unfasten his collar, and Stetson stopped him. "I want to do that, cowboy. Please."

Curtis met those pretty dark eyes and nodded, letting his hands fall to his sides. "You got it, Roper."

"Thank you. I dream about this, sometimes, baring you to my eyes."

His buttons popped free easily, and Stetson leaned in, kissed the hollow of his throat as Stetson worked to open up his damn soul.

He slid one hand behind Stetson's head, that cowboy short hair soft against his fingers. "I dream about you all the time."

"Liar." Stetson's moan, though, said his lover believed him, knew there wasn't a hint of a lie to it.

"Not one bit." He took a kiss because he'd waited long enough and he didn't want to miss the chance.

There was the strangest slide again—one where time stopped and Stetson was eighteen again, but at the same time not. This version was lean muscle formed from years of carrying sorrow and worry on those shoulders.

Curtis backed up a bit and helped Stetson undress as well, counting new scars.

"You're fine to me." Stetson's fingers smoothed his shirt down off his shoulders, the rough edges of Stetson's callused fingers better than any silken touch.

"Am I?" His ribs stood out and he knew it, but he was pretty well put together for a skinny bull rider. To hear Stetson tell him meant a lot.

"Yessir." Stetson knelt before him, and he shook his head. He didn't need…. A soft kiss touched his belly, and he gasped.

His muscles pulled up tight, his hips rocking. He panted, wanting more. *Please God*, he prayed. *Let this be real. Let this happen.*

"You're thinking too hard." Stetson popped the button on Curtis's jeans. "You know this. We were always so good at this."

"We were. This part was easy."

"Of course, we were both kids…." The sound as Stetson unzipped him was so fucking loud, almost drowning him out.

"Were we? We sure were wild for each other."

Curtis cupped the back of Stetson's head again and tilted so he could stare into those eyes. "Make no mistake, Roper. I still am wild for you."

"Kiss me, cowboy. I need you."

"Good." Was there anything better than this? He kissed Stetson again and again, until the strain on his neck made him pull the man back up on the bed.

As fine as it had been to see Stetson kneeling in front of him, Stetson straddling his thighs was a special kind of bliss. Curtis caught his breath, his body going on high alert.

"Lord, you feel perfect," he said.

Stetson chuckled for him, then leaned down to kiss him, giving him enough to drown in. They changed the angle and kept going, lips and tongues meeting, pressing, moving.

He held on to Stetson like a drowning man held on to a life raft.

Stetson clung to him the same way, the need flaring between them, the heat rising.

Damn, this was everything he wanted right now. Everything on earth.

He reached down, grabbing that fine, fine ass encased in Wranglers. Even skinny as Stetson was, it was a double handful of hard muscle, and Curtis squeezed. Stetson arched for him, rocked back into his body. Damn, but that made his mouth dry.

Trying to memorize every moment, Curtis stared at Stetson. He would never let this go, would hold it in the long months to come on the road. God, that was a thought. He was fixin' to have to get on his pony and ride, but he sure as shit didn't want to.

"Hey. Stay with me, huh?" Stetson cupped his face, stroked his cheeks like he was precious.

"Right here, babe. I swear." He snapped back to the present, and he kissed Stetson once more, an addiction forming, that mouth like heaven.

Stetson rocked into him, again and again, that hard promise in his jeans enough to make him dizzy.

"Need the rest of your skin, Stetson. All of you." He stood, lifting them both off the bed easily. Damn, he needed to fatten up his lover.

He was supposed to be the light one.

"Anything you want, cowboy." The jeans stripped off easy as pie, and soon they were bare as the day they were born, sliding under the cold, crisp sheets and pressing together.

They lay on their sides, hands sliding on skin, the kisses taking on a different note now they were completely bare.

He couldn't keep his eyes open, couldn't do anything but touch and touch, stroking Stetson everywhere his hands could reach. He traced the line of shoulder and arm, then skated one hand over Stetson's ribs, which stuck out too damned much.

Stetson chuckled, then pushed more firmly into his fingers, deepening the touch.

"Mmm. Hungry man."

"I am. Strange, considering how much we just ate."

Curtis chuckled, nipping at that swollen lower lip Stetson presented. "Dessert."

"Had that too. Wasn't good as this."

"This is so much better." He ghosted over the small of Stetson's back, then stroked one asscheek. "An embarrassment of riches."

Stetson chuckled for him, the sound deep and secret, something that belonged to him and him alone. "You know it."

Then Stetson's hand—that amazing, rough, scarred hand—found their cocks and wrapped around them both, measuring them from base to tip.

Curtis caught his breath, his body stilling completely for a moment. Even his heart stuttered, he figured. "Been so damned long."

"You know it. No more." Stetson stroked him, the touch as sure and wonderful as it had been the last time.

"Uh-huh?" Speech was becoming a luxury. He grunted, his hips moving slow and steady as he pushed into that touch.

Neither of them seemed to mind a bit, to be honest.

He pressed his hand hard to that tiny cowboy butt, keeping them in rhythm. Curtis wanted Stetson crazy for him, wanted to do all the things. This worked for now, though. They had all night.

Stetson groaned and leaned up, nipping Curtis's jaw.

"Mmm-hmm. Feels damned good." See him make words. Go him. He laughed, sheer joy taking him over for a moment. "Perfect, in fact."

"Yes." So simple, that word, but it was what he needed to hear.

He had all these other words trying to pop out, so he licked at Stetson's skin instead, because what good would some of them do now? He nibbled along one collarbone, tasting the tiniest bit of sweat.

"Damn!" Stetson's fingers squeezed, proving that he'd hit a hot spot and a half.

Yeah. Okay, he'd forgotten that and a thousand other things he needed to rediscover. Curtis scraped that place with his teeth one more time, damn near crowing when Stetson's belly rolled for him.

He did that. He'd made those muscles clench up. He reached down for a moment, pressing his hand around Stetson's just enough to give them both a thrill.

Stetson offered him a low cry that sounded damn near broken, so he lifted his head and swallowed the sound down, taking Stetson's lips as he did.

They gave up on thinking then. He knew it as well as he knew his own name. They moved instinctively, both driving toward the pleasure they needed so badly. The release.

The rest could come later. Right now they needed this most basic of touches.

Curtis rocked faster, pushing against Stetson's grip. "Harder, babe. More."

"Uh-huh. I got this." Stetson was true to his word too, tugging at him like he was pulling a bull rope.

He arched his back, his breath coming short. "Soon, babe. Too soon, but soon." Was he making sense at all?

"Shh. You're okay. I got you." Stetson nipped his earlobe, the tiny pain near unbearable.

"You do." He bit his lower lip, then squeezed them together more firmly, his hand still around Stetson's.

Stetson began to tease his slit with every single upstroke, and he wanted to scream. His balls drew up, his dick so hard a cat couldn't scratch it. He was so sensitive, the tiniest thing was going to set him off like a rocket.

He shivered like he'd taken earthquake pills, his whole world gone sideways.

"It's okay, cowboy. It's okay. Come on and let go." Stetson's voice was low, rough, but the generosity in the words stunned him.

"Need you like breathing, Stetson."

"I'm here. Right here. You can have anything you want." Stetson ran one thumbnail over his slit, which made a bright flash of lightning run up his spine.

That was all she wrote, he shot like a Saturday night special—fast and hard and without warning.

His breath left his lungs in a whoosh, and time stopped. He froze, then began to shudder, his body working through the fireworks in his brain.

When he finally blinked at Stetson, he felt like a real heel. His lover was still sawing back and forth, almost sobbing his breath in and out. Jesus.

Curtis slapped Stetson's hand away and grasped that long cock, jerking it with the rhythm he knew Stetson craved.

"Please." There was a world of longing right there, and he intended to answer it.

"I got you. I do." He watched every movement, every twist of that lean body. Stetson yearned like no one else; in fact, he begged with his entire soul. Curtis stroked and pulled, letting Stetson really feel his every motion, every callus. "Look at you ride."

Goddamn, he could see that over and over, at every angle.

"I—oh fuck, Curtis. Oh damn." Stetson's eyes went wide, and the man came apart in his hands, crying out as he shot, slick wetness easing the way of his touch.

Stetson blinked at him, and for a second Curtis thought his lover was going to lose it, but then Stetson just pushed in and leaned hard against him.

"That's it." That release of tension had been enormous for Curtis. He couldn't even imagine how Stetson felt, dealing with this situation for years now. "I got you. I promise."

"I know." The words came soft, almost sad, but neither one of them would say anything about it.

They would take what they could tonight, for sure, and let tomorrow wake them up only when they had to.

Then they'd get their collective shits back together.

CHAPTER NINE

STETSON USED up the final bit of the wood to build a fire for Curtis's last day here at the ranch.

It was colder than a witch's tit, and he'd left Momma sleeping so he could get the feeding done early. He didn't want to miss a bit of the time they had left.

It had been the best week in recent memory—riding and laughing, a couple of beers, and lots of loving and touching.

The absolute best.

It had almost felt real. Good thing he knew better.

Curtis padded out from the hall, sweats riding low on his hips, bare upper body sheened with a little sweat from all the push-ups and sit-ups he'd been doing. "Hey, a fire? Smells amazing."

"Yeah, I thought I'd use up that old wood. It's a mite chilly."

"It is. I'll be freezing once I stop sweating." Curtis came to him, leaning against his back, burrowing both hands under his jacket.

He managed not to start, but he knew Curtis felt his muscles jumping and shuddering under that chilly touch. "Be-be careful, now. Mine are like blocks of ice."

"Oh, payback!" Curtis kissed the back of his neck.

"You all packed for tomorrow?" He was gonna miss Curtis like a lost tooth. He'd forgotten what it felt like to not be lonely. He sure as shit would be regretting that come the morning.

"Mostly, yeah. Do I need to help feed the dogs or anything?"

"Nope. It's all done. All you have to do is sit with me awhile." *Just come and act like this ain't the last bit of wood, like you won't be gone tomorrow, and like I won't be sitting there in the home tomorrow, listening to Momma call me by Daddy's name. Like once you leave, you'll be well and truly gone.*

"I can so do that." Curtis grabbed a sweatshirt off the recliner, then tugged it on.

He shrugged off his coat, checked the fire, then went to sit with Curtis on the couch, snuggling close.

"Hey." Curtis kissed his chin, then his cheek. "Bristly. I wish I could stay, you know."

"I know." *Liar.* "It's the Finals. You have to go." He would go if he could.

"I do. I could—" Curtis bit his lip, cutting off whatever he'd been about to say.

"I have to stay. You have to go. Momma and I will be watching you ride, just like always."

"Always?" Curtis gave him the raised eyebrow look. "Well, now. I was gonna say I want to come back for Christmas. I just don't want to put a burden on you."

"I always watch you ride." A slow panic began to fill him. A burden? How did…. Curtis couldn't know how truly bad it was, right?

"I love that." Curtis leaned. "I mean, Christmas has to be tough. With Momma. I don't want you to feel like you have to let me come stay and deal with all your other stuff. I can help with feedings and all."

"I want you here." He wouldn't have the ranch next Christmas. This would be the old place's last hurrah, so why not make it a good one, with laughter and hot sex and even hotter posole on Christmas Eve.

"Then I'll come on as soon as the Finals are over. Do you want…. Should I bring a little tree?"

"Surely. We'll have a grand holiday."

"We will." Curtis was all smiles now, that famous cowboy mug wreathed in them. "Do you remember the first time I came to stay here?"

Stetson nodded. Curtis had gotten stepped on, right where it hurt, and Stetson had brought him home. He didn't have to worry about Momma accusing them of getting into something because all of Curtis's bits were bruised and broken. "I thought the drive was going to kill you."

"You're not the only one. Your mom had all these faith healers coming in."

"And that lady that drew on your cast." Stetson started laughing, and that was good, because he didn't think he had any laughs left.

"I'd never seen a ranch look like this. Never seen so many animals with so little grass."

"It's our way. Where are you staying in Vegas?" Stetson was desperately curious about the things he couldn't glean from the broadcast.

"Off strip. One of those places with the shuttle and the cheap-ass buffet. I get more sleep that way."

"Ah. Good deal." He felt like a bumpkin these days, which was mostly okay, because they all were. Everybody was hurting; everybody was broke-dick and running cattle through the dirt. Curtis had told him, all those years ago, that he'd hoped that holding on to the ranch was worth it. God, he didn't know how to answer that anymore. "I hope you have a good event."

"Me too. I've been having a good year. It would suck to fall down now." Curtis stroked his arm. "I wish you could come. I know, I know. If wishes were horses...."

"I can't leave Momma. Not now." She was fading fast. Hell, he wasn't sure she'd be with him by Christmas. He wouldn't leave her to do this alone.

"I know. I worry I've taken too much time." Curtis sighed. "I'm so sorry, babe. You know that, right? She's a fine lady."

"It's time. This ain't living. Not really. Not at all."

Curtis just hugged him close, not saying nothin' else. What was there to say about Momma?

Not a fucking thing. It wasn't fair and not much was, the end.

He leaned on Curtis and listened to the pinyon knots popping in the fireplace. Fair or not, he had this right now. This very moment was damned good.

"It'll be okay, honey. I'll ride and then I'll be back for Christmas."

He patted Curtis's leg. "Don't worry on me. I can hold down the fort, no stress."

After all, he'd been doing it for a lot of years. What was a couple of weeks if he got to spend another holiday with this man he loved so much?

"It's good to have someplace to come. Thank you." Curtis said it softly, but he thought it was true.

"Glad you came out." He looked at their fingers, loving how they looked twined together—a pair of scarred, tore up, tanned men just holding on in a world that liked to drown them as well as buoy them. "You're the good in a whole passel of crap."

"Am I?" Curtis's cheeks flushed. "Thanks, Roper. I want to be. I want to help."

"You do. You are. Whatever. You know what I mean."

"I do." Curtis hummed a little, and he thought it was a Christmas song.

He let it warm him. The ranch was fixin' to be cold tomorrow.

CHAPTER TEN

"HEY, CT! You ready for round one?" His buddy Miles popped up next to him by the rail, and Curtis damn near jumped out of his skin.

"You know it. I want to get it over with." He felt like he'd been out of the game forever. Hell, Curtis felt as though part of his brain was still back with Roper.

All his damn heart was, and that was the truth.

"Damn, you're jittery," Miles murmured.

"I am. I got all ants in the pants, huh?"

"Good on you. Ought to help you ride." Miles clapped him on the shoulder. Then his friend sobered. "How's Stetson's momma?"

"Dying."

Miles's face fell. "Shit marthy. I'm real sorry, man. I was praying for a miracle for him."

"Me too." Curtis sighed. "She's so mad when she knows what's going on, like she wants to beat down the world."

"I can't even imagine. How's Stetson holding up?"

"Stretched thin." He didn't want to talk about Stetson's lack of funds, but he knew it was a problem. Stubborn cowboy. Curtis wanted to pay off loans or invest or something, but how did he bring that up without hurting Stetson bad?

"Yeah." Miles nodded. "Thank God I got me some brothers to work the land, and they got me to make money."

"Right?" See, that could work, but they'd gone round and round about that already. Stetson would want him there, and if they were ever gonna make it work, Curtis knew he'd have to stay.

Curtis wasn't sure he could do that. Not yet. Soon. A year, maybe, and he'd be ready to retire. The ranch had felt more like home than anything since he'd left his folks' place in Texas, right? Shit, the ranch was... it was where Stetson was. "How's it going for you, man? You riding good?"

"Yep. Stampede pushed me over the top ten. Sitting in eighth now. I'll be in the big money, I keep this up."

"Fucking A." Curtis intended to take it all, but he was always glad when his buds made it to the top with him.

"Right? You can say you knew me when."

"You have to stand in line, buddy."

"You took time off. You'll have to work for it." Miles grinned at him, pure evil shining through. "You gained weight, man?"

"No." He had. Three pounds. It wouldn't affect his balance, and he'd worked out every day—crunches and sit-ups and push-ups.

"You sure?" Miles couldn't stop his grin for love or money.

"Positive. See?" He patted his belly, which was flat under his buckle, thank God. Hell, the way Stetson had petted him, he knew he had to look good.

"I do." Too bad that ship hadn't floated for a second. Him and Miles? Lord, that had been a wreck. One terribly bad night with lots of beer later, they'd decided friends was the way to go.

"You know I carry all my weight in my ass," Curtis said, trying to get Miles to hoot and slap his leg.

"You and your lead backside." Miles rolled his eyes.

"Keeps me in the middle."

"That it does. You going to ride in all three events?"

"Going for all-around," he agreed. "I have to. Got to beat out the ropers."

"You can have the bareback and the bulls; leave me the saddle broncs."

"We'll see how I score out. I want to win, Miles."

"Yeah? You feeling it?" Miles started rocking side to side, beginning to warm up, just a bit.

"I am." And suddenly he was. A plan was forming in his mind, a reason to get the job done.

He had a goal, and God help him, that was what he needed. A direction. A way to keep his mind in the middle.

Curtis rocked his head on his neck. Right. Time to warm up, get moving. Stetson wouldn't thank him for bucking off.

No, he had to put on one last show for Miz Betty. He bounced up on the toes of his boots, grinning at the cameraman who came by.

Somewhere Stetson would see that and know that smile was for him.

Chapter Eleven

"Look, Momma. It's Curtis. He's waving to you." Stetson didn't bother to look and see whether she was paying attention. He knew she wasn't. She sat there and breathed, in and out, in and out, gurgling. She was starving to death. She hadn't swallowed in three days.

He swore by all he held holy, he was going to find somebody to get him some insulin in a huge dose, and he was going to put her out of her misery. This wasn't fair.

Not a bit of it.

So instead of staring at her, he watched the streaming on his phone, here where there was Wi-Fi.

He watched Curtis.

Round three of the Finals, and Curtis led in bareback and bull riding. He was second in saddle broncs, and he was edging out one of the ropers for all-around by something like eighty points.

Every night Curtis called. Every night Curtis asked about Momma. Every night Stetson lied.

"Yeah, she's rooting for you, cowboy," he would say. "She went to bed right after the round."

Somewhere that was true. Momma loved Curtis to death. More than that, she liked him.

The bull riding came up, and he leaned his elbows on his knees, staring at the screen. "Come on, cowboy."

Miles Bend was pulling Curtis's rope; Hank Rogers had hold of his vest. That was like a top-three ice cream sandwich, and Lord it was a pretty sight.

"I swear, Momma, you better not be able to hear me thinking, because I'm a bad, bad man."

He grinned a little, then glanced at her. His smile faded. She needed to sleep. Maybe she was asleep. Who the hell knew?

Curtis was wearing his lucky shirt, the dark blue paisley looking fine on him.

Stetson clenched his hands when Curtis settled into place, then nodded.

The little Mexican bull turned toward the left, spinning fast as he tried to buck Curtis off. Curtis had ridden bulls twice as big and twice again as mean, but this one was quick as a wink, and that meant G forces.

"Come on, cowboy." He nodded with every second. *Four. Five. Six. Seven. Come on. You can do it. Eight.* "Yes!"

The score wasn't going to set the world on fire, but it was a score.

"Seventy-five, Momma! That keeps him above water. And this isn't his best event." He was so fucking proud. "That's our cowboy right there. He's going for it."

He glanced over to find Momma staring at the TV, and he knew she wasn't seeing what he was, but he hoped it gave her some solace.

At least her eyes were open.

He turned off the streaming video and tucked away his phone. "You ready for bed, Momma?"

She didn't answer, the weird gurgling of the tube the only sound. He told himself that it was a blessing, that the last thing she'd said to him was that she loved him.

That was all right.

He rose, then kissed her cheek. "Night, Momma." He would stay in the trailer tonight; he had people feeding, and the dogs were gonna forget who he was.

The night nurse was new, but he seemed kind enough, with an easy smile, a gentle manner. "You gone, Mr. Stetson?"

"I'll be out in the parking lot. Y'all holler if you need me."

"It's damn cold tonight."

It was damn cold every night. "Thanks, man. I'll bundle up."

"You need extra blankets, you holler at us," the nurse murmured.

"Thank you. I'll be in later to steal coffee, I'm sure." He headed to the trailer and climbed up into the comforting scent of animal and hay. He settled into the blankets and waited for his phone call.

It didn't take long, the buzz shaking his phone in his pocket. Curtis's name was like magic, making him smile.

"Hey, cowboy. Good ride."

"Hey, Roper." That voice flowed over him like warm honey. "Thanks. It was solid. That little bull turned me every which ways but loose, huh?"

"You handled it, though, even spurred a little."

"I did. Damn, I'm ready to come home."

His heart flip-flopped, and Stetson told himself not to read too damned much into that.

"You've got another six days, huh? How many rides do you have left?" He pulled the collar of his coat up.

"Three, I hope. Maybe four. Depends on Louis Dreyman." That was the guy chasing Curtis's dollar total.

"You want I should come hit him in the knee?" he teased.

"Yes. Immediately." Curtis chuckled. "Did you smoke today?" Curtis was giving him hell about the cigarettes.

"Yeah. A few." Half a pack.

"Stop it." All iron, those two words. "I need you all rarin' to go when I get back, not down with bronchitis or something."

"I'm looking forward to seeing you again. I…. You know."

"I know." Curtis lowered his voice. "I want you, Roper."

Oh, that warmed him a little. "You can have me. Whenever."

He was a little stiff now, a little sore, but he'd manage, if Curtis was here.

"Okay." Curtis chuckled, the warm sound keeping the cold night at bay. Then the inevitable question came. "How's Miz Betty?"

Dying. "'Bout the same. We were watching your ride today."

It was a lie, but a necessary one. Curtis needed to keep his mind in the middle.

"Damn. I keep hoping she'll perk up. I know it's stupid, but there it is."

"We're rooting for you. How're you feeling? Your body holding up?"

"Yeah, actually. I hate to jinx myself, but I been riding good, and I'm just a little bruised."

Maybe he was taking all the sore in Curtis's place. That would make a great story for some horror writer, huh? Lord have mercy.

"Did you have supper?"

Curtis paused long enough Stetson knew he was about to get the load of crap this time. "I had a bite with Miles."

"Liar. Try again."

"I had a bite or two off Miles's plate. I'll grab a salad from room service, I swear."

"Yeah? Because you have to keep your energy up."

"I do. Chicken Caesar. I promise."

Well, Curtis had never made him a promise, then broken it.

"Mmm. Eat the croutons for me?" He loved crunchy bread.

"I will. Acceptable carbs. I might even eat a few bites of a carrot cake."

He'd seen Curtis do that. Order a big slab of cake from room service and eat two bites before tossing it.

"Oh, man. I should be there to finish it for you."

"You so should. I'll stop and get one on the way into town."

"Fair deal." He shivered a little, pondering running in and grabbing another cup of coffee. It was shitty, but it was hot.

"You okay, Roper? Are you in that fucking trailer?"

"Huh?"

"Roper...."

"Don't you worry on this old cowboy."

"I worry about you every day. That hasn't changed." Curtis sighed, the sound like a gust of wind. "I hate thinking about you sleeping in the trailer. How cold is it, Roper? How cold are you?"

"I'm fine." If it got any colder, they would let him sack out in an unused waiting room.

"Let me get you a hotel room, Stetson. Just for tonight."

"I'm fine, cowboy. Let it go."

"I can't. It has to be freezing there. Shit, it's below freezing here in Vegas."

"Is it? Damn, you have your coat with you?"

"I do. Shearling and all." Curtis barked out a laugh. "Don't you deflect."

"De-whatzit?"

"Butthead. Don't you turn it back on me. Please, baby. Let me get you a room."

Stetson smiled, the care almost unbearable. "Tomorrow, huh? Ask me tomorrow."

"Okay. I will. I need you all healthy, okay? Are you eating? They feeding you at the hospital?"

"All the Jell-O I can eat!" They were good to him, honestly, bringing him the tray of food Momma couldn't eat.

"Okay. God, this hotel is loud. Even in my room. I got spoiled at the ranch."

"It's not loud out there, is it?" He had to chuckle, because there was nothing like being home and knowing no one was coming to bother you. That was a silence unlike any other.

"Nope. I mean, the coyotes let us hear them, but that's about it."
Curtis had the best laugh.

"I miss you, cowboy." He never let himself say it, but God knew
he meant it.

"I miss you too. It's a deep down hurt now I've been near you
again." Curtis hummed, the sound intensely sexual. Needy.

"Yes. Like I know now, how good it is." He whispered the words,
not out of shame, but because this was so raw.

"Right. We were so young before. Now we know what we're
missing, damn it."

That surprised a laugh out of him, the sound loud and raucous. He
stared up at the roof of the trailer, his body warming some at the thought
of what they'd gotten up to before Curtis left.

Curtis laughed with him, sounding happier than he had at the start
of the call.

"What's your plan for tomorrow?" He listened to Curtis ramble,
closing his eyes as he let himself live vicariously, pretend that his world
wasn't fixin' to come tumbling down.

It wasn't perfect, but he'd take what he could get.

Chapter Twelve

"You're up, Traynor!" The chute boss waved a clipboard at chute four, where a big, rawboned roan mare waited for his happy ass.

Of all his rides this week, he was dreading this one the most. Gale Force was a hell of a bucker, and his neck could only take so much more bareback.

Still, this was where he was in the money. This could keep him up there where he needed to be.

God help him, he wanted this bad. He wanted to win this bitch and then go home to his Stetson.

The thought was hard and fast and rang in him.

Curtis blinked but headed over to the chute. Two riders were set to go before him, but his rigging was in place, and they moved quick this late in the week.

"Good ride, cowboy." Old Vick grinned at him, half his teeth gone along with four of his fingers.

"Yep." He nodded shortly. No one would accuse him of being rude. Curtis zipped his vest, then adjusted his neck roll.

Please God, eight seconds. I need eight seconds and to mark out.

Curtis stepped up to the chute, grabbing the top rail. He took a deep breath, then grinned wildly. "Okay, lady. You. Me. Good score."

She rolled her eyes at him, but she knew her job, and she was daring him to do his. Her ears flicked, signaling readiness, and he climbed over the rail, Tim Halloway there to keep him from pulling a Pecos Bill's girlfriend. What was her name, anyway?

He got his legs set, his spurs above the shoulders. "Let's do this."

Curtis nodded, and the world set to rocking.

Gale Force leaped out, and he marked up on her shoulders until she began to buck four strides later. When she did, she went textbook, head down, back feet so high she could have kicked the moon.

He was either going to die or this ride was going to break records.

Curtis gritted his teeth, reaching back and up with his free arm, keeping the elbow bent on the other to hold the rigging.

"Come on," he bellowed. "Kick, you nag!"

For a half second, Curtis knew he was fixin' to go cartwheeling, but he stuck like a burr, and when that buzzer sounded, his happy ass was looking for a safety man—Nobert or James. He gave no shits.

The mare got real mad once the whistle went off, running along the fence line, and he got the feeling she was about to try to scrape him off. *There. Pick-up man.*

Of course, about the time he reached for that fast-moving man on horseback, Gale flipped her back feet up, sending him ass over teakettle.

Curtis landed so hard he felt himself rattle, heard it as his bones tried to find different places.

The crowd was roaring, so he climbed to his feet and took off his hat, waved it in the air. The scoreboard showed his score, which he'd missed with the bad get off. Eighty-two.

Goddamn.

"I hope you saw that, Roper. I hope you were watching."

He limped out of the arena, listening to announcer Dallas Ray shout him out. "Curtis Traynor for eighty-two points! That's a go-round winner, folks, and might just sew up Traynor's all-around win!"

Oh, praise God and Greyhound. He waved his hat again, then headed back. He needed to sit. He needed to breathe. He needed to see if it was true, if he was that close to taking the big purse.

Miles waited for him at the gate, pounding him on the back. "I think you got it, buddy."

"Math ain't your strong suit, Miles."

"Yeah, yeah. You need sport medicine?"

"Huh? Nah. I just need to sit—"

"Traynor. Get your ass back here and get your checkup."

Right. Sports medicine wasn't taking no for an answer. They always worried too much.

"Lord, Pete, you're a bossy fuck."

"I got nothing on Doc."

"True." He creaked back behind the chutes, grinning at the paramedic who doubled as Doc's assistant. "I'm not hurt, just shook."

"Let me feel better about it by looking. That was a great ride, man."

"Thanks." They did the handshake man-hug thing. He'd known Pete for ten years, at least. "Might have done the job."

"God knows you worked for it." Pete shone a light in his eyes. "Pupils look good."

"It's my spine, not my skull," Curtis teased. "Landed so hard on my tail I jostled my insides."

"Anything hurting in particular?"

"Just my ass." He winked, but it was true enough.

"Tailbone?" Pete was a smart man.

"Yeah. She bucked that last time and down I went."

"Come on all the way back and let me look. I promise not to get too personal."

Yeah, Stetson might just get grumpy about that. He followed dutifully, though, because Stetson would also get miffed if his ass was broken.

"Good ride, Traynor!" Folks were cheering him on, waving to him, all the way to sports medicine, where Bonner Nelson was lying there, arm at an awful angle.

"Well, shit, Bonner, you trying to get out of putting up the Christmas tree for your new wife?"

"How'd you guess?" Lord, that had to hurt. Bonner had pure agony written on his face.

"I know how lazy you are. Anyone go to get your lady?"

"No. I mean, I called her, but she's gonna meet me at the hospital. I don't want her seeing this. She'll see me once it's in a splint or a cast or whatever."

"Yeah. Jesus. They calling an ambulance?"

"They are. Andy had to get carted out earlier, so they had to call in another one." Bonner arched up off the gurney. "Christ."

"Let me give you something, Bonner," Pete grumbled. "Please?"

"I ain't gonna tell a soul, cowboy. I swear." Curtis knew that kind of pain. He'd broken his pelvis once, and thought he might keel over every time he moved.

"Okay. Okay, yeah." Bonner looked like he was gonna die.

"Just hang tight, Traynor. Let me help Bonner out."

"I'm good." He grabbed a doughnut doolie to sit on and settled in to call Stetson.

"You did it! Cowboy, you showed that mare!" Stetson's voice sounded so good to him.

"Right? She was trying to trip me up." He glanced at Bonner and said a little "there but by the grace of God" prayer.

"You landed hard. You okay? I saw they grabbed you from sports medicine."

"That's where I am. I landed hard. Just a precaution, though. Checking my tailbone."

"Ouch. I had a horse break mine three years ago. That's tender."

"I don't think anything popped, but I might be shorter." He lowered his voice. "That won't be a turnoff, right?"

"I promise not to even notice."

"I like how you think." He knew he was a banty rooster. Good thing Stetson didn't mind.

"One more ride, huh? You ride one more bronc and you've got it done, no question." That was his Roper, working the numbers. Stetson would say he was stupid, but Curtis knew better.

"Yep. His heeler missed in round three, and his calf came free in round five, so I bet he can't catch me. I'm pulling out of the bull riding and just doing saddle bronc."

"Good deal. Saddle is your sweet spot. Just don't break your butt no more."

"Nope. I promise. My butt will be ready."

"Promises, promises." Stetson chuckled, the sound so weirdly tired.

"What's up with you, Roper? How's Miz Betty?"

"I'm okay. Tired today."

"Yeah? I'm sorry, babe." He was. He wished there was more he could do, but he'd be back with Stetson soon.

"Eh. No worries. You need to just enjoy that score."

"I do. If I want to worry, I will, though."

"Bossy old cowboy."

"That's me. I miss you, Roper."

"I miss you, more than you know." Stetson's tone had changed, back to tense and tired.

"Roper, is everything—"

"I'm ready for you, Traynor," Pete said.

"I have to go. I... soon, okay? I'll be home soon."

"Soon. Just a few more days. Text me to let me know how your butt is. And eat something."

"I will if you do. Night, Roper."

"Love you. Night." Then the phone went dead.

He sat there a moment. *Love. Yeah. God.*

"Come on, Traynor." Pete beckoned him over to an exam table.

"Do I have to, Doclet?" Doclet. Oh, that was good.

"You do. Need that looked at. Drop trou."

"Don't let anyone video my ass, man." This was actually more fun than riding.

"Shut up." Pete snorted out a laugh.

Ah, there was nothing like letting someone check out your tailbone while you were in the middle of the room. Nothing.

Not to mention that Pete had damn cold hands.

Chapter Thirteen

"Stetson? Stetson, man?"

He woke up in a rush, every inch of his body ice cold, the world having turned into a long series of numb periods interspersed with panic. "Wh-what? What's wrong?"

"It's time." He didn't recognize the voice. It didn't matter. It was a nurse telling him Momma was dying. At this point, they'd said it more than once, and every time it was a lie. "Seriously, man. You've got to hurry."

God. Everything in him—every single cell of his body seemed to clench for a second, the sensation so fierce he couldn't even begin to feel anything.

"I'm coming." He crawled out of his nest of blankets and tugged on his boots, moving as fast as his stiff fingers would work.

"I'll pour you a cup of coffee."

"Thanks." Time. It was time. Christ. Why did people say that? It was always time for something.

They trudged back across the parking lot, and another nurse met them at the door. "You need to come on, Stetson."

"I'm here. I'm coming." He looked at her, his eyes feeling like they were full of ground glass. "What do I do?"

Helena patted his hand. "Tell her goodbye. Be there with her. That's your job now."

"Right."

He made his way to Momma's room, his boots ringing against the floor.

The lights were off, the machines silent here in the room. The only real sound was the sucker deal keeping her from drowning in her own spit. Stetson stood there for a second, then sat and took her hand. It was warm still, but it didn't feel like the woman who had run his world with an iron will. This was the frail hand of a stranger, and if he thought on it too hard, he would shatter like a cheap window. He didn't have enough in him to do that, to deal with this. He was only one man, and he was scared and cold and so tired, it wasn't fixable anymore.

"This sucks, Momma." His voice was so loud in the silence of the room that he jumped, Momma's hand falling to the bed in a lump. "God, I'm sorry, but I reckon you need to get on with this. You ain't got to worry on me. I'll be fine. Go on. Tell Daddy I said hey."

Wasn't that what he was supposed to do? Tell her it was okay with him? Because, God help him, it was. He was beginning to dream about putting her out of her misery so he could go home. Hell, they put dogs down for less suffering.

He was a bad man.

A bad, broke-dick man with nothing to offer and a dead momma. He just wanted to do this one thing right. *Please God, please. Let me do this right. I love her so much, but I need to lay her down. I can't hold her up no more. Forgive me.*

He picked up her hand and held it again, staring at nothing, as empty as he could be. At some point, Helena came in, turned the sucker thing off, and took it out of Momma's mouth. "You can stay as long as you need to, honey. We put a call into the funeral home for you."

"Okay. Thanks."

"Do you need anything?"

He needed to go home. He needed to take care of things. He had feeding to do.

For right now, though, he thought he'd sit for a second in the quiet and say goodbye.

"No, ma'am. I think we'll be just fine."

Chapter Fourteen

CURTIS SMILED for the camera as he collected his big old check and his brand-new gold buckle. He wished he got a saddle like in Cheyenne; he'd give it to Stetson, because God knew the man could use some tack…. Where was that Cheyenne saddle anyway? At his mom and dad's place in Colorado?

Who knew? Right now he didn't need to care.

All-around champion. The number one cowboy in the country.

God, he'd worked hard for this, and he hoped Stetson was watching. He hoped Roper was proud of him.

He smiled and nodded and did the glad-handing afterward, but he didn't linger for the party. He was already gone. His truck was waiting for him in the parking lot, packed up and ready. All he had to do was drive home. Ten hours and he could be there.

He hopped into the cab, then tugged out his phone. One last call before he got to see Stetson in person.

The phone rang once, and then he heard, "Congratulations."

"Thanks, babe." He frowned. "You sound pooped."

"I'm so proud of you. You rode like a dream."

"I did my best. It paid off finally." He had enough put back now he could pay off some of Stetson's liens.

"It did. I'm proud."

Was Stetson drinking? He sounded a little slurred and a lot repetitive. "Is it too cold out there, baby? Do you need that hotel?"

"I'm home. In Taos. At the ranch."

There was a dead finality in Stetson's voice that hurt him, made him wince.

"Is she sleeping finally?" He didn't think so. Dread settled in his gut.

"She's gone. Yesterday morning, early."

"Ah, Jesus, Roper. I'm sorry. So fucking sorry." He managed to get on the highway and gun it. "You didn't say, yesterday."

"Wouldn't have made her less dead, and you had a ride to make."

The words made him smile. That was his Stetson, cowboy to the bone. Christ, Curtis hurt for him. "She's in a better place, right?"

All of them believed that.

"Yes, God, yeah. You coming home?"

"I'm on the road now. Heading to you." Yesterday morning. Stetson had so many arrangements to make. All those people to call about insurance if she had any, and debts and tax notifications.

"Not going to the after-parties?"

"No, baby. I want to get home to you." He could help. He really could. Stetson would need him now more than ever.

"Yeah. Yeah, I'm all over that idea."

"I thought you might be." He would get that wee tree too, damn it. He could stop at a Target or something. Get a few sparkly garlands and some balls.

"I watched every second."

"Did you? That last ride was just okay, but the check was worth it."

"All you had to do was ride, and you did it."

"I did. I—I'm on my way, Roper."

"Thank God for that. I-I sorta…. I'm waiting."

"Sorta what?" Stetson sounded so damned defeated.

"I'm just waiting for you."

"I'm on my way. You got groceries?"

"I'll go pick some up in the morning. You make sure you get some sleep tonight. Stop somewhere halfway."

"I will." Not. He was driving straight through. He would sleep with Stetson when he finally laid down his head.

"Okay. You stay safe. Call if you need me."

"I'll check in." Hell, he would want to hear Stetson's voice about every hour on the hour.

"I'll see you tomorrow, huh?"

"You totally will." Curtis couldn't wait.

"Okay. Come home. I'll make you stew."

"Oh hell yes. Make biscuits? I'm off the diet until February."

"It's a deal, cowboy."

"I'll see you soon." He had to hang up because he needed to get the air going and get his head in the game.

He had a long way to go and a cowboy to get home to.

Chapter Fifteen

STETSON CLEANED the house up, did the feeding, his head down, the world quiet, still, the snow blanketing the ground.

God, his head hurt.

His heart hurt.

The horses and the dogs knew it, all demanding extra love. Trying to help. Even the ostriches minded their p's and q's, not going after his butt or his hat.

He gave all he had, the frigid temps pushing through his coat. His fingers stiffened right up, the joints swelling, and he told himself to breathe, to chill out.

Stetson needed to get the stuff to make biscuits and stew, so he needed to make a list and choke down some food.

He stomped off his boots at the back door, trying to get the bulk of the snow off them.

Lord, that made his toes tingle. He shook off his hat as well. Every so often he wished his people would have settled in southern New Mexico. Then again, the summers pushed up over a hundred degrees down there like they never did in Taos.

The sound of a truck pulling up into the yard surprised him. Everyone knew he was home. No need to come feed for him.

The pups barked and wagged up a storm on the porch, so Stetson stepped out to see what was what.

He blinked a second. Curtis had to have broken every speed limit on the book.

That was Curtis, for sure, hopping out of his truck and trotting around to run up the stairs.

"Cowboy." He felt like if he moved, he was going to crack down the middle like a dropped china plate. Boom.

"Hey, Roper." Curtis didn't break into a smile but came right to him, hugged him tight.

Stetson couldn't breathe. He held on, trying to remember how to do this, how to live. He'd known he wasn't okay, but this was shattering.

"Hey. Hey, I'm here. I got you." Curtis rubbed his back, up and down, warming him.

"You did good," he forced out.

"Thanks. Can we go inside? I'm froze."

"I have the furnace on." There wasn't any more wood, so he'd turned up the heat as much as he dared.

"Sounds grand. Shit. Let me get a couple things from the truck." Curtis moved fast, returning with some bags, one a big Target thing, the red circles on the bag unmistakable.

"You need help? I can help."

"Sure." Now Curtis did smile for him, handing him the big bag.

"I bet you got some laundry to do, huh?" He took the sack, then opened the door.

"I do, yeah. That off-strip hotel wouldn't even do my shirts!" Curtis grinned at him when his mouth dropped open. "I know, it's an outrage. They host a bunch of cowboys, they at least ought to starch shirts."

"No shit on that. They ain't cowboy people, I guess. I'll run them down to the laundry." Maybe this afternoon when Curtis was sleeping.

"Thanks, babe." Curtis dropped his shit in a pile, took the Target bag from Stetson's nerveless fingers, and then pulled him into another hug.

Stetson's eyes dropped closed, and he told himself that crying was right out. He was a cowboy. Dammit.

Curtis never said a peep, just rubbed his back, really letting him lean.

"You—you want breakfast? I didn't go to the store yet, but I can make you eggs."

"I would love that, babe. If you're not too tired."

"I ain't tired." He was exhausted. That was totally different.

"Then bring on the food. For you too." Curtis kissed him, just a soft brush of lips and stubble.

"Tell me about your trip?" He opened the fridge. There were seven eggs, a half stick of oleo, five Coors, and a container of half-and-half. *Okay. Eggs.*

"Long. But productive." Curtis laughed, the sound happy as all get-out. "I won, Roper."

"You did." That was why he hadn't called and told about Momma. What good would it have done? Curtis wouldn't have been on the ball, and she was dead. That news could happen any time.

"I still can't believe it. It was close there for a bit."

"I was damn proud. Still am." Hell, at the end of Curtis's last ride, Stetson had been on his feet, jumping up and down and shouting.

"Thanks." Curtis sobered. "I'm so sorry, Roper."

He didn't pretend not to know what about. "It was time. She hadn't been there for days. She couldn't swallow, she couldn't speak. She didn't even cry no more."

"God." Curtis closed his eyes, lips pressed together. "Then it's a blessing. She would hate living like that."

"Yeah." He'd thought of smothering her with a pillow, of just holding her nose and mouth closed and stopping her suffering, but he couldn't do it. He wasn't a big enough man.

"Have you—uh, do you need help? Making arrangements?"

"They're cremating her. Everyone will start coming day after tomorrow, you know?" It was polite to wait for the full four days before coming to the family, especially up here in Taos. It was the way of half his momma's family, the Pueblo side.

"Sure. Are you doing a service?" Curtis shifted in his chair, seeming uncomfortable.

"I don't know. I ought, huh? For her friends? I don't know how."

"Well, I can make some calls."

He nodded slowly. Curtis was good at arranging shit, and Stetson was tired of dealing. "I just... there's enough life insurance to cremate her and stuff. Did you know they have to put her in a box to do it?"

"Nope." Curtis stared at him, eyes wide. "They burn the box too?"

"Uh-huh. I had to pick one out." No one should have to do that. No one. Ever.

"Damn. That's crazy."

"It is. I—" No one but him had to know he picked cardboard, right? He didn't have a choice, moneywise. The wood ones, even plain pine, made everything too expensive.

"Hey. Breathe, baby. It's okay." Curtis stopped sitting and staring, and moved to take the egg carton from him.

"I'm sorry. I'm not—I'm sorry."

"Shit, Stetson. You've had a hell of a time." Curtis cracked eggs into the bowl he'd pulled out of the cabinet. "You're upright and moving, and that's a lot."

"I guess so."

"Now we're both upright and moving, together. Even my tailbone, which protested the drive."

"Yeah." He took a deep breath. "I don't know if there's bread."

"No biggie." Curtis dug around in cabinets. "There's Pop-Tarts and hamburger buns. Buns?"

"If they're not moldy, go for it. I think they're partially made of trees."

"Tree bread? Eek." Curtis put the buns back. "Pop-Tarts it is. Told you I'm off the diet."

Stetson started laughing, the noise tearing out of him, sounding more hurt than happy. God. God, he loved this son of a bitch.

Curtis grinned wide, like he'd done something amazing.

Tears were hiding behind the laughter, so he went for another hug, smashing them both in the hard muscle of Curtis's shoulder.

Curtis held on, going to sit at the table, breakfast ignored for the moment. He perched on Curtis's lap, feeling weirdly huge.

"I miss her. I knew I'd never bring her home again, but...." But she was his momma, and she'd never let him down before. Some part of him had believed she'd beat this, somehow, because she was his momma and she loved him.

"It blows, baby. It's shitty. I know there's all sorts of shit about better places, but she was fierce, your momma. She loved you."

"She did. She does." Some things were bigger than dying. This he knew.

"Yep." Curtis hugged on him until someone's stomach growled. Stetson thought it was Curtis's.

"Eggs and Pop-Tarts." The important things in life.

"You know it. I'm sorry, babe. I'm starving."

"Don't be sorry! I'll feed you." He was being a titty-baby.

"We'll feed each other. Egg duty or toaster manning?"

"I'll scramble the eggs. My pan is cranky."

"Works for me." Curtis set to tugging Pop-Tarts out of their sleeves and popping them into the toaster. "You even have the good kind. Cinnamon and brown sugar."

"That's the only decent kind."

This was an old argument. A wonderful one.

"Oh, I dunno. I like cherry. Frosted."

"Ick. Those are unnatural." He grinned because his argument didn't even make sense, but it felt good.

"They are not. Now, those blue-and-pink things? Bad mojo."

"They have blue and pink?"

"Some kind of fake berry." Curtis shivered dramatically.

"Fake… ew. No. No no." The eggs stuck. They always stuck in this pan since Momma left. Maybe he didn't use enough butter. She never used nonstick anything.

"We need to get you new pans, baby."

"Oh, I make do."

"I know, but you're losing the money in eggs you'd put into a new pan." The Pop-Tarts came up, and Curtis grabbed them, put them on plates.

He chuckled softly. "Spoken like a man that has cooked a few eggs in his time."

"I have. Protein, and you can cook them in a camp skillet on Sterno."

Oh. Camping. He hadn't gone camping in a while….

"What's that smile for?" Curtis bumped hips with him.

"Huh? Oh, I was just… wandering."

"Mmm. It looked like a good wander."

"It was. I was thinking about camping, with you."

"Yeah?"

"Yeah. Like for fun."

"We could do that, for sure. We could go down toward Las Cruces in the spring."

"Do you want to, though?" God, that would be fun. And cheap too. He had an old tent; all it would cost was gas.

"Hell, yes. You know I love to fish."

"Uh-huh." Curtis liked to nap in the sun while they fished. The fishing was his best excuse.

"Then we'll do it."

His grin felt odd, stretching cheeks that hadn't smiled much lately. "Eat your eggs." He'd given Curtis the lion's share.

"Thanks." Curtis dug in, eating with the kind of mechanical precision only athletes managed to attain.

He watched, drinking Curtis in. This was his last hoorah, the last one here, and if he was honest, the last one with Curtis. They'd only ever had that one big blowout fight; then Curtis had just stopped coming home, and he'd stopped going out, and suddenly he'd seen Curtis on the TV with Danny Gonzales and he'd known everyone had moved on.

"You okay?" That sharp gaze never missed much.

"Fine as frog hair." He ate one of the Pop-Tarts and a couple bites of eggs, then pushed his plate over. "I'm full, cowboy. You ought to eat 'em."

"Stetson, you need to eat. We need to go get groceries." Still, Curtis took the food. "We'll get you some grapes."

"I'll pick some stuff up." While Curtis was sleeping.

"Cool. I'll come with. Just to see what town looks like."

"Yeah? It looks like Taos. Cold and snowy." And beautiful. Because it still was so goddamn beautiful.

"Yeah, but it's been years since I spent any time." Those lean cheeks went pink, and Curtis ducked his head.

"We'll have a good time, huh?" Momma would be tickled.

"We will." Curtis stood, then gathered the dirty dishes. "Man, it's good to be out of the truck."

"I bet. You want a shower? It's clean. The tub." He hadn't even been able to go to Momma's side of the house yet.

"I do. Don't suppose you wanna come with?" Now, that was purely naughty.

"I do. I most definitely do, cowboy." He wanted to touch, to remember how to feel.

"Yee-haw. Come on, baby." Curtis took his hand after putting the dishes in the sink, their calluses scraping where they touched.

Baby. Curtis had called him that so much back in the day. Hadn't called him that much recently. Or maybe he had, and Stetson hadn't heard it. He didn't know. All he knew was he heard it now and it heated him right up. He supposed he ought to feel guilty, with all the stuff he had to deal with, going off to play with Curtis.

He didn't.

He wanted what he could get. He needed all he could get.

Curtis dragged him into the bedroom, then the bathroom, got the water going with a few quick motions.

He toed his boots off, then stripped off his heavy shirt and hooked it on the door. He moved like he was underwater, stripping down while he waited for Curtis to plop his ass on the pot so Stetson could work the man's lace-ups off.

Curtis sat, lifting one leg, and he unlaced and tugged and pulled, the motions familiar as breathing.

"God, you're hot."

The words made him look up, blink. "What?"

"I mean it, Roper. You're stunning. Make me so damned happy." Those blue eyes burned for him, staring right into him.

He leaned in, bracing himself on those ropy thighs and taking his kiss. What else could he do? Curtis's words touched him soul-deep, where he needed that balm.

Curtis kissed him like there was nothing else on earth he'd rather do. Slow and easy, hands on his hips to hold him up.

"Come on, baby. I need you to love on me some."

"I'm ready." He straightened up, then pulled Curtis up with him, working on those drove-all-night clothes.

Together they managed to get naked, both of them standing there for a second, staring like goats at a new fence. Curtis was bruised from one end to the other.

"Hot water, cowboy. It'll help."

"I hope so." Curtis laughed. "I'm not broke, though."

"Nope." That was him. "Thank God for it too."

"Yeah?" Curtis kissed him again, and they stepped into the shower, locked together like that. That mouth could make a man forget his own name, let alone all his troubles.

He grabbed the Irish Spring and started rubbing, relearning every inch of Curtis with a careful hand. No hurting.

Curtis leaned on the wall and let him have at all that skin. It didn't take long for Curtis to take the soap, though, and return the favor. Impatient cowboy.

"You're fixin' to dry up and blow away. I need to cook for you. Spend some long days in bed together." Curtis traced the hollows under Stetson's ribs.

"Been a hard little bit. Don't worry on me. I needed to tighten up."

"Bullshit." Curtis said it fondly, but that jaw was set like steel. He knew who would be buying the groceries this time. No arguments.

He traced that angular jaw, his body telling him that maybe he wasn't as old as he felt, that there was something about Curtis and his hard body that made Stetson want to go to his knees and beg.

Not that he needed to. Curtis gave him everything. Touches and kisses and words. All of it.

"Want everything, Roper. Want you now and tomorrow and the day after."

The bite to his earlobe made him twist and sob. He wanted all that and then some. He wasn't sure he could believe anymore.

"Hot motherfucker." Curtis growled for him, the sound hard and needy, not a bit of softness in it. "Now."

"Yeah." He didn't even care what he was agreeing to. He just wanted it. Now.

Curtis took him in hand, fingers closing around his cock. The tugging sent a shock through his balls.

"Cowboy, fuck, you make me—" He went up on tiptoe, swallowing down his cry.

"That's the idea." Breathless as hell, Curtis worked him, never letting him down for a moment.

Time stopped and he stared, those blue eyes like lasers. No one had ever been Curtis Traynor. No one.

"Stetson." His name. Just his name, but Curtis said it like a prayer.

All he could do was nod and try to suck in one breath, another. Well, and not drown. He laughed, the sound rough and harsh, because Curtis tugged his balls at the end of the latest stroke down.

"Want to watch you shoot for me. Want to see you scream."

Somehow he didn't think that was going to be a problem. He was only as quiet as he was because he lacked breath.

Curtis gave him even more then, bending to kiss him, free hand sliding down to cup one asscheek.

Lightning hit him, and he shattered, coming so hard he forgot everything but his cowboy's name. That he knew, and he shouted it to the air, his body sawing back and forth.

"Fuck, baby. Look at you. Just look. So damned pretty."

He felt shattered, bone-deep. He slumped against Curtis, holding those strong shoulders to keep him upright.

"Sorry. Sorry." He needed to take care of Curtis. He knew it.

"I'm not." Curtis nibbled at the side of his neck. "That was fucking amazing. Better than any ride I've ever had."

Stetson chuckled. "Than any ride, cowboy?"

"Even the gold buckle, Roper." That tone.... He glanced up, finding Curtis staring at him, not wavering one bit.

"Well, then...." He eased himself down on the bath mat, letting Curtis's body protect him from the spray. He didn't wait, because he didn't know how long the hot water would hold out.

"Oh, damn." Curtis stretched up tall, cock bobbing in front of him.

"Mine." He licked a line from the underside of Curtis's cock all the way to the tip.

"Yours," Curtis agreed, hips bucking just like he was riding in the short go.

It was easy to lick again, try to get more of that amazing salt, that taste of pure need. The water held a hint of soap, but it wasn't bad at all.

Stetson closed his eyes and wrapped his lips around Curtis's thick cock, tongue moving restlessly over the heavy shaft. He worked up to trace the head, the flared ridge fascinating him, the slit so delicate, so sensitive.

Those muscles worked under Curtis's skin, and Curtis started babbling at him, love words and swear words and finally grunts and clicks.

That was what he needed, what he wanted, to make Curtis crazy. He wanted all the sounds and touches. Everything.

Curtis cupped the back of his head, encouraging him to move faster, take more. Not forcing; Curtis would never do that. That was what made Stetson work harder, bobbing up and down, sucking deep.

He heard a strangled sob, a low, needy cry, and he swallowed, needing to pull Curtis over the edge.

Bitter, salty heat filled him, Curtis shouting when he came, one hand on his head, one on his shoulder. Look at that man ride....

The water stung his eyes, and he blinked it away, wanting to see.

"Jesus, Roper. You're gonna make me fall down." Curtis had the goofiest grin on his face.

"You don't get moving soon, you're gonna freeze. That hot water's going to give up the ghost soon."

"It already is a little." Curtis tugged him upright to rinse them both off.

He turned the faucets before Curtis became a Popsicle, then grabbed the towels.

"Brrr. Damn. I need to get you a towel warmer."

"Oh, I had one of those once. Used it 'til it died."

"Well, see?" They both shivered and ran. Clothes. They needed clothes.

"Bed. Come to bed. I got an electric blanket."

"I can get into that!" Curtis grabbed his robe off the hook, and they hopped into bed, sliding under the covers. Curtis wrapped them both in the robe, holding him tight.

He turned the blanket on high, then pushed close, sharing warmth.

"Woo. This part of the house is like ice."

"Yeah. Come snuggle. I'll grab more blankets in a few."

"You got it." Curtis blew a raspberry on his neck.

That meant war.

Chapter Sixteen

Curtis woke up late. He knew it because the sun slanted across the floor and not the end of the bed. Damn. Damn it all.

Stetson was careworn and skinny, and he needed food and rest. Trouble was, Curtis would bet anything the man had been up and working for a few hours. Maybe he'd even gone to the damned store, and Curtis wanted to buy the groceries.

He looked out the window, shaking his head at the sight of his lover hauling wood in a wheelbarrow, up from God knew where. He knew the regular woodpile was long gone. *Stubborn ass.*

He dressed for warmth and made a mental note to get some damn longies in Taos.

There was a piece of paper on the counter, along with a wrapped-up peanut butter sandwich and a bag of Fritos.

Coffee's in the thermos. Found bread in the freezer. I'm trading for some wood.

Huh. Well, looked like the trade was done, so Curtis tugged on his coat and headed outside.

There was most of a half cord in the back of Stetson's truck. God knew what the man had traded off. A kidney? His soul?

Curtis didn't ask any of the questions ready to leap off the tip of his tongue. He just found a pair of gloves in the console of his truck and got to work unloading.

"You want to take the wheelbarrow? I wanted to be able to have a fire tonight after groceries."

"Sure." He was stiff and sore enough not to argue. He could help more this way, anyway.

"Did you eat? I left you a sandwich."

"Not yet. I'll grab it when we go in. Then I'm taking you into town and buying us something decadent."

"Yeah?" Stetson grinned at him, the look going all the way to his eyes. "You were sleeping good."

"I feel amazing." He really did. Working was stretching stuff the long day in the truck had bent.

"You look good in my bed."

"You think so?" That tickled the shit out of him. "It's warmer with you in it."

"The fire tonight will help warm everything up, and I promise to snuggle."

"I'm better now than I was last night. I just need to hit the nearest store where I can get some long undies." Snuggling was one of his superpowers and a great joy.

"You can borrow mine if you want. I'll take you in a bit."

"No problem, babe." He huffed and puffed by the end, but they got the wood stacked in no time. Curtis felt pretty accomplished.

"You need that sandwich, cowboy, and a bottle of water." He loved how Stetson said "sangwich."

"Huh?" He wiped the sweat off his face, trying to make sense of what Stetson was saying.

"Cowboy. Move. Now." Stetson muscled his ass into the house and sat him down. Then a PB and J appeared in his hand, along with a glass of water.

"Thanks." He stared at it until Stetson took the water away, then brought him apple juice, sticking the little straw right between his lips. Curtis sucked, the cold juice shocking him.

"There you go. Drink some more."

"Oh." That hit bottom, and he rolled his eyes. "Altitude. Shit, Roper, sorry."

"I know, cowboy. Eat your food now."

"Yeah." He took a bite of the sandwich, feeling better right off the bat. "Oh, that's good jelly."

"Rose hip from Mrs. Javes."

"What did you trade for the wood?" He popped the question out, hoping to surprise Stetson into answering.

"My motorcycle. I don't ride much no more. He gave me the wood and a couple hundred for feed."

"Oh." *Oh, damn.* "Well, I hope he gets some use out of it, huh?"

"Yeah. Someone ought to." Stetson took off his coat and poured himself a cup of coffee.

"Did you eat?" Curtis asked. "I really do want to take you to the diner or the pizza joint or something."

"I'm in." Stetson turned and leaned back against the counter, offering him a smile.

"Good deal." Curtis drank his water before a headache set in. He forgot how high Taos was. He didn't have altitude problems, but it did take a few days to adjust.

"You feeling better now?"

"Mmm. Yeah. I just got stupid." He didn't have any damned body fat, and he should have eaten that sandwich before he went out to work.

"You need some more to eat, honey?"

Hell, he wasn't sure what else there was in the house to feed him. Stetson's place was worn to the nub, cupboard to floor.

"Nah. I'm good. Will you come over here and kiss me good morning?" He held out one hand, not wanting to feel like strangers.

Stetson cackled, came right to him. "More like good evening, but I'll take it."

"Hey! It's not that late. Is it?" Shit, he didn't even know where his phone had ended up.

"It's four thirty, give or take."

"Christ, baby. Why didn't you get me up?" They would lose daylight in what? Half an hour? "Sorry."

He pulled Stetson down for the kiss he wanted so bad.

"For what? I can drive in the dark. I know how."

"I do too, you dork." Curtis laughed. "I just feel like you had to do twice as much without me helping."

"You deserved your rest." Stetson kissed him again, and again, and then again.

That was far better than food or sleep or even long underwear. The weight of Stetson on his thighs was pure magic; their bellies pressing together made him ache.

He hugged Stetson around the waist, hanging on tight so he could keep this moment. Right here.

"You're okay, cowboy. You can rest awhile."

"You want to share my Fritos?"

"I'll take one or two, sure."

Curtis opened the little bag of chips so they could share. They really did need to get groceries, but Stetson was in no hurry, so he could sit. The Smith's was open until eleven.

They could eat and then get their groceries on.

"You okay?" Stetson asked finally, stroking his hair.

"I am. Much better. You about ready?"

"Ready as I'll ever be."

"Let's do this, then."

Stetson stood, giving him a hand up, and they both put on their coats to head back outside. Stetson paused to give all the dogs a giant bowl of kibble.

He handed Stetson his keys. "We'll take mine if you want, but I'll let you drive since I was so wonky."

"Sure. Come on, I'll show you off."

"Hey, now. I ain't no trophy cowboy." He laughed right out loud, though, pleased as punch.

"You're mine."

That he was, sure as shit.

CHAPTER SEVENTEEN

THEY ENDED up at the pizza place, where they could carb load. Curtis·
needed the illusion of something healthy, and they had salads he could
have with his monster calzone.

Stetson wanted to tease, but he figured it was still too soon for that.
Curtis had that whole love-hate thing with food. Making a big thing of it
would make Curtis shut down and eat nothing but poached chicken and
egg whites. Maybe frozen grapes.

Him? He ate food when there was some around. Didn't when there
wasn't. Watching Curtis eat was still on the top of his wish list, though.

That lean pocket cowboy could flat-out moan and lick his fork.

Thank God for sitting down and jeans that were holding
everything back.

"You okay?" Curtis asked, nibbling at cheese he pulled off Stetson's
pizza.

"Just admiring the view, is all."

"The view—oh." Curtis flushed. "It's good shit."

"It is. I used to come a lot, just to hang out." Then he'd gotten old,
right along with Momma.

"It seems like a happening place." The little dining room was
packed, the noise and scent of garlic almost overwhelming.

"Yeah, it was, once upon a time. Still, I guess."

"I like the calzone. And the pizza."

"Hey, Stetson." Angela Hollis stopped by the table then. She
worked back in the kitchen.

"Hey, Angie honey. How've you been?" He stood, held out one hand.

"Good. Good. Lula said you were here and, well, I wanted to
say...." She took his hand. "I'm sorry about your mom."

"Thank you. It was time, I think." Hell, he knew.

"I know it must be hard, though." She patted his hand, her
expression all sympathy.

He nodded, trying to remember how to breathe. He didn't want
to do this, stand here and try to understand what the fuck he felt. If he

started thinking about how Momma was gone, then he had to think about bills and taxes and how he was so fucking happy not to go back to the fucking hospital and be able to sleep with Curtis in his bed, and that made him a bad man, and he knew it.

"Hi, I'm Curtis." Curtis stood as well and held out a hand to Angie.

"Hey there. You don't remember me, but we met a long time ago. It was four kids ago."

"Well, heck, I'm sorry." Curtis beamed. "I'll remember from now on, I reckon."

"You staying out to the ranch?"

"Yes, ma'am. Stetson needs me." Curtis didn't bat an eye.

"I bet he does. That place is big, and it needs about four more hands."

"It's not that bad, Angie." Stetson waved off that concern. It was his place. He knew every inch of that land and what it needed.

"Uh-huh. I'll come by tomorrow with food, huh?"

"That would be a kindness." Stetson hugged her, smelling basil and tomatoes and bread.

"You have a good night." She kissed his cheek before leaving them.

"I don't remember her, babe. Who is she?"

"You remember that girl that worked at the diner? The one that used to wait on us early?"

"No shit?" Curtis glanced back to the kitchen. "Huh."

"I know. She's changed. We all have."

"Sure we have. We're all old as fuck." Curtis winked.

"Yeah, damn near what? Thirty for you?"

"Yep. Long in the tooth for the rodeo game." Something pained crossed Curtis's face, so fast he hardly had time to see it.

"Stop it. You're the best in the world." Surely Curtis got that, believed it, knew it.

"I am this year." Curtis shook it off visibly, reaching for the last bite of his calzone and drenching it in sauce.

What was he supposed to say about that? Nothing, he guessed, so he didn't. He just picked at a bit of pizza until Curtis took it away from him and ate that too.

"You okay?" Maybe the better question was, was *he* fucking okay? He wasn't sure. Not at all.

"I'm fine, baby. I am." Curtis nudged his foot under the table.

"Stetson? We just wanted to say how sorry we were to hear about your momma." Mr. and Mrs. Apodaca stood there, Ralph's hat in hand. "Can we stop by tomorrow? Bring food?"

He stood again, feeling like he was in church. "Yes, ma'am. Thank you. She's at peace now."

"Finally with your papa again, hmm?" She was such a dear lady, but he wasn't sure he could hack this.

"Yes, ma'am. I'm sure he came to get her." Please. Please, he just wanted to scream. He didn't want to think right now.

"Well, I'll bring Flora by with food tomorrow," Ralph said, clearly more in tune with the cowboy way.

"Yes, sir. Thank you. I appreciate it." He sat, his hands fisted in his lap. These were good people. His people. They just wanted to mourn with him.

"You want to get a box for the rest, Roper?" Curtis asked quietly.

"Yeah. I'm done, and it's too good to waste."

"It is." Curtis rubbed his belly and winked, then simply turned to look at their waitress, which brought her running.

"You guys ready?" When Curtis nodded, she leaned and whispered, "It's on the house. We're so glad to have you back, and so sorry for the reason."

"Thank you." His throat closed up. Stetson wanted to go get groceries and never leave the house again.

"Hey, this is for you, then." Curtis tugged out his wallet and handed her a five. Good man. "Can we get a box?"

"Of course."

As soon as she left, he stood. "I need a…." Shit, he was supposed to have stopped smoking. "I'll be outside."

Then he took off and headed to the parking lot to light up. It was a crutch, one he couldn't afford, and a poor one at that, but it calmed his nerves.

Curtis joined him just a few minutes later. "That's nasty, Roper."

He guessed the grace period was over. Curtis had been good about the smoking when Momma was in the hospital.

"Uh-huh." Didn't mean he wasn't gonna finish this one.

"I mean it, baby." Curtis took the smoke and crushed it out. "So not good for you."

He didn't know whether to snarl or be pleased that someone cared enough to notice. Stetson settled on pleased and just nodded, then handed Curtis the half pack he had left.

"I can't promise not to hunt them when I'm desperate," Stetson murmured.

"You won't find them. As high as we are here, you don't need them."

"Butthead." He sighed, rolling his head on his neck. "Let's hit the Smith's, huh?"

"Yeah. We need snacks and things we can eat around all the enchilada casseroles and tamales we're fixin' to get."

Stetson smiled faintly. "We ought to get a ton of tortillas too. We should grab some of that grilled chicken and a bag of beans."

"What do you want that's decadent, baby? Seriously, something you want bad?"

"Swiss Cake Rolls." He said it immediately, no thought necessary.

Curtis stared a moment, then laughed softly. "You remember that weekend we spent snowed in over in Cedaredge in Colorado? We survived on dry roasted peanuts and Doritos and Swiss Cake Rolls."

"And those weird olives. God, those were so good. Salty." He'd had so much fun. They'd made love over and over, keeping each other warm.

"Yeah." Curtis got them going, driving to the Smith's. "We'll definitely get those, then."

"Maybe a little container...." They cost a damn fortune.

"Don't worry about it, babe. I got this trip. You know I'm picky about my coffee and creamer."

Oh, didn't that make him laugh. "You and your fancy-assed coffee!" For whatever reason, that made Stetson happy as a pig in shit.

"All that time spent on the road. I swear, they put crack in Starbucks." Curtis grinned across the cab at Stetson, and his heart clenched. Fuck, there'd never been anyone so beautiful in his eyes. No one.

Curtis hummed with the radio, something on the new country station on Sirius that Stetson had never even heard. They got parked at the grocery store and headed in, and he wondered if he should tell the pharmacy folks Momma was gone. Too late tonight, anyway, and she hadn't filled anything there in a long while, not since she'd been down in Santa Fe.

"Come on, baby. It's late and no one's about. Let's goof off a little."

"Pretend that we're kids again?" Pretend that everything was okay?

"That's it." Curtis hit the produce first, zooming the cart across the floor.

"Don't forget to grab grapes!"

"Whoops!" Curtis spun in a tight circle, the cart wheels squealing.

"Ride 'em, cowboy!" Oh sweet Jesus! He held his belly and laughed so hard, he damn near choked.

Curtis squealed to a stop, then bowed for him, dramatic as hell.

"That—you." Stetson wheezed. "Old Mrs. Ramirez will call the cops."

"What fun is that?" Curtis chuckled. "I'm not hurting nothin'."

"She's just a fan of orderliness." He winked. "Grapes?"

"And a couple of bananas." Curtis started putting fruit in the basket.

"Perv," he whispered.

"I am." Curtis nodded easily. "You are what you eat, after all."

Stetson blinked, and then he started laughing, the sound tearing out of him.

Curtis pushed to the veggies next, adding bagged salad, radishes, and avocados.

It was more fun to follow, watch in fascination as Curtis shopped. They moved on to meat, and he noticed Curtis mostly trolled the outer ring of the store where most of the health stuff lived. They did get ice cream. And Swiss Cake Rolls. Nuts. Doritos. Lord.

Then Curtis stopped by the pharmacy and picked up lube—the warming kind.

"Curtis Traynor!"

"What? Trust me. It's amazing. Do you want me to get condoms?"

"Do we need them?"

"Not unless you been doing skanky things, baby." Curtis went serious. "I haven't been active. In a while."

"I—you were the last, that I'd let in." The only.

"Well, there you go." Curtis left the rubbers on the shelf. "We got toilet paper and stuff?"

"I'll grab some. Folks will be coming."

"I bet. There's lots of folks who want to pay respects. I'll make some calls tomorrow about a service like I said." Curtis was so willing to help. That really made him feel better.

"Yeah. You're good to me." He went to grab a thing of Charmin.

Curtis started singing, some silly Chris LeDoux thing that suited the man to the ground.

God, when was the last time he'd been here? A year? More? Christ. Suddenly he felt like he was going to scream.

"You okay?" Curtis took the toilet paper out of his hands. "You look all froze up."

"Sorry. Woolgathering." Considering a total breakdown.

"We're almost there. We just need some Cokes and we're out."

"Good deal." It would get better, he knew. It had with Daddy. The hurts showed up less and less often, and then one day it was more bittersweet than awful.

He knew, but his heart didn't really give two shits about what all he knew. His heart ached, and all he could do was look at Curtis, because at least that made him smile.

"Come on." Curtis hefted two twelve-packs onto the bottom rack of the cart. "Let me take you home."

"I—yeah. That would be good. Sorry, cowboy, I'm just...." He spread his hands, his shoulders rising.

"Hush, Roper. I got you." Curtis wheeled up to the checkout. "You want to go wait in the truck?"

"You going to be pissed if I smoke?"

"Yep."

"Then I'll stay with you."

"You got more smokes hid somewhere?" Curtis gave him that look, the one that meant stubborn.

"Probably." Stetson could do stubborn.

"Butthead."

"Stetson. Hey. How are you?" Margaret was a sweetheart, and she and Momma had always gossiped together during checkout. "So sorry about Betty."

"Thank you, ma'am." Yeah, everyone was sorry she was dead. Everyone, but they hadn't been there the last, terrible few weeks.

That wasn't fair, was it? Those days were for family and nurses, so that everyone else could remember the dead fondly, not be fiercely glad it was over.

And what kind of fucked-up was he? To be glad the pain and starvation and loss was done. Shit.

"Hey." Curtis took his arm and moved him out of the way. "Can you bag up some stuff, Roper?"

"Huh? Yeah, sure. Sorry." He started bagging, head down. Man, they had bought the damn store.

"You're that rodeo friend of Stetson's," Margaret was saying. "Congratulations."

"Thanks." Curtis smiled his for-the-fans smile. "It was a good season for me."

"It was. You must be proud." Margaret got skinnier every time he saw her.

"Yes, ma'am." Curtis started bagging as well, and soon enough they were on their way, Margaret promising to drop by with soup.

Good thing they'd bought Saran wrap.

Curtis loaded the truck while he stood there, wishing he had a smoke.

"Baby, come on. You need to just sit a bit, I bet." Curtis bundled him into the truck.

"I'm sorry. I just...." He had spent months sleeping in his horse trailer.

"I know. No. I mean, I can see how bad this hurts. No platitudes from me." Curtis reached over to squeeze his leg.

"I thought it was never gonna end. It felt like I was never going to be able to breathe again."

"Starting to breathe again is the hardest part." Curtis chuckled. "I remember that from a certain breakup."

"Yeah. I—I thought I'd never see Danny Gonzales's face again without wanting to wipe the floor with him."

Curtis whipped his head around so fast, Stetson thought it might fly off and roll to the floorboards. "What?"

He looked over at Curtis, one eyebrow raised. "You didn't think I'd notice? I watched every single second of footage of you that was ever uploaded. I know when you're knocking boots."

A dark flush stained Curtis's cheeks, so hard he could see it by the glow of the dash lights. "I did a lot of stupid shit. I never once cheated on you, though. I swear."

"I believe you. I don't blame you or nothin'. I'm just sayin' I may have hated Gonzales a little bit." It had been what it was. He was married to the land, to the routine, to the idea that his life was in this high desert dirt. Curtis had wanted to live. He hadn't understood then, but he did now.

"Well, I would have hated me too." Curtis glanced at him sideways again. "It wasn't fair to him either."

"No?" He hoped Curtis had dumped him like a bushel of rotten potatoes. "How long has it been since y'all broke it off?"

His money was on five and a half years.

"I reckon you know that, Roper. We never. I mean, it was never serious enough to—well, shit. I never had to get tested after him, if you get me."

"I hear you. I don't want you to think I was stalking you or nothin'. I just missed you." He'd missed being part of an *us*.

"I missed you too." Curtis made a raw little sound. "I'm glad you called me. Even if the reason sucked."

"She loved you. Hell, she thought I was an idiot. You? She thought you were amazing. You made her happy, coming to see her."

"I'm glad. She was always good to me." Curtis turned off at the ranch. "We need to get you a new TV."

"Whut?" Curtis's mind worked faster than his, always had.

"We can put it on top of your momma's if you want, but there's no reason not to have one in the front room now."

"I guess not." Curtis could take it with him and…. "Where do you live, cowboy?"

He knew all of Curtis's sponsors, where his fan club was stationed, all the stats—how did he not know this?

"Huh? Oh. Uh." Curtis shrugged. "I have a storage thingy in Grand Junction, where my folks are now. I have a few boxes at my cousin's in San Angelo."

"Real estate's real pricey Colorado way, I hear." But those hot springs… Lord, Lord.

"Yeah. I mean, Mom and Dad would let me stay up at their cabin, but that always comes with strings." Curtis had an uneasy relationship with his folks. At best.

He watched the outline of Curtis's face in the dashboard lights. "If there's anything you've never needed, it was strings, cowboy. You deserve to be wild and free more than anybody I've ever met."

"I've done my share of rambling, for sure." A tiny smile curled Curtis's mouth. "I'm actually tickled as a pig in shit about Christmas. I haven't had a real one in a bit."

"I haven't either. It'll be ours."

"It will." That had Curtis grinning again, then leaning to kiss him once the truck was parked at the kitchen door.

"Hey, cowboy." He took one more kiss, because the truck was still warm and it was dark and he wanted to.

The contact settled him some, eased him deep inside.

Now he could unload the truck and maybe make up a little fire for them.

Just something for them.

CHAPTER EIGHTEEN

CURTIS SET the alarm on his phone so he wouldn't sleep in and make Stetson do all the damned work this morning.

He still managed to miss a good many of the chores, judging from the fact that Stetson was gone when he got up and still wasn't back after he had a shower and tugged on every bit of clothing he owned.

Jesus, was the furnace broke or just....

Fifty. The thermostat was set to fucking fifty.

Curtis stood in the hallway, torn. Stetson had his pride, and obviously he was having trouble making ends meet. That was clear as glass. But damn. Curtis turned it up to sixty-two. Happy medium.

"Shit, it's bitter out there." He heard Stetson stomping and clearing his boots of snow, and then he heard Stetson chuckle softly. "You pups hang out and I'll find everyone a couple more blankets."

Curtis moved to the kitchen and the coffee maker, which, wow. Ancient. Gross. Okay, he needed to make a trip to Target down in Santa Fe. Was there a Target in Española? He couldn't remember. "Morning, Roper."

"Hey, cowboy, you sleep good? Everyone's fed and snuggled up out there."

"I did. You need me to help with the dogs?"

"Nah, I'm just going to make sure they've got enough to keep warm. Fixin' to dump snow again this afternoon."

"It's amazing up here. Shit, I'd forgotten the winter." He'd acclimatize again, but right now he needed to carb load and mainline water.

Stetson chuckled for him, then disappeared into Miss Betty's part of the house and returned with a pile of old blankets. "You want to start coffee, and I'll bring in some wood."

"I'm on it. You want pancakes for breakfast?" He knew he'd gotten all the stuff last night.

"Oh, that would be a blessing. Please, thank you."

"You got it." Coffee. Pancakes. Chicken sausage. He snagged Stetson for his good morning kiss because he wanted one.

"Oh—" Stetson's lips were icy, but the kiss wasn't. Not at all.

No, the contact warmed up real quick, Stetson wrapping those long arms around his neck and holding on. He hummed, a happy noise that kinda surprised him.

He stepped right into the curve of Stetson's body, holding them tight together. They both tilted their heads the other way, the kiss going deep in another direction.

Jesus. Good morning to him. He worked the buttons of Stetson's shearling coat open, hunting that tight body that waited for him. Life was short. He was gonna start with dessert first.

"Curtis! It's morning!"

"Mmm. Broad daylight, even." He grinned at Stetson, feeling his face stretch with it. "God, I want to lay you out in the sunshine one day, watch you arch for me."

Stetson moaned, the sound damn near pained.

"You need loving, Roper. You scream for it." He nipped Stetson's exposed skin, just above the starched shirt collar.

"For you. I need your loving. No one else's."

"Now, that's the perfect thing to hear." He smiled up at Stetson, tickled to death.

"Just the truth, huh?"

"God." He kissed that hot mouth again, mainly to keep himself from saying all manner of sappy shit. They were still adjusting.

The sound of tires crunching on gravel sounded, and Stetson sighed. "It's day five. It's time, huh?"

"Well, and you were out and about yesterday." Curtis dropped one more short kiss on Stetson's mouth. "Lots of coffee. I'll help any way I can."

"You are. I'm not very good at this part."

"Bullshit." He remembered his Roper out there carving vigas and haggling with folks, about how you couldn't go to town for a beer without someone wanting Stetson to do something with them.

Hell, he'd been there last night. These folks were ready for Stetson to come back.

Maybe Stetson didn't think he was ready, but time waited for no man.

The dogs set up a ruckus, so Stetson buttoned back up and stepped outside.

Curtis got to making coffee. They would need it.

The door opened and two women came in, one carrying fry bread, the other a covered dish. "Stetson told us to come in. He's on the porch with Matt."

"Hi. I'm Curtis." *Who's Matt?*

"I'm Denita. This is my daughter, Aliya. Matt and Stetson went to high school together. He's my brother."

"Oh. Pleased to meet you, ma'am. Here, let me take that. Something smells amazing."

"Just carne adovada." She smiled, her face changing completely with the expression. "How can we help? Do you know?"

"Not yet. I know he took care of some stuff at the hospital, but I need to make some calls about a service. As far as around here, I think what Stetson really needs is stuff he's just had to let go with the traveling back and forth. Firewood. Riding fence. Cleaning. That sort of thing." Was that presumptuous of him?

"Aliya, call Anthony, eh? Tell him that Mr. Stetson needs wood. I'll tell Gina at the feed store about the fence. We take care of our own. We're glad he's home."

The door opened again, and before Curtis could breathe, there were fifteen women in the house and an equal amount of old men building a fire in the horno outside and pulling up chairs.

One of the older ladies—who looked weirdly like a carved apple person—grabbed his arm, handed him a cup of coffee, and sort of forcibly pushed him out of the house.

"I was gonna make pancakes...." The door shut in his face. "Or not." He glanced around at the chorus of chuckles he heard from the men.

"Might as well come sit. I'm Darby." A round man with long braids stood and held out a hand. "The fire is warm, and we have breakfast tacos."

"I'm Curtis."

"We know. We heard congratulations are in order. Glad you're here."

Suddenly he was sitting in a circle, listening to stories about Betty and Parker Major, about how they'd built the ranch.

"I remember Parker wanted nothing more than to ride, though. I swear to God, I worked with him building this place for six years, but the bulls called him." Tom Harrison had damn near raised Stetson, and Curtis had always thought, quite privately, that Betty and Tom had been having an affair for years, even before Parker passed.

The man looked old today, lines carved deep in his face, and Curtis reminded himself that Stetson wasn't the only one mourning Miz Betty.

"It will make a man crazy," Curtis agreed. "The ride, I mean."

One of the younger guys with a prosthetic leg and a crew cut grunted. "It's adrenaline. I know about that."

The men nodded and murmured, like a group of ravens.

"You in the service?" he asked.

"The 82nd. I was a warrant officer. Came home eight months ago."

He reached over to shake the man's hand. "Thank you for your service."

"Miguel Torres."

"Curtis Traynor." They nodded like old men sitting around a checkerboard at the feed store. "Someone said tacos?"

"Egg and bacon or egg and sausage?"

"Bacon. Go big or go home, right?"

"Stetson? You ain't no more than bones and skin. Eat. Eat, now." That man had to belong to the lady who'd shoved him out the door. Lord have mercy.

"Here, Roper." Curtis picked two foil-wrapped tacos out of a basket someone shoved at him. "Breakfast."

Stetson took them, then offered him a smile that he hadn't seen since Thanksgiving.

This was good. This was what Stetson needed, to know he wasn't alone. Curtis opened up a taco. "We got any green chile?"

A little tub was tossed at him, and he grabbed it. Someone added another log to the fire. Men left and new ones came, and they sat there, talking and telling stories as the day got colder and colder.

As the clouds rolled in, a huge trailer pulled up, full of firewood and hay, sweet feed and salt licks, and the propane truck showed up a few minutes later.

Curtis stood there, teeth in his mouth. He'd be goddamned.

Stetson got a little wild around the eyes. "What's going on? Curtis? I didn't order a feed delivery."

"Don't worry on it." Tom patted Stetson's arm with that three-fingered hand. "We take care of our own."

There was a crack in Stetson's armor, his face crinkling up, and everyone looked away. Everyone but Curtis. He got that part of Stetson too.

He touched Stetson's arm and got a tiny smile.

"I don't know what to say, guys."

"How many times have you been out at dawn looking for a horse or fixing a door?" Tom snorted gracelessly. "Hell, you dug out a sewer line for my mama two years ago."

"Well, she needed it."

"Right. Now we can do for you." Miguel thrust a Navajo taco at Stetson. "Shut up and eat lunch so we can go unload."

"How about we all unload and then have a bite?"

Curtis knew there was no way Stetson was going to let a wounded warrior unload and him sit.

"Sounds good." Tom climbed to his feet, joints popping like rifle shots.

"Come on, boys! That snow's not going to wait on us!"

They fell on the pile, unloading and feeding and laughing at each other, their breaths turning to smoke in the cold. Curtis warmed to the whole situation, which was a damn sight like being on tour. Without all the dick measuring.

By the time it was all done, people started heading home, beating the weather, and suddenly it was him and Stetson and Tom, standing there in the kitchen.

"I came to see her, before Thanksgiving, you know, but... she didn't know me, Stetson. I've been her... her friend for thirty-plus years, and she didn't know me. I didn't know how to be with that."

Stetson nodded, jaw tight, but meeting Tom's eyes. "I know that, Tom. I'm grateful you were her friend. She wouldn't have wanted you to see her like that."

"No. No, she probably wouldn't. She was a proud woman. I just... I feel like shit, not coming more."

"You fed for me, more than once. You did what needed doing."

"I wish it had been more." Tom held out a hand to Curtis, shaking first his, then Stetson's hand. "If you need me at all, you call."

"Yessir. You go on. I know you have things to do. This storm's supposed to be a stone-cold bitch." Stetson walked Tom to the door, gave the man a back-pounding hug, and then showed him out.

Curtis looked around. The kitchen was spotless, more food than they could ever eat stacked on counters and in the fridge. Funny thing was, he still wanted pancakes.

Stetson locked the door, then moved to put another log on the fire.

Curtis watched him for a few moments, just checking in, seeing how Stetson moved, where his shoulders sat in relation to his ears.

"What a day, huh? Can we still have pancakes, man? Please?"

"I was just going to ask." Curtis grinned, the pop of worry breaking like a bubble. "I'm still craving."

"Me too." Stetson stood up. "I'm going to take off my boots and all, find you some heavy socks."

"Sounds good." He headed for the kitchen to start assembling supper. Bowl, milk, eggs, pancake mix. He'd even heat up the syrup.

It didn't seem long before Stetson's hands were on his shoulders, a pair of heavy socks and sweats appearing. "I'll get the griddle out while you change."

"Thanks, baby." He sat in the kitchen chair, pretty sure his boots were frozen to his feet. Still, when he took them off, his feet were there and his toes weren't weird colors. Cool.

"We need to get you better socks."

"We do. I can get them at the Walmart, but I might need a Target run."

"That's in Santa Fe."

"We can go down, have lunch, come home, and never go near the hospital."

"Sounds like a plan. I'd love to go to the Plaza and see who's at the governor's palace." Stetson knew every Native American artist from the Four Corners to Oklahoma. Seriously. He loved that, that Stetson believed in the art. Who would believe that about his stern cowboy lover?

Curtis hoped to hell Stetson got back to his wood carving soon. He needed his hands on the wood, making it into what it wanted to be.

"I got the griddle heated up. You want bacon or anything?"

"I was thinking that chicken and sage breakfast sausage, but I'm easy." He stirred the buttermilk into the mix.

"In the freezer?"

"Yep. We can eat a whole box."

"A whole box, huh?" Stetson started rummaging.

"Yep. I love that shit." He'd had bacon for breakfast, and God knew what was in that taco at lunch....

Whatever it was, it had tasted like spicy heaven.

Together they put together a great breakfast for dinner. Buttery, rich, sweet—Curtis felt like he was going to have a foodgasm.

He patted his belly. "That's probably more than I've eaten in one day in three years or more."

"Me too. It was so good. I love pancakes."

"God, yes." He would cheat on his diet for IHOP on the road. "What's on the agenda tonight, baby? Just resting?"

It had been a long day.

"Sit, rest, watch the snow fall. It's nice in here tonight, warm."

"It is." Jesus, how long had it been since Stetson ran the heat? "All that cooking."

"Uh-huh. It smells good and everything. Maple syrup candles should be a thing."

"It totally should." Maybe it was. His mom loved that candle place in the mall. She bought them in sugar cookie and pumpkin pie smell.

"Thank you for being here, cowboy. I appreciate it."

"I'm glad I was. You have an amazing group of neighbors." The stories, the faces.... They'd all fascinated him. He did love a good bullshit session.

Curtis finished drying the last dish. "Come on. Let's sit."

"Sounds good."

There were heavy blankets piled on the sofa, just perfect to snuggle under. Curtis slid deep in the couch cushions and tugged Stetson down before covering them up. Lord, that was nice. Warm, but also cuddly.

"Hey." Stetson rested against him. "We're gonna be snowed in, if we're lucky."

"Well, we got groceries and wood and feed." And a Christmas tree that was still in the bag. Tomorrow he would get out the little wreath and some of the goodies.

"What else do we need?"

"Each other." He was convinced that could cure any ill.

"Romantic." Stetson kissed his jaw.

"I'm a cowboy. We're all hearts and roses." He winked, wrapping an arm around Stetson's shoulders.

"I'll keep that in mind."

"You better, baby. I'm also into sex." He wanted to make Stetson laugh out loud.

"Hearts, roses, fucking." The soft chuckles started. "Anything else?"

"Mmm. Bacon. But sparingly. And you know my secret obsessive food."

"Sopapillas. With extra honey," Stetson said immediately.

"Uhn." He wasn't even hungry and he would eat those.

"See? I know all."

"You do." He leaned over to take a long, slow kiss. "There's no one I'd rather be snowed in with, Roper."

Stetson reached up to touch his cheek. "Ditto, cowboy. It's really coming down. I think it will happen."

"I can't wait to see it in the morning." Curtis grinned. "Though I have some thoughts about the kind of snuggling we can do in bed tonight."

"Perv." From the light in Stetson's eyes, though?

His cowboy knew exactly what he was thinking.

CHAPTER NINETEEN

STETSON WAS hiding.

Like a giant yellow-bellied coward in the back bathroom with the door shut.

They'd done the funeral; they'd sprinkled Momma's ashes over a piece of ground that they'd cleared of the snow. The deal was done.

Now he needed everyone to leave him the fuck alone.

Too bad there were all these freaking people. As many as there had been the day everyone had decided to finally come see him. More. People he didn't like as well as Tom and all....

Lord help him, he needed a little breather. Maybe a lot of breathers in a row.

There was a part of him—a mean, bitter part of him—that pointed out that none of these folks were here when Momma was here. Not even Curtis.

Hell, Curtis would still be happily wandering around if Stetson hadn't called.

That was so not fair. Curtis had come right off the bat when he called. And stayed to help a goodly bit.

A soft knock sounded on the door. "Roper? You okay?" Speaking of Curtis....

"Yeah. Yeah, I'll be right out." He washed his face and smoothed his black shirt. He'd had to dig it out of the closet, and it didn't fit so well anymore.

"No worries. I was just checking. Hang out in the bedroom if you want. The only folks left are Tom and the Martinez peeps, though, if you want to say bye."

Now, how had Curtis accomplished that?

"Okay. I'll be right there." Tom. The Martinezes. He could do this.

He walked out, glad as hell that he didn't have to paste on a smile.

"Hey." Tom gave him a half hug. Very manly. "I know I need to get out of your hair. You need anything, you call. Jake and I already did your feeding."

"Y'all rock. I appreciate it."

"No problem." Jake Martinez pumped his hand. "Belinda left you more tortillas and some horno bread."

"I'm gonna get fat."

"You could use a couple pounds." Tom grinned. "Come on, Jake. I'll buy you a beer."

"Nah, you'll buy me a margarita. On the rocks." Jake chuckled, following Tom out the door.

The quiet that descended was a balm to his frazzled nerves.

He stood there, just feeling like a shattered window that was holding in the frame. One touch and he'd just turn to shards.

Curtis stood a few feet away, looking at him. Kinda cautious, and how could Stetson blame him?

He didn't know what to say. *My momma's dead? I just poured the remainder of her onto the ground, and she's gone, for sure? I'm tired, and I'm scared because now I'm supposed to just go back to real life again, but I'm not sure I remember how?*

"Did you see Jake brought you some twisted cedar? He thought you might be able to use it to carve some."

"Did he? I haven't done that in a long time." He looked at his hands, wondering if he even knew how to carve. "I think I have to get the fuck out of here."

He stopped, tilted his head. He hadn't intended to say that.

"Okay. You want me to come with?" Curtis wasn't smiling, exactly, but he had that knowing look about him.

"Please. I just want to go away." Anywhere. Everywhere.

"You got it." Curtis moved around, gathering coats and keys. "We fed the dogs a bit ago, so we're good. Come on."

He let Curtis lead him out the door and into the truck, let him drive out the long, icy ranch lane and into the early darkness.

Stetson had no idea where Curtis might take him. He didn't care. He just had to go.

They got on Highway 64 and started driving, Curtis singing with Luke Bryan on the radio.

He leaned his head back, his brain rattling a little in his head. Lord, he was tired.

The car kept going, and for a second Stetson thought they were going to stop at Angel Fire, but they kept going on. He wondered if he should text Tom and ask him to feed again in the morning....

Hell, he could get someone to come in. The dogs had plenty of shelter. He would just trust Curtis.

Right now, he needed someone to take care of him a minute.

"You need anything, Roper? Cup of coffee or a candy bar?"

He took a deep breath, trying to see if there was room inside him for food yet, and he found out there was. "I could handle a drink, yeah."

"Cool." Curtis pulled off at the next gas market dealie. "You want to sit?"

"No. I want to come with." He wanted to see something different, even if it was the same.

"Good deal." Curtis shot him a relieved smile. "Man, this place looks quiet, huh? If we held hands, the clerk might have a heart attack."

"They might. Although, this is ski country. They might not care."

"True enough." Curtis took his arm, which he thought was a nice compromise.

They bought stupid shit—Funyuns and Dr Pepper, Sixlets and a cappuccino from a machine. They pondered the many flavors on chicharrones before deciding that was too much like Funyuns and going for the hot fries and Corn Nuts instead.

"Why do I suddenly want a Slushie? It's like eight degrees out there," Curtis said.

"It's instinct. You come in a place like this and see the machine, and eight-year-old Curtis says, 'Gimme.'"

"Right? I used to con Ally, the lady who worked at the Go-Fer, to let me mix Coke and cherry."

"I like the Coke best. Always have."

"Purist," Curtis accused, and Stetson couldn't argue the point when it came right down to it. "I need a Big Cherry too." Curtis swerved off to the candy aisle.

"I like the peppermint ones."

"Peppermint Pattie it is." Curtis grabbed Slim Jims, and by the time they got to the register, they had a feast of junk.

"Y'all heading to Colorado for your green?" The guy behind the counter looked like he knew all about that.

Curtis cackled like a big bird. "I wish. Nah. Just an impromptu road trip."

"Road trips are cool, man. Seriously. We all need more of them."

"You know it. What's the best thing to see around here?"

"Angel Fire is cool, but there's a wicked haunted hotel in Cimarron."

"No shit?" Stetson blinked. He'd never heard that.

"Well, it's just a cool hotel too, but that's the rumor. It's like Old Westy."

"I think I saw that on *Haunted Collector*." Curtis grinned when they both raised their eyebrows at him. "I'm on the road a lot. I watch marathons."

"Dude, that's cool. You should check it out. See if you have an experience."

"Totally." Curtis paid for their shit, and they were outside again, laughing breathlessly.

They tumbled into the truck, sharing a piece of chocolate and a kiss.

"Mmm." Curtis touched his cheek right above the corner of his mouth. "Chocolate."

He reached up, wiped it clean. "Did I get it?"

"Yeah. Rats." Curtis winked before settling behind the wheel. "Cimarron, then?"

"Let's go. I haven't had an adventure since...." He shrugged. "I don't know."

"Well, we can't have that." Curtis got the wheels moving again, back on the state highway.

"I'm not boring. I just had a lot of work to do."

"Baby, I'm not judging. I'm just saying we need to get you out and doing now that you can. Easing you into things, well, you know that's not my style." Curtis glanced at him, clearly checking in.

"No. No, it's not." It was one of the things he'd fallen in love with. Curtis was take charge, full speed ahead. So full of life it hurt.

He was... steady, he guessed. Strong, for sure.

"Anyway, you got good friends who will help if we have a wander." Curtis jerked his chin at the bags of food. "Slim Jim, please?"

"Absolutely." He unwrapped one and handed it over. "Lord, nothing smells like those."

"Yeah. Kinda like a three-day bull rope." Curtis wrinkled his nose. "They're addictive, though."

"No carbs. Portable. Smell like ass. The perfect gay cowboy food."

Curtis burst out laughing, slapping the steering wheel with one hand. "Fuck, yes. I love that, you know?"

"What's that, cowboy?"

"How you're funny. I fucking love that."

Stetson snorted. "I'm a giant dork, but I'm glad you like it." He touched Curtis's leg, just resting his fingers there. Connecting.

"I do. I want to take you a thousand places, you know that?"

"Like where?" He wanted to listen, to hear Curtis talk about his travels. Rest his head.

"We should go to Galveston, to Disneyland. To Hawaii. You know how much fun we'll have in Hawaii?"

"Hawaii?" He'd never even dreamed that far. "I would love Disneyland." He had this desperate need to ride Pirates of the Caribbean. He blamed *Jurassic Park*, which he watched every time he saw it on.

"Which one?"

"Are they different?"

"Well, one is Disney World, I reckon, and it's in Florida."

"Oh, California is far enough." He'd never been east of Texas.

"We could do LA while we're there. Pretend we're famous."

Stetson chuckled. His cowboy was as close to famous as he needed to be. "You know where I hear is real pretty? Reno. Lake Tahoe."

"It is. We can go there too. We can plan things, if you want."

What did that mean? Did it mean plan to visit while Curtis was on the road? He had no idea, and he wasn't going to ask. Right now he lived on the fantasy that Curtis was going to hang around past stock show season.

"Sure. I want. I—" He was fucking overwhelmed, is what he was. He grabbed his coffee and drank deep.

"What do you want, Roper?" Curtis asked the question gently, but not hesitantly at all.

"To plan things with you."

Planning didn't cost a dime.

"Good." Curtis covered his hand for a moment, squeezing. "I just got you back, and I'm not ready to let go."

"Would… would you ever have called me, do you think?"

"I don't know, Roper." Curtis sighed, the sound a little sad. "Truth be told, I was ashamed of the way I slunk off. I was afraid if I called you'd tell me to fuck right off, so I told myself it was better to let you move on."

"You ought to have known I wasn't going anywhere." That had been the whole thing.

"I—I never have been real bright." A soft chuckle sounded. "I'm learning shit all the time."

"Momma would tell you that meant you were still alive."

"I guess so. Some lessons come hard."

"There's the exit. Cimarron."

"That didn't take long." Curtis guided the truck off the exit. "So, we'll get us a room, maybe have supper. Then we might have to wander around and look for ghosts."

"I appreciate this. I know you don't have to humor me."

"What? I get to take you out and show you off. You got no idea how ready I am to do that."

"Doesn't look like there's much to Cimarron to show me to." The main drag was mostly shut down.

"Lots of galleries and such for tomorrow. You might make a contact or two."

"A contact? What for?"

"Your carving. I know you. You'll get the itch to start again."

"You think so?" He sure as shit hoped so.

"I do. It's tough to make art when you're hurting, Roper. You have to get back to yourself first, but I know you."

Curtis kept saying that. Over and over. Stetson wasn't sure he was the guy Curtis thought he knew. They'd see.

They pulled in by the hotel, which looked twinkly and festive in the snow.

"Oh, now that's fine." He could imagine it a hundred and fifty years ago, serving settlers, folks heading to California.

"It is. I was a little worried rolling into town, honestly."

"I guess it's a little like a hidden gem deal."

"I'm in. Let's see what they got in rooms." Curtis hopped out, whooping a little. "Cold!"

"Listen to you! Ain't you from Texas? I hear Texans spend all their time in Colorado." He was putting on a face, though, because it was bitter.

"Yeah. I stay in Glenwood Springs when I'm there. Forty-five hundred feet, tops." Curtis trotted to the door, opened it for him.

"Thank you, sir." He tipped his hat, feeling daring as all get-out.

"You're most welcome." It was Curtis who got him back fast, pinching his butt when he passed.

His steps hiccupped a bit, but that was it. He was smooth. Suave. Debonair.

"Evening, gents." The lady who ducked out into the lobby smiled for them, looking a bit harried. "What can I do you for?"

"I don't suppose you have any rooms?"

She shook her head. "I just got the one, and it's a king. I'm sorry, fellas."

Curtis's cheeks went pink, but he cleared his throat. "Is it gonna get us kicked out if I say that's what we would have asked for?"

One eyebrow lifted, and Stetson considered getting his back up, but the smile she gave them was warm. "None of mine, boys. If the ghosts protest, I'm not to blame."

"No, ma'am. We'll take our chances." Curtis gave her that gold-buckle-winner smile.

"Good deal. Restaurant's open for supper. Y'all are welcome."

Curtis handed her a credit card, signed the papers, and they were heading upstairs, the steps creaking under their boots.

"You feel like we ought to whisper?" Curtis asked.

"I know, right? It's like… I don't know. Like folks are hearing you."

"Or maybe you're waiting to hear them." Curtis unlocked their room, and darn, it was pretty.

"Is it wrong of us? To come and stay after just an hour's drive?"

"Nope. This is a getaway. Just a night or so. Nothing wrong with it at all." As soon as the door closed, Curtis reeled Stetson in for a kiss.

It was so easy to let himself pretend that they were in the Wild West, together in this room that smelled of wood and old dust. No bags or TV or clock radios. Just them in their hats and boots.

Curtis cupped his ass, the touch gentle and solid, all at once. They rocked together, rubbing their belt buckles.

He felt naughty, like they shouldn't be kissing and humping here, but it felt so good. No way was he giving this up. No way in hell.

"Relax, babe. Let yourself go, just for a second."

"I'm trying." He laughed, linking his hands behind Curtis's neck. "I'm just a little crazy."

"I know. I swear to God, Roper, you think on things, so much."

"Is that bad?" He leaned back just enough to meet Curtis's eyes.

"Only when I feel dumb." Curtis shrugged a little. "That sounds asinine. I mean how is it about me? But sometimes I do wonder if I'm just not that deep."

"I don't know how to answer that."

"Then don't, babe. Breathe. Be here with me, just for a little while." Curtis leaned against him, forehead and nose pressed to his. They shared the same space, the same breath.

His shoulders shook as the tension tried to let go, the muscles trembling.

"Oh, baby." Curtis reached up to rub his shoulders.

"Sorry."

"Don't be. You've held the world for years."

"I feel like it." He leaned, goose bumps rising on his arms. "Who was that guy that carries the earth around? Atlas?"

"Isn't that a map book?" Curtis waggled his eyebrows at him, teasing him like the butthead he was.

"Right. Ass."

"Yeah, but I'm yours and you reckon to keep me." Curtis kissed him once more before heading to the bathroom. "Sorry, baby, all of a sudden...."

"When you gotta go, you gotta go." He shucked his coat and went to sit next to the window. Did he think too much? Did he stress things too bad?

The toilet flushed; then the sink sounded. Curtis came back into the main room. "Whew. Man, all that cappuccino...."

"You got warm and your bladder unfroze."

"I guess so. Want to go down and explore? The dining room was the saloon once. I saw the brochure."

"Kiss me one more time?" Then they could rejoin the world at large.

"Hell, yes." Curtis came right to him, grabbing him for a kiss, holding him tight as if he understood.

Maybe he was losing his shit, but they weren't home, they weren't lost, and he wasn't alone.

Dammit.

CHAPTER TWENTY

CURTIS LOVED the old saloon feel of the restaurant. They had steaks and burgers and New Mexican stuff, so he didn't feel like he was pushing Stetson to eat anything weird. That could wait for California.

The tin ceiling made him grin. He thought maybe those were bullet holes up there.

"You think those are bullet holes?" he asked, nudging Stetson with the toe of his boot under the table.

"If this was the saloon? I do. This was the Wild West back then, you know?"

"Yeah. Gun law." Curtis didn't pine for those days like some guys did on the circuit. He liked his smartphone and his pickup. "This place is amazing. Smells good too."

"Meat. It smells like heaven." Stetson looked around, eyes following the carved wood frame of the mirror over the bar. Stetson kept acting surprised when Curtis said he would want to go back to wood carving, but that creative streak would pop right back up now that Stetson had the time. It was sunk deep into him. He used to be able to watch that for hours—Stetson and his chisels and knives, focused totally on the wood and what it was telling him.

"Hey, folks. What can I get you to drink?" A cheerful older lady came to wait on them, handing them menus.

"A light beer?" Curtis asked.

"A margarita on the rocks and a glass of water, please."

"Salt?"

"Please." Stetson smiled, and finally, blessedly, it wasn't strained.

God help him, he wanted to see that smile every goddamn day. He wanted to wallow in it. He dreaded the rodeo season starting up again, because if nothing else, he'd be expected to go sign autographs at some of the big events, and he wasn't wanting to leave Stetson.

Maybe this time Stetson could come with him. At least to a few places. He wanted to show Stetson the world.

Stetson dragged his fingers over the table. "This isn't old like the bar is. Pretty solid, though."

"I like it. Dark wood. It has a nice patina to it." Hell, he had no idea what he was babbling about.

Stetson chuckled for him, shook his head. "I do too. Can you imagine traveling out here in the olden days? Stagecoaches and horses."

"No. I mean, that had to be wicked uncomfortable." Stuffed in a tiny space with a bunch of smelly strangers.

"I would have had to ride, even in the worst weather. Outside is better than in."

"You and your horses." Curtis loved to ride too. They'd go a lot once the weather was better, he reckoned.

"Yeah. Spring is coming, and they'll all want their exercise."

"Christmas first, though, right?"

"Yeah. Christmas first."

He fist-pumped the air. "Yee-haw." He winked at Stetson, then leaned back to let the server put down their drinks.

"Y'all ready to order or do you need a few minutes?"

"I haven't even opened my menu, ma'am." Stetson smiled up at her, and she melted a little bit. "Do you mind giving me a couple?"

"Not one bit. I'll bring you some bread."

Stetson looked at the menu, and Curtis did the same, his eyes stopping at the chicken, just like always, but he wasn't on tour right now, and that steak smelled like pure heaven. Steak it was. He'd make the baked potato plain and have a salad with it.

"What are you going to get, Roper?"

"I think the...." Stetson looked again. "They got a burger, it looks like."

"With all sorts of add-ons. You don't want lamb?" He had to tease.

"No, sir. No, even if it wasn't as much as a steak, I wouldn't order it."

"Well, I'm buying, so if you want steak, splurge. You fed me the whole time I stayed before. It's my turn to pick up the tab."

"Are you sure? You got the hotel room and all...."

Curtis nodded easily. "I got that check with the gold buckle, and I got a good bonus from my hat sponsor, baby. We're good." He just wanted Stetson to stay relaxed and happy.

"I'll be back on my feet soon, I hope."

"I know you will. Medical bills are tough. Remember how I sent home all my checks that year my dad broke his leg? Mom thanked me, at least, but it was ramen noodles for a while."

"Yeah. I remember that. You're a good son."

"Shit. I was just scared she'd ask me to come home." His mom loved him, but if he heard "hate the sin, love the sinner" one more time in his life, he might snap.

Stetson nodded, the look sympathetic. "At least Momma never got onto me for being the way I am, not even at the end."

"She was your staunchest defender." Curtis smiled fondly. Miz Betty had been fierce.

"No. She was disappointed in me. She wanted me to be more like you."

"Oh, baby, she was so proud of you. She liked me 'cause I reminded her of your daddy, I guess, but you were her boy." Curtis knew that, deep down. Betty had told him so.

"I was. Am. Whatever. I can't be more than I am. I'm just a...."

"You're a cowboy. You're more of a cowboy than ninety percent of those 'rodeo athletes' that have never strung a foot of fence or pulled a calf. Don't even go there. You got it in your bones."

Stetson blinked at him, and then a slow smile spread over his face. "Thanks, cowboy. That means a lot coming from you."

"You folks ready?" The server was back, but she wasn't being intrusive.

"Steak, baked potato plain, salad with oil and vinegar, please."

"I'd like the same, please, but with butter and sour cream and ranch dressing." Stetson winked at him. "I ain't worried about fitting into my jeans."

"It's the belt buckles." Curtis hooted, and so did their server.

"You ride the rodeo, I guess," she said.

"I do." He didn't elaborate.

"Excuse me." An older gentleman stopped at their table. "I don't want to be a turd, but are you Curtis Traynor?"

"Yessir." Curtis stood, holding out a hand to shake.

"Bill Mackey. I saw you win the Finals. It's a pleasure. A real pleasure."

"Thank you. I wasn't sure I'd ever win it." He let Bill pump his hand, always tickled to meet a fan.

"Are you in town long? I'd be pleased to buy you a beer later."

"Oh, well, that would be real nice, but we've been on the road...."

"Sure. Sure. Well, do you mind if my wife gets a picture on her phone?"

"Not at all." He posed with the man, and Stetson even took a picture of the three of them.

"Thanks so much, Curtis. We appreciate you." The couple left the dining room, and he plopped back in his chair.

"Lord. Cimarron of all places." He chuckled.

"My famous Mr. Traynor."

"I'm all that and a bag of chips."

"You're all of it to me."

He flushed with pleasure, then reached out to touch Stetson's hand where it lay on the table. "I'm glad."

"Me too." There was a little shadow in Stetson's eyes, but the man had just lost his momma. It had to hurt in waves.

They got their food, and Stetson perked up. Now, that smile was worth all the work.

"Damn, that looks fine."

Stetson was right. In fact, that butter and sour cream looked like heaven.

Curtis licked his lips. Damn it. "Ma'am? Can I get some butter and sour cream?"

Stetson's grin was knowing, teasing, but he didn't say a word.

"Yeah, yeah." He drizzled oil over his salad, then liberally applied vinegar. "What can I say?"

"What? I judge not. Butter is a great thing."

"It looks so good." He dumped it all on the potato once it came, mixing it all in. Smell that. Damn.

"Salt? Pepper?"

"Please." He went light on the salt, heavy on the pepper. Just the simple act of sitting down to a meal without counting calories amazed him.

They ate, taking their time, laughing and telling stories. He had a second beer and ordered another round for Stetson. He was addicted to the sight of his lover with his shoulders relaxed.

"You boys want dessert?"

They looked at each other, then at the waitress. "What have you got?"

"We have a pecan pie, an apple pie, a brownie sundae, and a tres leches cake."

"You want to split pecan pie?" Curtis asked. He knew Stetson loved pecans.

"I'd love to. Absolutely. It's damn near Christmas, after all."

"It is!" He nodded. "Pecan it is."

"Ice cream?"

"God yes." Curtis was gonna need a cart to wheel his ass back to the room.

If he was lucky, Stetson would push it for him.

Pie and ice cream made Stetson moan happily, and they had coffee to boot. Maybe they would wander out in the snow and work it off.... Or go upstairs.

Stetson licked the ice cream off his spoon, humming low.

"That might be the best part so far, Roper." Curtis knew it was for him. Stetson. Licking.

"The ice cream is good, huh?"

"Uh-huh. The pie stuff makes it taste like butter pecan."

"Mmm. I have a bit of that in the freezer at home."

"I'll remember that, you know." Reddi-wip. He would get that on the way home.

"I'll share it with you."

"We'll get whipped cream and more candied pecans to go on top." He'd have to order one of those little trampolines on Amazon and start jogging. Hell, he'd bet Stetson could put him to work.

He found that idea surprisingly perfect.

He was going to have to unpack that a little, but there was something so right about thinking about fixing up the house, the barns, exercising the horses.

"You sure you can go that decadent?" Stetson teased.

"I think maybe I can, Roper."

"Good deal." Stetson leaned back and groaned, patting his belly. "Oh, I'll sleep good tonight."

He would take that. He thought Operation Distract Stetson was working.

If it stopped, he had more than one surprise in his proverbial bag of tricks. Including, but not stopping at, a blow job. Wait. Was that skeezy?

Eh. If it was, Stetson would forgive him. Or just tell him.

"What are you thinking about so hard?" Stetson asked, bringing him back to the half cup of cold coffee and sticky plate.

"Later tonight."

"Oh. Those are good thoughts, then. I'll leave you to them."

"Nah, you can join me." He held out a hand, wanting Stetson to touch. There were only a few other people around, all ignoring them.

Stetson took it, fingers wrapping around his, holding them.

Warm, callused, that grip sent tingles up his arm. He loved this man so much.

"Come upstairs with me, huh? Tell me what all you were pondering?"

"You got it." He rose, grabbing the bill to see if he could charge it to the room. Score. Curtis scribbled his name and room number, along with the tip, before he signed.

"I'll thank you for supper later, cowboy."

"Promise?" Curtis stepped aside at the stairs so he could follow Stetson.

"You got my word."

Well, all right, then.

CHAPTER TWENTY-ONE

"ARE YOU sure it's not sacrilegious to decorate the house, Curtis?" Stetson ducked the pillow that went flying past his head.

"It's just a little tree and some garland, Roper. It's not like we're doing Santa's workshop in the kitchen."

"Which is a shame." He did love the way the lights looked, sparkling against the walls.

"Next year we'll do it up right." Curtis wrapped a bit of garland over the mantel.

"Yeah? You thinking you'll be hanging your hat next to mine, still?"

"Hell, yes." Curtis glanced over at him, biting his lower lip. "I figure if I have to ride, I'll do the Cowboy Christmas this summer and maybe Rodeo de Santa Fe. I can miss the stock show season now. I might have to go a couple of places to sign at the sponsor booths, but you could come with."

A pang of hope hit him, right in the breadbasket. "Yeah? You think?"

"Yeah. I worked my ass off last year so I could win that buckle before I got too old. I—I like having a place to be home."

I'll do my best to keep it here for you. "You know you always have a place with me."

"I do now." Curtis hung this crazy little felt reindeer on the garland. Examining the tree, ornaments, and decorations Curtis had bought on the way home had made Stetson laugh until his belly hurt. There was a flocked beaver, hand to God.

A flocked beaver, a llama in a rainbow tutu, and a glow-in-the-dark Kokopelli.

He grinned, stringing the weird little fake popcorn doolie around the three-foot tree.

Curtis kept bringing in things—a speaker thing that filled the house with Christmas music, a bunch of new lightbulbs for the lamps, even a new television came in a UPS truck.

Stetson would open his mouth, then close it, not even sure what he would say. He'd told Curtis this was his house too. How could he tell the man not to spend money to make it homey for them?

Especially when he had to admit that big-screen was sort of amazing. You could count the hairs under people's noses.

Right now the TV was playing crackling log....

It went real nice with the fire in the hearth. The whole thing seemed utterly unreal.

"It's dueling fires," Curtis whispered, coming up behind him, one arm snaking around his middle. "Like dueling banjos, but with flame."

"You're a nut." He leaned back, letting Curtis hold him up.

"Nuts! I bought nuts in the shell. Where did I put them? For the stockings."

"You did? I picked up candy canes."

"Oh, we're rocking it." Curtis kissed his neck.

He'd traded for a tooled wallet for Curtis's stocking and a three-year-old paint that was looking to be broke. Stetson grinned a little, hoping Curtis was gonna be tickled.

They stood there, Christmas music sliding through the air around them, and he said a little prayer of thanks for what he had right now. Right here.

It was the best he could hope for. He'd worry about the rest of it tomorrow.

"You want hot chocolate?" Curtis asked, sliding around to hold him.

"I do. We'll make some up, huh? Together?"

"Totally." They held hands and wandered to the kitchen. The dogs all thumped tails on the floor, because Curtis had brought them in. It was supposed to get down to eight degrees tonight. He thought Curtis didn't approve of them being out at night, especially with them housebroken.

Curtis hummed along with the music, always moving, always making noise. Stetson adored that, and he found them dancing, two-stepping back into the front room, nice and easy.

Who needed hot chocolate? Curtis kept him plenty warm.

The house phone started ringing, and he sighed, shook his head. "Let me grab that."

Curtis let him go. "Okay, baby."

He grabbed the phone in the kitchen. "Hello?"

He needed to pull out milk, cocoa mix.

"Is Mrs. Betty Major available?"

"Nope."

"Do you know when she'll become available? We have questions about some medical bills."

How the hell did he answer that?

"I'm her son," he finally settled on. "I have her power of attorney." He had no idea if it was okay to tell them she was dead until he knew who this was.

"She's late on a number of bills. She's been sent to collections."

Could you send a dead woman to collections? "I see. Are you a collections agency?"

"We are, and any information we gather will be used by—"

He hung up the phone. He couldn't deal with this shit right now.

Curtis was frowning. "Who was that, baby?"

"No one." He handed Curtis the milk.

"You hung up on them. Salesman?" One eyebrow rose to Curtis's hairline.

"Something like that, yeah. Bill collectors are unwelcome folks, for sure." The phone started ringing again.

"So we'll unplug. It's unnatural to call anyone this close to Christmas." Curtis walked over to turn off the ringer.

"Yes." That was a good idea. Anyone who needed it had his cell number. He ought to just turn the damn thing off altogether.

"What were we doing?" Curtis grabbed his hand.

"Dancing. We were dancing and making hot chocolate." Good things. Not worrying.

"We were." Curtis pulled him close, then stepped him in a fast swing to "Rockin' Around the Christmas Tree." Lord, he hadn't known he'd remembered how to do that. Curtis could cut a rug.

They ended up laughing and breathless on the couch, the fire burning low. That was the Christmas spirit. Not some stupid bill collector.

This was real. This was love.

CHAPTER TWENTY-TWO

THE PHONE had been ringing off the hook.

Curtis hadn't said anything before Christmas, but they were fixing to get into the New Year, and he didn't want Stetson to drag this stress with him if he didn't have to.

So when the phone rang next and Stetson was out shoveling the path to the barn, Curtis answered.

"Hello?"

"We're trying to reach Miss Betty Major."

"I'm sorry, she passed away. What can I do for you?"

"I'm sorry?"

"She's deceased. Can I ask who this is? What are you calling in regards to?" He could remember his mom handling these calls when his grandpa died, and he kept his tone calm. He was gonna have to call a lawyer about what Stetson needed to do.

"Are you the executor?"

"Yes, ma'am." Curtis hedged his bets. He knew enough to lie until he could get some names and numbers.

"Well, this is a creditor, and I'm required by law to tell you we're trying to collect a debt."

"Yes, ma'am, I understand that. What debt and who's calling?"

"We've got a hospital bill here for $39,549, sir. Are you going to make this bill right?"

"As I'm sure you know, I have a right to a statement of my mother's account in writing. Once the estate has all the information it needs to proceed, then action will be determined." He said it by rote, grateful to his mom and to his contract lawyer, Paul, who'd told him over and over never to agree to any damn thing on the phone.

Forty thousand dollars. Damn. That was a chunk of change. He listened to the little voice on the other end of the line, getting more and more aggravated.

"You send that bill on in the mail." He hung up, because, damn, those people were a nightmare. Then he found his favorite contacts and keyed up Paul Davidson. The lawyer lived and worked in Dallas and was a shark in a cowboy hat and Wranglers.

Curtis kind of adored him.

"Paul Davidson's office."

"Hey, Shelly. It's Curtis Traynor. Is Paul in?"

"Let me make sure he's not on a call, honey. He's always in for you." She put him on hold, the strains of a Muzak version of a George Strait song making him groan.

"What the hell do you want, Mr. Traynor? Aren't you supposed to be on break?"

"I am on break, buddy. I Christmassed until my jeans don't fit. I just need to pick your brain."

"Surely. Shoot."

"A friend of mine just had his mom pass away. He's got bill collectors trying to get medical bills. A passel." He rubbed the back of his neck with his free hand.

"There any life insurance? Any assets?"

"Uh." He had no idea. Stetson had said there was enough life insurance to bury her. "I know she was sick a while. I bet she turned it all over to Stetson a long time ago."

"You find that out first. Find out the details and then holler. Assuming your buddy wasn't stupid, we can take care of this easy."

Relief flooded him. "Thanks, buddy. I appreciate it."

"No problem. Congratulations on the win, by the way. You did it."

"I did." He let himself feel the pride of it. "I didn't really think I would."

"I never doubted you. Holler when you have all the details, buddy. I have another call coming in."

"You got it." He hung up, tickled as a pig in shit. He could help Stetson with this. Ease the load.

Speak of the devil, in he walked, covered in snow and shivering.

"Hey, you. Get in here by the fire." Curtis trotted over to tug Stetson all the way in.

"I was sweating my ass off until ten seconds ago, swear to God."

"Right. You stopped working. That's the danger zone." He tugged off Stetson's jacket so he could start rubbing those cold arms.

"No shit on that. I got it cleared, though."

Damn, were Stetson's lips blue? "Jesus. You need a shower. I'll start the hot water."

"I just got the path shoveled. That's all. I do it every year."

"Honey, last year you had another thirty pounds on you. I've seen pictures."

"I guess...." Stetson shivered, and that was that. He took Stetson back to the bathroom, getting the water going.

"Sit on the pot. I need to take your boots off."

Stetson sat. Blinking at him.

He eased off the boots and rubbed those red feet. God, that was ridiculous. He was going to get them better socks before Stetson lost his toes. The winter was bitter this year, as if the earth knew about Miz Betty.

"Oh, burns. Damn." Stetson began to pant softly.

"Yeah, and we got to get the blood flowing again before we stick you in hot water." He didn't think they needed lukewarm foot baths or anything, but damn.

"I wasn't out long."

"Uh-huh. It's bitter and fixin' to snow again." Once he felt like Stetson's heart wouldn't explode the minute he got them in the water, he hauled his lover up off the pot and stripped him down. *Socks, towel warmer, maybe a portable heater for the bathroom. Fuzzy towels and the world's softest bath mat too.*

He didn't figure Stetson would mind him redoing the bath a little. The guest bath, now, it needed a total overhaul. All those roses.

"What are you thinking on so hard, cowboy?"

"Roses." He got naked so he could push them both under the spray. "And about how we need some new bath stuff."

"Roses? It's too early to plant more, and God knows Momma has a bunch in the ground."

"More like the ones on the shower curtain in the guest bath." He didn't want to overstep, because Stetson needed time, but man, those were old roses.

"You mean the scary bathroom, huh? That's been there since I was in elementary school."

"Oh." He scrubbed Stetson's arms gently to keep the blood moving. "Is it special?"

Stetson looked at him, shrugged. "You don't know what it was like there, before I took her to the hospital." Stetson never called it a nursing home. Never. "If you moved anything—anything at all—she'd start screaming. Then she wanted things moved back like they'd been twenty years ago. It got to where I was scared to touch anything. I blocked off my side of the house so she wouldn't go tear my things up while I was working."

"Oh, Roper." He couldn't even imagine that. Constantly having to tiptoe around your own home for fear of upsetting someone you couldn't even be mad at....

"Part of me wants to burn this fucking house to the ground. Part of me wants to leave it like she did. Part of me wants to have a huge yard sale and make it something new." Stetson's eyes went all shimmery, and he lifted his face to the spray. "All of me hates how it ended up with her. It ain't right. I wanted her to go, by the end. She starved to death."

Curtis just took Stetson in his arms, holding on tight. Christ, he should have been there. But Stetson needed what Curtis could give now too. He needed a new start.

"I think this—you, you being here, loving on me—I think this was the last thing she gave to me."

Now it was his turn to feel the sting of tears. "Then she did good by both of us, baby. Real good."

"Yeah. Yeah, I think so." Stetson rested them together, relaxing against him and trusting Curtis would hold him.

He would. Curtis so would, for as long as the good Lord let him.

Maybe longer. He was a stubborn son of a bitch, after all.

CHAPTER TWENTY-THREE

"ROPER, WE need to talk."

Stetson looked up from the piles of bills on the table, and this time he was too fucking sad to even turn the top page over and hide them. "What's up?"

"We got to deal with this shit. All these papers and stuff."

"I'm trying." Stetson's head began to throb.

"I know you are." Curtis pulled out a chair and sat. "I got a lawyer friend willing to help. But I need to know what's what."

Lord, he didn't know. He didn't. At this point, there was so much paper with red letters screaming that he didn't know what was important, what they were going to get him for. What to do. "I...."

Fuck, how do you tell the current number one rodeo cowboy on earth that you ain't been paid for anything for fifteen months? That you don't know what's gonna happen now that Momma's SSI is gone?

"Well, first we need to sort out the medical bills." Curtis nodded, as if that was that. Maybe it was. They needed a direction to go, right?

"There's tons of them. Boxes. This pile's from this month."

"Okay." Curtis stared at the pile. "You got any old file folders?"

"Uh. Yeah. Yeah, I do. From when my business was going good." Stetson got up and went to the coat closet and pulled down a box. Lord, the dust.

Curtis grinned. "I bet that picks up again."

"I sure hope so. I got nothing else to offer." Nothing else felt as good either.

"Hush with that. That's a lot. You're good at it. Okay, so we need a folder for the medical bills, one for house stuff, and one for anything else." Curtis must have been reading organizing shit online.

He pulled out a couple of the files, smiling as he found sketches, notes on vigas and mantels and custom work.

"Can we combine these into a few bigger folders?" Curtis asked, watching him, those blue eyes happy.

"Sure. They're old. I don't know why I kept them, you know? Just notes." Just happiness.

"Hey, I love how you look when you see them."

"I did good work." It wasn't what Curtis did, but it lasted longer than any ride ever had.

"Yeah." Curtis took the folders he handed over. "I'll start with this stack."

"Okay." He sorted, a dull shame filling him. He should have been able to do this, to cope with this shit. He wasn't an idiot, dammit.

"Hey." When he glanced up, Curtis was staring at him intently. "Stop it. I can see your lips all pursing."

"Shut up. I am not."

"Are too."

He stuck out his tongue. That ought to keep his lips from wrinkling up.

"Don't put it out there unless you want to use it," Curtis said.

"That's way more fun than sorting bills...."

"It is. Let's get this one month done and I'll reward you."

Now, that was an incentive.

"Yeah, I could handle that." Hell, he felt like they both spent hours fixing the barn or feeding or hauling wood, not playing. Curtis was having a ball playing rancher, just like all rodeo folks did when they could.

The best part was that Curtis was good at it. Genuinely. He cowboyed right on up, dragging his ass through the mud right alongside Stetson. Curtis was adjusting to the altitude and the cold, and a few days ago, he'd made Stetson go down to Santa Fe and go to the Target. Socks. Long undies. Bath mats and a shower curtain. New towels.

New coffee maker and pans.

Curtis was spoiling him.

Stetson knew how quick the prize money could go, though, so he was trying to keep Curtis—"Ow!"

Curtis pinched the shit out of his arm. "You need to get your mind in the middle, baby."

"I was! It wasn't the same middle, maybe, but...."

"Nope. Sorting. Then bedroom. Keep up."

"Sorting. Then bedroom. Right. Got it." *Butthead.*

Curtis beamed. "That's it."

He leaned over to try and get a kiss, when the sound of tires on gravel sounded. "I'm going to chain the gate across the drive."

"No shit. It's like a madhouse around here still." Curtis swept the papers and folders into the box to tuck it away. *Good man.*

Stetson peered through the front room window, frowning at the sight of the little Smart car in the driveway. "Isaac?"

What in the world was Isaac Key doing here? He hadn't seen that man in... four years?

Isaac stood there, shifting foot to foot. It had to be cold in those sleek Italian leather loafers.

"Lord, man. What are you doing here?" Stetson asked after he opened the door.

"I heard about your mom. I brought doughnuts and beer." Isaac held up a six-pack of Fat Tire.

"Well, come in before you freeze."

"Thanks. I had an unexpected day off, so I thought, I'm coming to see him."

Isaac stepped inside, almost going ass over teakettle when he hit the floor. Slick.

"Take those ridiculous shoes off, huh? I'll get an extra pair of socks."

"Babe?"

He smiled at Curtis, rolling his eyes dramatically. "I don't know if you remember Isaac. We went to high school together, and I think when you and I were hooked up, he was in his crazy Rocky-Mountain-high artist phase with these rainbow-colored dreads."

"I know, right? I went all corporate. My mom is so ashamed." Isaac held out a hand to Curtis. "Curtis Traynor, right? I'm Isaac Key."

Curtis smiled easily, but it was his fan smile, not his deep eye lines one. "Pleasure."

"Well, probably not. But someone isn't answering his phone, and someone is a butthead, and this is what you get, ignoring your best friend. You get boyfriendus interruptus. Suck it up. Seriously, man. I was worried you'd.... Well, done something stupid."

Christ on a crutch, listening to Isaac was like having a tropical bird in your house.

Curtis relaxed a little. "Come on, seriously. I'll get the socks; you get some coffee, babe."

"Oh. Oh, I have doughnuts, which totally go with coffee!"

Stetson started chuckling, and that turned into deep, hard laughter.

Isaac patted his shoulder, looking more than a little worried, but Curtis just snorted at him before heading to the bedroom. Shit, that felt good.

"So, seriously. You cannot just fall off the face of the earth. I worry."

"I didn't mean to. I'm sorry, huh. It's just been a... rough time."

"You didn't call me at Christmas, even."

How did he say that he hadn't even thought of Isaac? That his entire brain had been Curtis, Momma, and bills?

Finally he just spread his hands. "I suck. I'm sorry."

"No. I mean, no feeling sucky. I was just scared." Isaac came to him, hugged him tight. "I'm so sorry, man. I am."

"Go take your coat off, Isaac."

"Okay. Should I go? I don't want to—"

He put a hand on Isaac's chest. "Go. Take your coat. Off."

"Right. It's good to see you. You need to eat more. I love your hair."

"Okay." His hair? What was different about his hair?

"Dude, you don't even know? It's all shaggy and streaked with silver. I love it."

"Oh." He clenched his hands to keep from reaching up to feel his hair. Wouldn't do any good.

"It's a great look for him, huh?" Curtis returned with socks, herding them into the kitchen.

"Totally. I bet it makes a great handhold in bed too."

He whipped around, staring at Isaac, who just fluttered his eyelashes. "What? Just making an observation."

"Well, stop it." Curtis scowled, a damn intimidating look on his cowboy, which, okay. Hot. Like nuclear. Like he was going to have to stand in front of the fridge or step outside for a second.

"Sorry." Isaac tried for contrite. Not convincing.

"Liar." Curtis handed over the socks. "I'm not sure what your situation was, but Stetson's activities in our bed are not yours to worry on. We clear?"

Stetson just sat there with his teeth in his mouth, his dick taking a marked interest.

Isaac, God love him, blinked hard a few times before nodding slowly, a huge smile spreading over his face. "Got it."

"Good."

"You know how to work one of these fancy-assed coffee makers, man?" Stetson had better things to do than make coffee right now.

"A Keurig? Indeed I do."

"Cool." He grabbed Curtis's hand and muscled his lover down the hall, slamming their mouths together as soon as they got near to the bedroom door.

Curtis kissed him back, giving as good as he got. Those lean hands landed on his ass, holding on.

Fuck yes. He didn't know, exactly, why he was on fire, but he was, and Curtis wasn't spraying him with cold water, so he'd go with it.

Hell, Curtis was pushing him into the bedroom and closing the door behind them.

He moaned for his man, one hand working between them to cup Curtis's balls. Curtis went up on tiptoes, grunting, the kiss going a little toothy. Someone really did like that touch. So he did it again, then once more.

"Damn, baby. Damn. So fine." Curtis plucked at his shirt. "Off."

"Uh-huh." He yanked at it, tearing at the buttons. How stupid, to be so wild. He didn't care. He just wanted Curtis. Now.

Curtis struggled with their jeans, yanking at buttons and zippers, cursing when they didn't give right away.

He stumbled to the bed, dragging Curtis with him.

Landing on top of him, Curtis kissed him hard, lips and tongue pressing on his.

They were mostly naked, totally erect, and rubbing together like teenagers—all clumsy and heavy-breathing. They couldn't figure out where to touch, what they needed beyond this contact, this sudden, urgent desire.

Curtis slapped against him, the connection fierce, and Stetson nodded, encouraging it. Hell, begging for it.

"Uhn." Curtis finally got enough coordination to bring their cocks together in one hand. "Yeah. Like that."

"Uh-huh. Just like that. Good." He was reduced to grunts and clicks.

They rocked, staring at each other, the color high in Curtis's cheeks. Those blue eyes blazed for him.

"Mine, Roper. All mine." Curtis's voice sounded blown out, gravelly and hard.

"You know it." *Also ditto.*

"Uh-huh. No city boys, not anymore." Curtis tugged at them, hand moving fast, up and down.

"No. Just you. More."

"More," Curtis agreed, bending to gnaw at his neck.

"Jesus!" He hurt, all the way to his balls, and he let himself holler.

"Mmmm." Curtis just jacked him and licked that little bruise, giving him more than he could handle and everything he wanted. "Love that I can do this."

"Me too. I love it so bad. Harder."

"Listen to you." Curtis kicked his legs apart, grinding them together, and his cock ached with it.

Stetson panted, rocking his hips to get closer, to get more friction. To get Curtis to give him what he needed.

"Close, baby. So close."

He believed it. Curtis was hot as fire and hard as nails.

He grabbed Curtis's ass and pulled. Hard.

"Stetson!" Curtis's eyes went wide, his hand clamping down around them both.

They shot, one right after the other, staring at each other. The smell of them mingled, hot and sharp and perfect.

This whole fucking thing seemed pretty damn perfect.

They slumped together, and it wasn't but a few seconds before they were both snorting with laughter.

"Oh, Roper, that was rude."

"I'm sorry! I am, but I needed." God, he was going to be in flames when he had to go face Isaac again.

"I know." Curtis gave him this slow smile that meant the world to him. "Me too."

"Yeah?" Then maybe that wasn't so bad.

"Mmm. Can we just sit here a minute before we wash up?"

"Isaac is pretty self-sufficient." And there was no way the bastard hadn't heard them either. He was going to tease Stetson unmercifully.

"Cool. I don't need to worry about him, right?"

"Worry about him? He said he knew how to make coffee."

"No, baby. I mean as competition."

He almost laughed, but Curtis was serious. Worried.

"Well, we've given the rare hand job when one of us was in need, but no. He hates it here, hates everything about this place, and me? Well, he knows I've been stupid over you forever. There's no competing with that."

Curtis kissed him then, slow and deep and purposeful. "That sounds good, baby. Real good."

"Yeah. Excellent." He felt a little giddy, a little like the world was spinning out of control. Maybe it was, or maybe he felt free for the first time in months, as if something had cracked down the middle and he could breathe.

He closed his eyes and hid his face in the curve of Curtis's throat. Just for a second. He just wanted to float here, just a second.

CURTIS WOKE up maybe an hour later, jolting, his heart pounding. What the hell was that—

Shit. Isaac the high school friend.

Okay. Okay, he'd just wake....

Stetson was sound asleep, sprawled out, those stress lines faded. He couldn't disturb that.

Instead, he slipped out of bed and dressed in sweats, his thick socks eating up the sound when he left the room.

He smelled coffee and something else, something breadlike. Fresh and hot. Yum.

"You two suck. Totally, Stetson. Leaving me to hear you two yodeling like hysterical calves." The guy was tip-tapping on his computer so fast it damn near blurred. "Still, I'm glad he finally came down to roost."

"He's right here. Stetson is still asleep."

"Oh." Isaac spun around, eyes huge. "Jesus, I'm sorry. I just assumed. You must want to hit me with a hammer."

"Nah." Curtis stretched. "I am home to roost. And we were rude as hell. Sorry about that."

"It's cool. I've never... I mean, who knew he could be all grr?"

"Mmm-hmm." Lord, that had been fine. "Do I smell bread of some kind?"

Isaac flushed. "I bake when I'm nervy."

"That's a great quality in a man." And this one was a keeper.

"Thanks. Uh, you want a cinnamon roll? I used the cans in the fridge. I'll totally buy you more."

"You totally don't have to. They smell like heaven." He sat down next to Isaac. "Seriously, though, I apologize. Stetson needed a break."

"Is that what we're calling it in New Mexico these days?"

"Yep. Afternoon delight." He winked, but that was all the sex talk he was gonna take. "So you live in…?"

"Boulder. I'm a graphics guy." Isaac leaned back in the chair. "I was chatting with my sister, and she mentioned Betty had passed. I needed to see him."

"I get it. You can have plenty of time once he wakes up." He grabbed a plate and loaded it with frosted goodness.

"So, are you… I mean, are you living here?"

"Yep." He had nowhere else to call home, and he meant to be with Stetson as much as he could.

"That rocks. Congratulations."

"Thanks." Isaac really seemed like a decent guy. "You eat bacon?" Curtis asked.

"Are you kidding? I'm a hipster. I love bacon. I would marry bacon."

"I'll cook some up. I love bacon with sweet rolls."

"Cool. Does… do we need to have a bake sale for Stetson? A GoFundMe? Something?"

Curtis blinked. "I don't know. We're starting to get medical bills, but we really haven't dealt with the estate yet."

"Well, my sister said… that it's bad. I can help a little."

Curtis fought to keep from bristling. Any help might be good. "I might take you up on the bake sale if we do it in tourist season."

"Whatever. No one wants Stetson to lose the ranch."

That had him blinking some more. The thought hadn't occurred to him. Oh, he knew Stetson was in a bad way, but lose the ranch?

"No. No, I reckon not."

"You okay? You sure you don't want help?"

"I'm good." He would have to really poke Stetson, though. Curtis got to making bacon and Isaac made him a coffee, which was just what he needed.

Stetson came wandering in, cheeks all pink. "Sorry, y'all."

Isaac popped up to hug Stetson hard. "I made cinnamon rolls. Do you want coffee?"

"Please. It's good to see you, buddy. I appreciate you coming out."

"Thanks." Isaac bounded to the Keurig. "I missed you, man."

"So, you're still in Denver?"

"Boulder. Way more my people, you know."

"Right." Stetson smiled faintly, and Curtis bit back a laugh. "Santa Gay was never big enough to hold you."

"No way. I need room to bounce off mountains. Hell, I need to be around artists less talented than me."

"That's true enough."

The byplay fascinated him. Stetson was so easy, teasing and playing.

He knew Stetson had lots of local friends, but this was new. This was different. Curtis didn't want to be a butthead, but he had to admit he was a little jealous.

This wasn't the Stetson he understood, he guessed. He knew two forms of Stetson as of late—sad and worried.

"You want sugar and cream?" Isaac asked.

"Just black, man."

"Dude, Stetson! When did that happen? You were a sweet and light guy."

"I got used to it, I reckon. Last few years I've needed more caffeine and less stuff."

A few years? Had it been that long since Stetson could afford the little luxuries? Curtis felt like a blind idiot.

"There's heavy cream, though, and sugar. Let me spoil you two, us three, I mean."

"Okay, sure." Curtis grinned at Isaac. "We got caramel creamer too."

"Oh, dude. Yes, please. Sit. Eat bacon and rolls, and I will provide sweet, creamy goodness."

Stetson sat.

Curtis wandered to the table and sat next to him, putting the plate of bacon on the table.

"Mmm. Bacon." Stetson smiled at him, and the temptation was huge, to lean over and take a long, hard kiss.

He glanced at Isaac, who was shaking his butt and singing, and gave in to the urge. Stetson opened, letting him right in.

When they came up for air, Isaac was watching them, this goofy smile on his face. "Oh God. You're so pretty!"

"Stop it." Stetson chuckled. "Come on and eat with us, you dork."

"Uh-huh. Seriously. I want to take pictures."

Curtis gave Isaac a look. "That was your free one."

"No pictures. This belongs to us." Stetson didn't look like he was joking a bit.

Isaac nodded easily. "You know I'm just joking. No sex tapes. Got it."

"No sex tapes, no art photos—well, maybe one for me."

"Curtis!" Stetson's cheeks went bright pink.

"What?" Curtis loved that shocked expression. "If I had a lick of talent, I would do like that fella in that *Titanic* movie. Draw you."

Stetson fluttered some, expression a fine mix of pleased and embarrassed.

"Drink your fancy coffee," Isaac said.

"Curtis loves fancy coffee. We might have to come up to Boulder, and you can take him to all the swanky coffee places."

It was Curtis's turn to go wide-eyed. "I'd love to do Boulder with you, babe."

"You would?" Stetson gave him a happy grin. "Cool. I mean, as soon as we dig out a little."

"You guys are welcome to stay with me. I have a pull-out couch."

"That would be great." Stetson looked happier every damn second. Traveling with him. Imagine that. Although Curtis thought he'd spring for a hotel. Something on the decent end.

Stetson deserved room service. Some pampering.

"Just let me know, huh?" Isaac blinked and drank deep. "Y'all are going to let me spend the night, aren't you?"

"You can stay as long as you want," Curtis said. "Well, for a few days, anyway."

Stetson nodded. "We got the guest bed in my old office. It's all made up."

"Thanks." Isaac's cheeks flushed. "I just sort of mounted up and rode down."

"I appreciate it." Stetson grinned at Isaac. "It's good to have friends."

"It is." Isaac grabbed a cinnamon roll. "Call me next time something bad happens."

"I will. Hopefully I'm done with that for a long while."

"We're gonna bank on it," Curtis said. If nothing else, he knew the power of a positive attitude.

"No shit on that." Stetson touched his thigh under the table.

That touch sent all sorts of tingles right through him. Lord, he did love Stetson with all he was worth.

Enough to let this too-pretty old friend stick around a few days. Probably not enough to let Isaac take sexy photos, though.

Yeah, no. Not enough for that.

STETSON GRABBED another couple logs for the fireplace and got them going while Curtis loaded the dishwasher. They'd made spaghetti and meatballs, goofing off and enjoying the hell out of each other.

He hadn't realized how good it was to see an old friend.

Isaac looked good. Older. A little nervy, maybe, and Stetson had no idea what that even meant. It was just an impression. An expression? Whatever.

It was good to know someone cared.

Curtis, now, he was a hoot, circling Isaac like a big wolf might a very small coyote.

Still, it hadn't been so bad, Curtis having a little competition. In fact, it had been damn hot.

"You're smiling. That's really cool." Isaac sat on the couch, watching him. Curtis had gone to the bathroom, which was always when Isaac snuck in bizarre conversation.

"Do you think it's too early?" Should he not be happy yet?

"What? No way. You just haven't had much to smile about, I bet."

"No. No, it was—it was just hard."

"Have you cried?"

"Shut up." *Asshole.*

"It's good for the soul, Stetson."

"You learn that in therapy, buddy?" Stetson teased, trying to go for light.

"Art school," Isaac shot back, deadpan. "My film instructor would give me a whole grade level up if I produced the perfect emo tear for him."

"Did you have to suck him off too?"

"No, I did that voluntarily. He was a cold bastard, but he was amazing in bed."

"Really?" He knew his eyes were big as saucers, but damn. Curtis laughed at him, shaking his head as he came back and moved them both toward the sofa.

"Yep." Isaac gave him a crooked grin. "It ended badly."

Well, shit. He didn't know how to respond to that. At all. So he just sat.

Curtis just chuckled a little. "He was probably too old for you, buddy."

"Probably, yeah, but I swear, guys, he turned me inside out." For a second, Isaac looked sad, tired, but it disappeared with a pop.

"So, you're footloose and fancy-free?" Curtis asked. "I know a couple of cowboys...."

Stetson grinned, pressing his lips together to keep the wild laughter in.

"No shit?" Isaac flushed a deep red. "Oh. Uh. Wow."

"Oh, Lord. Not Trey or Oscar, either one. I like Isaac. His ass couldn't handle it."

"No? Well, if you say so...." Curtis waggled his eyebrows.

"Shut up, Stetson. Sit there and shut up. You know what I'd give for a real cowboy?"

"Mine's not available."

Curtis blinked over at him. "You think I'm a real cowboy?"

"What? Of course you are. Don't be any dumber than you have to be." The son of a bitch was the number one cowboy in the world.

"You know how many folks think rodeo is trash." Curtis looked pleased as punch.

"I know. People are stupid."

"Trashy? Hot as hell, you mean." Isaac poked him. "Let Curtis fix me up."

"You'll have to come down for the Rodeo de Santa Fe. All the guys will come in for that purse," Curtis said.

"It's a deal. I'll even spring for us all to have separate hotel rooms so I don't have to listen to you two howl like monkeys."

"I'm fixin' to have to beat you, Isaac," Stetson threatened, and Isaac simply snorted.

"Curtis already kiboshed that, man."

"Really?"

Curtis nodded slowly. "No touchy."

Well, then.

He warmed up, balls to bones. "Fair enough."

"Not fair at all." Isaac grinned. He'd forgotten how Isaac liked to laugh.

"Fair or not, that's nothing to me." Curtis ran one hand down his side, petting him.

They could be themselves with Isaac, though Stetson had to admit a bit of surprise that Curtis was so open and relaxed. It felt like… well, shit, like Curtis really meant to be with him.

"You two want dessert?" Curtis had outdone himself, throwing a dump cake together.

"Oh? Cherry?" Isaac was such a slut.

"With whipped cream," Curtis agreed.

"I am most totally in. Thanks." Isaac blew Curtis a kiss, and Curtis rolled his eyes.

Stetson pinched Isaac, forgetting the hands-off rule.

"Hey! No pinching!"

"You two are gonna get separated." Curtis waved a big spoon at them.

"But Da-ad!" Stetson protested while he got Isaac in a headlock for a noogie.

Curtis tickled him with the hand not holding the spoon, making him shout with laughter.

He let Isaac go and went after Curtis, both of them grinning like fools. They made laps around the kitchen, but he finally caught Curtis up against a counter, then blew a raspberry against his neck.

God, he loved how this fine son of a bitch smelled—leather and black pepper and soap.

Curtis kissed his mouth one more time, hands on his butt. "Dessert. Need to fatten you up."

"Shh. I'm at my fighting weight. Isn't that what you tell me?"

"Yeah, but I'm all muscle." Curtis laughed out loud when Stetson bared his teeth.

"I'll show you muscle—" *Wait, did that make sense?*

"Please!"

They both turned to Isaac. "Hush!"

Isaac rolled his eyes. "Then feed me cake, for God's sake. Please."

"You got it. Get the spray cream, baby." Curtis sent him off to the fridge before spooning up dump cake.

Lucky. It took him a second to understand what he was feeling, but he was lucky. This was his now, and he had to figure out how to keep it going. He could do this.

He had to.

CHAPTER TWENTY-FOUR

ISAAC WAS a hoot, but Curtis was glad when he finally headed back to Boulder.

Some of the things Isaac had said about the ranch being in deep financial trouble made him dig a little into all those bills while Stetson was off helping someone fix a frozen pipe.

This was serious. The electric bill was a month behind, the taxes were four thousand dollars behind, and apparently Stetson's good truck had already been repossessed.

Christ.

That didn't account for the medical bills. Those numbers were enough to make him nauseous.

He emailed a bunch of stuff to his lawyer buddy, Paul, knowing they had to sort out the estate first.

Still, Christ. Stetson hadn't been eating to feed the horses and the dogs and the llamas and the donkeys....

The next thing Curtis did was sit down and tally up his finances. Lucky for him, his folks had never needed him to send all that much money home, so he'd always taken enough off the top to live on, then put the rest into savings. It had been years since he'd had to scrape up the loose change in his truck to pay his entry fee.

His sponsors paid for his living expenses, so he wasn't hurting. Hell, he could help with the taxes at least. Just pay them. The house was paid off.

Now, he would never do that without talking to Stetson first, and he had no idea what else needed to be paid....

Still, how long had it been this bad? How long since Stetson had done his art?

Curtis reached up to rub his temples. Jesus. He knew why Stetson hadn't called or anything, but he felt like he should have been helping.

He wanted to... to what? What was he doing here? Seriously. What did he need to do?

"Hey, cowboy." Stetson stomped off his boots, a cold wind whooshing through the door when he came in, barely giving him a glance before asking, "What's wrong?"

Jesus, his man was sensitive as hell. Stetson didn't need a nickel to buy a clue about what Curtis was feeling.

"How about a cup of coffee?" He didn't want to just get all up in Stetson's business because he was at a loss. His dad did that all the time, flew off the handle at the smallest thing, and Curtis didn't want to be that kind of man with anyone, especially not Stetson, not now.

"Okay...." Stetson put his coat in the closet, his hat on the hook, then went to start coffee without a word.

Shit. He teetered on thin ice, not sure how to start.

"What did I do?" The coffee appeared in front of him, and then Stetson stood by the sink, eyes like coal.

"Nothing. I mean, I just been digging into that box of bills. I want to help, but I'm afraid you'll tell me no."

He swore Stetson got smaller, the look on the beloved face still as stone, but Stetson didn't say a word.

"Have a sit?" He didn't want Stetson closed off, but they had to hash this out.

Stetson sat across from him, watching him like he was going to attack or something.

Curtis tried for a smile. "Hey, it's not all that dire, baby. I just think we need to talk on it."

"Okay." Stetson looked for a second like he was going to burst into tears or something, but instead those near-black eyes focused on the table. "I tried my best. I fucked up, but I didn't waste a dime. I swear to God. If... I'll go wait in line for day laborers tomorrow. I've been lazy because of Christmas."

"Look at me." Curtis laid his hand over Stetson's. "I got to tell you, Roper, I'm not one of those people who believes suffering leads to redemption or some shit. I'm not asking you to go sit in the damned work line."

"I don't know what to do. I haven't for months. I just keep trying."

"I can see that." He really could. The stacks of bills were prioritized. The electric bill wasn't paid because him being there had driven it up. He wasn't stupid. "I'm not here to punish you."

"What do you want, cowboy? I feel like shit about this, but I can only apologize for being a fuckup so much."

"What I want is for you to stop acting like a martyr," he snapped. Then he gritted his teeth for a moment, breathing deep. "Dammit. Sorry. I just need you to go over with me what's been paid and what hasn't, what's the most pressing thing."

"Don't you worry about it. I'll figure it. I got shit to do." Stetson stood, shoulders stiff as a board, and he could feel Stetson pulling back, pulling away from him and hiding. Fuck, he hated this stoic shit. "I been dealing with my mess for a while now. You're on break and all."

Then Stetson just went for his coat again. Curtis considered throwing his coffee cup right at the stubborn fucker. Maybe if he beaned Stetson in the head, he'd listen.

"So you're saying you don't want me to stick around, then?"

"What?"

"You seem pretty all-fired ready for me to get on my pony and ride, man. Stop pussy-footing around about it and be honest about what you want." He reckoned he might as well be hung for a sheep as well as a lamb. "You want me to go, I'll fucking go."

Stetson whipped around, eyes blazing. "Who asked you to fucking leave? I said I'd deal with my own fucking mistakes! I'm not a martyr, you fuck. I'm just a stupid fucking cowboy that can't tell my ass from a hole in the ground no more!"

Curtis stepped right up, pushing into Stetson's space. "You're not stupid! What is wrong with you?"

"Back off, man."

"Make me."

He could see it in Stetson's eyes, a flash of a wild fury that reminded him for a second of staring into the mad eyes of a bull. Good thing he wasn't smart enough to be scared. "I swear to God, Curtis. I don't want to hurt you."

He fought his smile, because he knew better. Stetson Major wouldn't hurt him again for love or money. This was about shame, and it didn't belong to him, even a bit. "You can sure try, Roper."

Stetson grabbed him by the upper arms, roaring with a pure rage, but his lover didn't throw so much as a punch. "Jesus fucking Christ, I'm not going to be uncomfortable in my own motherfucking house anymore! I didn't say I wanted you to leave. I didn't mean it if I did. I'm fucking scared, you motherfucker! I can't fix this!"

"Then let me help!" Curtis crossed his arms, covering Stetson's hands with his own. "I just want to help."

"Did I say no, you asshole?" Christ, Stetson could beller.

"No, you just got up and walked off. We got to do better than that this time."

Stetson stared at him, and then it was like all the air went out of him in a rush. "Christ, my head hurts."

That didn't surprise Curtis at all. Stetson had to learn to breathe all over again.

"We need to have lunch." He'd done some work on the porch this morning before settling in with the paperwork, and his stomach was growling. "We'll think better with some food in us."

Stetson blinked at him, then took a step toward him. "Yeah?"

"Yep." They were both going to have to learn this part—arguing without it being the end of the earth. Lord knew they were both stubborn assholes. They were going to fight.

Last time they'd let that be a wedge between them. Curtis was determined to do better this time around.

"You want to make sandwiches or warm up soup?"

"I'll do the soup, I guess." Stetson was still blinking a little, but he made himself a cup of coffee before he pulled out a can of vegetable beef and a chicken noodle.

Curtis grabbed bread, then opened the fridge to grab turkey and cheese. He surprised Stetson with a kiss when they passed in the open part of the kitchen.

"Hey."

"Hey, baby. I missed you this morning. How did the pipe go?"

"I dug it out, and Doug and Tom helped me replace it. Chilly out there." Stetson shivered a little.

"Just thinking about it makes you cold, huh?" Curtis chuckled, then set aside the sandwich fixings in favor of rubbing Stetson's upper arms. "We're okay, you know, Roper. We are okay. I should have started with this—loving on you and lunch."

"Well, then, we both learned something. Go us. Old dogs, new tricks."

Curtis swatted Stetson's butt, because the words were sarcastic but the tone wasn't. "Smartass."

"Better than a dumbass, I guess...."

"Uh-huh." He got the skillet on the stove next to the soup pan. He didn't mind his soup microwaved, but Stetson liked his heated up the old-fashioned way. They worked together, and he could see it as Stetson relaxed, skinny shoulders coming down from his ears.

A grilled sandwich and soup brightened his outlook for sure, and they didn't chat much until after they ate.

"Better?" Curtis asked.

"Yeah. That's hard work, digging."

"It is. I shouldn't have hit you with shit like that walking in the door. Sorry." There. He said it, and he meant it.

"Thanks. I know it's stupid, to be so ashamed, because I didn't make any mistakes."

"Proud cowboy." Curtis winked. "Can you pencil me in a time to take a bite out of it here and there?"

"I'd pencil you in for anything, Curtis."

That was good enough for him. Curtis actually felt better than he had since Isaac showed up. They'd had a snarl, and neither of them had run off.

Looked like they were going at this relationship thing as adults this time.

"I want to help. I mean, if I'm living here with you, not just staying here."

Stetson met his gaze, so serious, and he almost—almost—groaned. He wanted Stetson to hear him, not get all pissy and....

"I don't want you to think that I have you here for your money. I would have you if you didn't have a dime."

"You did." Curtis grinned, grateful he hadn't been a butthead. "I didn't have any sponsors back when."

"Yeah. I loved you when you were borrowing your entry fees. I just needed you to know that."

"I do." That much he did know, straight-up. Sometimes he was uncertain about Stetson actually wanting to *live* with him, but he knew the man loved him. Had loved him all along.

"I don't know how to fix the money part. I'm getting some work, but I sold all my tools and traded my wood to pay for stuff, so I'm starting from scratch. You know how it works up here, anyway. You trade this for that. It's what happens."

He nodded slowly. Sold all his tools.... *Damn. Just damn.* "Well, I can help. I really can." Curtis held up a hand before Stetson opened his mouth. "I'm gonna live here, I have to be able to pull my weight."

"I get that, but you've sorta done that. You did Christmas, bought food."

"Short-term thinking, baby." He winked. "We'll do it like eating a bear."

"I feel so fucking ashamed. People do this all the time and manage. Why couldn't I?"

"Stetson. You're one man. You don't have brothers and sisters to help out. Your mom was sick a long while." Stetson needed to stop being so down on himself.

"Yeah. Yeah, she was." Stetson's head bobbed, and that weight was back on those shoulders, so this time Curtis stood and went to rub a little, ease the tension. See? He could learn. He could figure this out.

He grinned a little now that Stetson couldn't see him. Stetson was totally worth it.

Curtis got that now.

"Feels good."

"Jesus, Roper, you're tight."

"Shoveling frozen dirt bites, man."

"I know it." He did. Actually. Their pipes froze in the winter all the damned time because his folks' house was a hundred years old and up on bois d'arc stumps. "But you got something out of it, huh?"

"Back of the truck's full of junk—wood, some copper wire, a couple of windows."

"Well, there you go. We need to get your workshop back up and running." No one around Stetson's place had any more money than Stetson.

"Yeah. I'm gonna fix those windows and trade them to Tom for parts to fix the pellet stove."

"That's even better than windows." Lord. Stetson bartered for everything. That owed as much to the Pueblo way as anything, he reckoned, but Taos was full of artsy types who did the same thing. Too bad you couldn't barter for taxes. "How do you feel about me running some broncs out here?"

"We got plenty of room. You thinking on bucking 'em?"

"I am, yeah. I mean, Miles and I have talked about it a million times. He would run them to events...." That such a dream could become a reality was weird but wonderful.

"Good deal."

Just like that, easy as pie. Good deal. He dropped a kiss on Stetson's head.

Stetson chuckled. "We got about a million things need doing."

"I'm on it." The bills could wait another half a day. One bite at a time.

CHAPTER TWENTY-FIVE

JESUS, MARY, and Joseph, Stetson was pooped. He'd been working his ass off, running back and forth to make a few deals and get things together again, get things going.

He had to make the money for the taxes. He knew Curtis wanted to talk about it, and he knew he'd have to take some help, but he wanted to earn half.

Christ, two thousand dollars seemed like an impossibility.

When Momma had first started to slip, he'd taken her to three different doctors to get second opinions. That was when he'd sold his tools, knowing the bills would pile up.

Now he wished he'd had a little more faith in his work.

His head throbbed, and he took himself to the back of the house where it was dark and cold and he could close his eyes.

Curtis was on the couch when he came in, curled up under a quilt, sound asleep. Waiting on him.

Gorgeous son of a bitch. Seriously.

He smiled, watching Curtis's chest rise and fall. Curtis had fed for him tonight, and had probably frozen his nuts off.

Did he wake Curtis up? Let him sleep? What?

Curtis sat up, blinking hard. "Did I miss supper?"

"Miss is a strong word. I just got in."

"Shit, baby. It's…." Curtis checked his phone. "Nine."

"You want… meatballs?"

"Sure. I can make garlic bread, and we can have sammiches."

"Works for me. Beer?" He grabbed one for him, wincing as the blisters on his hand tore. *Dammit.*

"Let me see." Curtis stood, tossing the blanket aside. He walked right up and grabbed his wrist.

"Just from the cold."

"You're bleeding." Curtis tugged him to the sink, then turned on the water, letting it heat up some.

"Am I? I'm just a little sore…." God, it felt good, the way Curtis loved him.

"What were you doing? Stringing wire in the dark?" Curtis washed his hands in the mild pump soap that had appeared next to his soap dish of Lava.

"Electricity to the workshop. Mice did a number."

Curtis's face broke into a smile. "You're working on the workshop?"

"Yeah, I didn't see you when I got home from working at the Bexar place, so I went to get some work done at the shop. Once I save enough for taxes, I want to buy my tools back."

"I was down at the organic grocery store. You must have parked back at the shop, huh? I missed your truck coming in." Curtis dried his hands off, wrapped them up.

"I did. Did you get anything neat?"

"I got some protein powder, but I also got us a rotisserie chicken and some fruit and some of those fancy-ass granola bars I like. And coffee."

"Protein powder? On purpose?" *Ew.*

"I need a protein shake. As much as I'm eating, I've still lost two pounds. You're working me to the bone. Here, sit down, will you?" Curtis pushed him into a kitchen chair.

"I'm sorry. Am I?"

"Teasing, Roper. I'm having a ball. Look at all my new calluses!" Curtis had plenty of them before, from riding, but now he had them on his fingertips.

"Sexy son of a bitch."

"Huh?" Curtis looked at him, then grinned slowly. "Why, thank you."

"It's true." He leaned against Curtis's hip, the scent of his lover filling him. "I got five hundred saved, after I pay the light bill."

"That ought to be enough to get most of your tools back, yeah? I mean, I don't know who you sold them to, but it ought to work."

"Tom. Tom Harrison. I got to pay the taxes. I know I'll have to borrow some from you, but I want to get half."

Curtis bit his lower lip, that expression impossible to read for a moment. "I paid them today. The taxes."

"What?" He stood, the chair tipping over in the rush. "But…. You did?"

His heart throbbed, the whole world stopping. He wasn't sure if he felt crushing relief or just shock.

"I did. I mean, I did go to the store, but I went to the assessor's office. There were penalties and interest, and it was just better to pay it. I figure…." Curtis stopped, taking a deep breath. "I figure it's an investment for me. In the bucking broncs. And you can put that five hundred in savings for our trip to Boulder or in tools. I'm easy."

"God." He reached out for Curtis's hand, the sudden loss of pressure around his shoulders enough to make him sick. He wasn't going to lose the ranch.

God.

He wasn't going to lose his home.

"You okay?" Curtis took his hand and pulled him into a hug. "I could have made a payment plan, but I just had to transfer some money from savings."

He couldn't breathe.

"Baby? Are you okay?" Curtis muscled him into another chair, kneeling before him.

No. No, he wasn't. He wasn't okay. He couldn't fucking breathe. He blinked at his lover, just staring.

"Stetson?"

Curtis had to think he was the worst kind of broke-dick asshole. All Curtis had to do was transfer money around. Shit. He didn't even have a checking account right now.

"Talk to me." Curtis looked stressed out as all fuck, and Stetson didn't get it. What did Curtis have to be stressed about? He came out here because he felt sorry for them, for the poor ranchers, and saved everything.

"What do you want me to say?"

"Thank you?"

Stetson stood up so fast, the chair went flying, and Curtis went the other way. "Thank you?" Fuck, the words felt dry as the dust that made up the land. "You did it, cowboy. You rode in, you made Momma happy, you saved the ranch. You did it all in a couple of seconds."

And he hadn't been able to.

"Oh, for fuck's sake! Stop being a baby, Roper. I came out here to help you! To do this with you. You act like… like I've stepped on your fucking toes. Did you want to lose the ranch? Is that what this is about? You tired of working for it? God knows you act like it's the most important thing on earth for you, this fucking land." Curtis rolled his eyes, and God help him, he hated that look. "You left me for it, so I figured you liked it."

"You're the one that walked away. You're the one that left." And he'd never once gone anywhere. He'd been... right here.

Right here like the worthless dirt farmer he was.

"I had to. I had a life."

"You still do." And he knew it. "You still got yourself a life, and it's not here."

Curtis stared at him like he'd thrown a punch. "What? Stetson, what the fuck...."

"Get on. Go find yourself a rodeo and ride it." *Go now, before I lose it, because I don't know how to do this anymore. I don't know how to breathe good no more.*

"I'm not...." Curtis reached for him, and he shoved the man away.

"Go on! You came because she asked! This whole thing is a fucking lie!" He could hear himself screaming, hear the sound of his control shattering like one of Momma's crystal plates hitting the floor. "Get out!"

Curtis stared at him a second, then nodded, just the once. "I can do that."

The sound of the door slamming behind Curtis was the loudest thing he'd ever heard, and the silence left behind hurt as bad as the void left when he'd told Momma goodbye.

CURTIS DROVE down to the diner like his ass was on fire, took the turn into the parking lot on three wheels, and sat in the parking lot, hands white-knuckled on the steering wheel, wishing he was still smoking.

He breathed for a second or two, and then he called his momma, needing to hear her voice, to just... hell, he didn't know. To connect with what Stetson'd lost, maybe.

"Well, hey, baby!" God, she sounded happy to hear from him. "How goes?"

"It goes." *I'm back with Stetson, except he's mad at me, and I don't know how to make it right. Help me?*

There was a pause, then, "What's wrong?" She always knew. Always.

"Stetson's momma died."

"Oh shit. Thank God. I mean, it's a shame, but a blessing. Poor Stetson. I bet he's lost as all get-out."

"I guess? He's just.... I don't know, Momma. He's just such a...."

"Cowboy?"

He barked out a short laugh. "How did you guess?"

"You love him, so he must be. You ain't never suffered fools worth a shit, boy."

No. No, he didn't figure he had. "I keep making him mad, Momma. I swear to God I'm not trying, but I am."

"Well, of course you're not trying. He's not mad at you, son. He's mad at the good Lord, at the world, at his momma for leaving him. You're the one he can be mad at, because he believes in you. Losing a parent is hard, and he's lost both."

"I know, but...." Dammit. Dammit, he hated that she could do this, be such a... a mom.

"But what?" She chuckled softly. "Son, you want easy, don't love a cowboy. You want easy, go hook up with some suburban schoolteacher with a concern list that involves what to get at Starbucks."

That made him laugh, made his fist unclench. Right, because he could live with that. He wanted Stetson, for all he was an asshole.

Fucking prideful asshole.

Fucking stubborn butthead.

Fucking *cowboy*.

The thought had Curtis smiling, even though he didn't want to.

That was it, wasn't it? Everyone on the big circuit wanted to be a "real" cowboy. Everyone wanted to be so deep into a piece of land that you could see it writ in the lines on his face. Every single one of them wanted to be salt of the earth, wanted to be a working cowboy with scars from bleeding on land that was theirs.

Every one of them wanted to know what was wrong with them that they didn't have it.

Fucking stubborn, prideful, willful, hidebound cowboy.

Curtis loved him more than life.

"You know I love you, right, Momma?"

"I've never doubted it a second, son. Go on home and hug him tight. His soul hurts, I bet."

"Yes, ma'am." He would grab a couple of pieces of cherry pie and some burgers and fries. That would taste good, even if they had to tie it up before they ate.

STETSON STARTED with the motherfucking TV, the explosion when the old thing hit the ground outside hugely satisfying. Then he started on the furniture that she'd never let him move, never let him replace, even when they'd been flush.

No, Stetson, this was your daddy's favorite.

No, Stetson, this is my home. Leave it.

No, Stetson.

"You never let me change anything, and you bitched at me for being tied to this land!" He screamed the words as he tore the top off the ancient recliner that smelled like old woman and piss and death. "You never let me out of here, and now I'm all broke! Now I cain't find my way out, couldn't if I wanted to."

Now Curtis was gone, driven away like before, and he was here in this place that he'd given his whole life to, and for what?

Moving into her bedroom, he tore the rod from the closet, Momma's clothes going flying. The first swing put a hole in the wall; the second shattered the ceiling fan, glass raining down on him. "I wanted to go with him! I wanted to go, but you needed me here! You needed me, and I stayed!"

He swung again, and the third blow was stopped short, Curtis standing there and staring at him. "Roper? What the fuck?"

"Leave me alone!" he screamed, yanking at the wood dowel. "Go away."

"Yeah, I don't think so. You been busy, huh?" Curtis didn't pull the wood from him, but he didn't let Stetson have it either.

"I—" *Oh fuck.* One of the blades of the ceiling fan sat there on the floor, held together by nothing but dust.

"Yeah, looks like you're starting on redecorating without me. Good job."

He let the dowel go and stumbled into the front room, staring at the destruction.

His momma's house. Oh, God forgive him.

What had he done?

"Hey. You—you need some water."

"I—" His voice broke, and he hiccupped, staggering forward. He liked to hit his knees if Curtis hadn't caught him, easing him down to the floor.

"You stay there."

Curtis disappeared, and Stetson did just that, stayed there, the shame and pain flooding him and leaving him stupid.

"Drink." A water bottle was pressed to his lips, and he drank, afraid it was going to bring him to his senses. Curtis was here, back like the wind had blown him in off the range.

Stetson gulped down the water, which made him gag, so Curtis took it from him, going to his knees next to Stetson. "Oh God, I'm sorry I let you run me off, even for a minute. You were just so mad."

He was shaking, his body feeling frozen solid. His fucking teeth were chattering.

"I know this isn't really about the taxes," Curtis went on. "I know it. I'm sorry, baby. I am. I just knew it needed doing, okay? I mean, we talked on this some, whether or not it seeped through your thick skull. We're partners, right?" Curtis was asking for him to be coherent, and he couldn't do more than grab hold and squeeze.

Then he nodded sharply, more than once. He knew. He did. God, he was going to explode. The fucking pressure inside him kept getting bigger, and all the damage he'd done.... God. Stetson had been so scared for so damned long. "I thought I was going to lose it. This has been in Momma's family for a long damn time, and I thought I was fixin' to lose it."

"No. No, we're gonna build it back up." Curtis chuckled softly. "Looks like you done started renovating all on your own."

He looked around at the damage, at the utter chaos he'd created, and then he looked into Curtis's eyes, just horrified. "Oh God."

He searched for disappointment, for anger, for shame. All he could see in his cowboy's gaze was home.

"Curtis. She's gone. She's really gone." He grabbed his lover, shook him, let himself trust that Curtis could take it, take the full weight of this agony. "You aren't listening to me, goddamn it! She's gone, and I was going to lose her house. I wanted her to die at the end! I wanted her to go away and leave me the fuck alone and let me sleep in the warm."

"I got you." Instead of pulling away from him, Curtis pulled him in, just hugged him and held him close, arms like steel bands.

"Didn't you hear me?"

"Yes, sir, I heard you. I got you, Stetson."

He tried to pull away, and Curtis held on, so stubborn, so fucking stubborn that finally he howled out his rage at the universe and let the tears come. He cried and railed for all of it—how scared he'd been, how she'd hurt, how much they'd lost in the last few years.

He missed her. God, he'd missed her for so long that he couldn't even get rid of those fucking roses in the bathroom.

Curtis held on, not saying a word, not doing anything but holding on and letting him know he wasn't alone.

Not anymore.

He whooped for air, trying to get breath into his lungs, trying to stop, but now that he'd started, he couldn't staunch the flow.

Stetson thought maybe Curtis was singing to him.

When the storm faded, Curtis stroked his hair away from his forehead. "Hey."

"Hey." He caught his breath finally. Yeah. Okay, he could do this. Stetson sat very still, his hands clenched in the fabric of Curtis's shirt. His head pounded, his temples throbbing. "I—Christ, I didn't mean for that to happen."

"That's good, though. I remember how Mom was when Grandma Miller died. You have to let it out." Curtis rose, then moved to get the box of Kleenex for him.

"I'm not pissed about the taxes. You're my fucking hero. I'll make sure to make it worth it."

"You already do, baby. I—knowing I have a place? I haven't had that since I left high school." Curtis smiled for him then.

"Did we say what we were going to do for supper?"

"Well, we had talked meatballs, but I got that chicken and some potato salad and rolls. Why don't we just do that?"

"Works for me. I... I miss her. God, I do. The her when she was still Momma, you know?"

"I can't even guess, baby. I don't see mine much, but I know she's there if I need her. It's got to be killing you. I love you."

"Love you. God. I love you."

"You'll love me more if I feed you."

"I bet I will." He could actually crack a smile. Lord, he felt old. His joints creaked.

"Let's eat, baby. Seriously. Food. A bath. The good stuff."

"Yeah." Tomorrow.... God, tomorrow he could call Tom and get his tools back.

Thinking about that might just make him break down again.

"Food, baby. Focus. Food. Bath. Rest. Tomorrow is another day."

Stetson rolled his eyes. "Tomorrow might have to be a late day."

"It can be." Curtis's grin changed to something slow and heated. "We can cuddle."

"I like that. I like knowing you're in my bed."

"Our bed now," Curtis reminded him, and yeah. Theirs. They even had new sheets.

"Yeah. Our bed. Our ranch. It works for me."

"Good deal." Curtis just nodded, like that was that.

He grabbed the chicken and the potato salad from the fridge. Maybe it was.

Maybe it was going to be okay.

CHAPTER TWENTY-SIX

WHEN HIS phone rang in his pocket, Curtis damn near jumped out of his skin. Shit. It had been a good bit since anyone but Stetson even texted him.

He tugged out his phone and clicked the green when he saw Ty Berry's name pop up.

"Curtis? Hey, son. It's Ty, from Cinch."

"Hey, old man. How's it going?" Ty was his sponsor liaison with the jeans company.

"Good. Good. Are you going to make an appearance at the Dallas event? We'd sure like to see you."

"Dallas?" He wasn't sure what that even was. "Uh."

"Normally we've had a sit-down by now to work out your schedule, but I figured you were taking it easy after your win."

"Yeah. I am. I've been working on my ranch. Thinking about investing in bucking horses."

"Woo, son. You got you a ranch already? Look at you, becoming a real cowboy."

"Hey, I grew up that way." Sometimes the rodeo attitude got to him, even though he knew better. "I've settled on a place outside of Taos."

"Pretty country there. I come up to ski sometimes with my kids."

"Well, you should come up to see the ranch. It has amazing bones." And Stetson. "Remind me about Dallas?"

"They're doing that big Ride of the Champions deal. You're going to be the big draw. Twenty different champs. You ride in rounds until there's one left standing."

"All roughstock? What's the purse?"

"All bulls, all the way. Million bucks at the end."

"Fuck." A million dollars to the winner? His heart kicked into a hard rhythm. "Any payout for runner-up?"

"Fifty thousand for fourth up to a hundred for second."

"Goddamn. When do I have to be in Texas?"

"Valentine's Day weekend."

Oh, man. He would just have to take Stetson with him. They could celebrate together.

"All right. I'm in. I'll call Barb and have her make arrangements."

"There you go. She probably already has you signed up."

"Yeah, well, if she does, she should have told me. I need to work out some." He chuckled, but he was already dreading the grueling regimen he'd have to fit into the next three weeks or so. "Is there a meet and greet?"

"Yeah. VIP package deal too. You know the drill. We'll bring the stand-up cardboard bigger-than-lifelike Curtises."

"Fuck you, man. I ain't that little."

"Uh-huh. Still...."

"Okay. Well, like I said, let me get Barb on it, and she can call you."

"Good deal. Send pictures of the ranch."

"I will." He knew Ty would want to know if the place was worthy of a photo shoot.

He wondered what Stetson would say to a casita. Something they could put company in. Of course, there was a full side of the house they weren't using.

Still, a casita would let them put business guests out somewhere with a little kitchen and their own bath and only have to deal with them when they called ahead....

He realized all of the sudden that he didn't remember telling Ty goodbye. Huh. His mind was on what all they could do with a nice big purse.

He pondered tracking down Stetson, but he didn't want to interrupt workshop time. Those tools had just come home today. He didn't imagine he'd see his Roper until supper.

So he could make some calls and get the plan set. Better to ask for forgiveness than permission. Stetson would balk at him doing four or more rounds of bulls, and he knew it.

It was too soon, but the money was too good to pass up. With that kind of purse?

Shit.

He could take off the rest of his damn life. Well, except for Santa Fe. That was like a state pride thing, if he was gonna be a New Mexican now.

He could buy horses and settle down, actually be the working cowboy he wanted to be.

Curtis stopped right there in the kitchen, his scalp prickling. Holy shit. He really was ready to retire.

Jesus. He stared out the kitchen window, at the barns—his barns.

His and Stetson's. The whole world had tilted on its axis in just a few short months. The perfect storm had thrown them back together, and now was the time.

His heart had damn near stopped when Stetson broke down. He'd never seen that from his lover, but it was like, all of the sudden, Stetson could breathe.

Curtis clicked some buttons on his phone to call his sports agent, Barb. He needed to be in on that ride of champions. Even fifty thousand would be a lot of improvements on the ranch.

Hell, showing up would make a nice nod to his sponsors and possibly a commercial or something. He could glad-hand and sign autographs and wear his gold buckle. Then he could come home. To Stetson.

Maybe he'd even be able to bring Stetson with him. He was sure gonna try. Stubborn cowboy.

Okay. Time to make a plan. It felt good. Real good. He knew where he was going for the long haul.

Now he had to figure out how to tell Stetson so he didn't feel like Curtis was running out on him. Maybe he would make an engraved invitation.

Curtis laughed out loud.

That just might work.

HIS WORKSHOP looked… like his again.

Stetson sat on the stool and breathed, surprised that he couldn't see his breath. That little heater did its job. His tools hung on the pegboards or lay neatly in the workbench drawers. He had some twisted cedar and a big hunk of ironwood Miz Ivy had traded him for a bonus llama that had appeared on his land last year.

She was out there with a leaf blower once a week, grooming the llama so she could shear him late in the spring and make yarn.

God, was it true? Was life coming back together?

He stared at his hands, trying to decide if he should feel guilty. Momma had passed on, and suddenly his world was spinning again. Did that make him an asshole?

He didn't think so. He'd stopped everything to be there for her. He'd given her his best.

Okay. Okay, so he had his shop. His tools. The lights were set up. Maybe....

Stetson picked up a piece of twisted cedar.

By the time he looked away from the wood, it was dark outside and he had a rose in his hand, heavy and eternal. The grain of the wood worked its way around the outer petals and spiraled into the middle, and he thought it looked pretty damned good for a first try.

He put it on the table, staring at it. "Not bad. Not bad at all."

Grinning, he tugged out his phone, took a picture, then sent it to Curtis.

It only took seconds for him to get a *Beautiful. Now come eat* back.

Curtis was kinda obsessed with learning to actually cook. Stetson had seen him looking online at cooking classes in Santa Fe.

Weirdo.

He cleaned up his shit and put his tools away, then locked up. The snow was falling again, looking like fairies where the flakes caught the lights from the house.

Turning up his collar, he headed out, two of the dogs joining him, dancing around his legs and begging to play.

"Hey, y'all." He bent down, scooped up a handful of snow as he walked, then threw it, the silly beasts tearing after it.

They barked and leaped and rolled each other in the white stuff all the way back to the porch, where Curtis met him. "Hey, baby."

"Hey. How goes it?" He made another snowball, threw it hard.

"Good. I like your rose."

"It's okay. I need practice."

"Good thing you have a heated workshop." Curtis winked. "I have to practice. I have to get out in the cold."

Stetson snorted softly. "You're working on getting those barns gone up so good that you'll be in shirtsleeves in there."

"Is it ridiculous to want an indoor practice arena?"

"I don't see why?" He stomped his boots off. "We'll save up and build one between the two big barns."

"Sounds grand." Curtis grabbed him once they were inside and two-stepped him through the mudroom.

Stetson laughed, blowing an icy cold kiss on Curtis's throat.

"Oh! Damn, that's freezing! I hate to think what your hands feel like."
He feigned a grab at Curtis's fly. "You want to know?"

"No!" Curtis danced away. "I made lasagna."

"For real? That sounds good, man." He loved anything that involved noodles and cheese.

"Yep. I had a wild hair. Real, not Stouffer's."

Hmm. Okay, what did Curtis want? Stetson grinned, ready to stretch it out a little, make Curtis sweat.

"You and your wild hairs." First a practice arena, now lasagna—had the man bought a load of horses?

"I do get them." Curtis wouldn't quite look at him, and that sent a little ball of dread to his belly. "So, I got a call from a sponsor."

"Yeah?" Was that bad? Back in the day, that was good.

"Well, you know how I said I would skip stock show season, maybe just do some events around Cowboy Christmas?" Curtis warmed to his topic, meeting Stetson's gaze with his. "There's an event in Dallas over Valentine's weekend. Last man standing kinda thing. All bulls. The purse is a million for first, and Cinch wants me to headline."

He'd known that this was coming. This was the nature of the breed, and there was no way Curtis was going to spend the rest of his time on the ranch. Stetson would take what all he could get. "Good deal."

"Even if I just place, it's good money. Fifty K for fourth. That's our initial investment for the horse operation, and I could just let the rest of the year go."

"Damn. That's a good purse." He wouldn't make that all year, unless he lucked out and got a huge job on a house or a church.

"Yeah. We can do Dallas together, huh?" Curtis grabbed his hand, clearly excited now. "I need to work out some, but I got a few weeks."

"Yeah? You want company?" That sounded even better. He hadn't been anywhere in an eon.

"Of course I do." Curtis squeezed his hand. "I told you, this is the long haul. No more running off without you."

"Well, I like that." He liked it a lot, to be honest.

"Cool. I'll get Barb to arrange the tickets and hotel, then. They're thinking it will be a big crowd."

"Dallas folks do like their bulls." And they'd be on fire, as short a distance as those bastards would have to travel. Curtis would have to be careful, because really the NFR bulls had nothing on some of the bulls who went to the pure bull riding events. Lord, his neck hurt.

He rolled his shoulder, trying to loosen the kink.

"You okay?" Curtis frowned slightly before turning him around to rub him good right where it hurt.

"Not used to carving so long any—there! Oh damn. Right there." He wasn't sure if it hurt like all get-out or felt so good. Goose bumps popped up on his arms, and he went up on tiptoes. "Damn."

"You'll get it back." Curtis kissed his neck. "Get the garlic bread out of the oven?"

"Surely can." He toddled over to the oven and pulled it out. "Let me go take my boots off and change my socks and I'll be out."

"You got it." Curtis hummed, setting the table, sounding happy as a clam.

He liked that. He liked that Curtis wanted company. That he wanted to go. It felt damn good, and even better to say yes. Years ago he would have turned it down.

Years ago Curtis wouldn't have asked.

He guessed they had both grown up a little.

He could live with that. Now, the cold feet in his boots? Not so much.

He stripped out of his cold, damp clothes, threw on his comfortable jeans and a sweatshirt and heavy socks. Better.

Now, about that lasagna. The whole house smelled like garlic and red sauce, and he was suddenly starving.

"God, I'm hungry." He walked into the kitchen with the heavy table where it always had been, the casserole dish the one Momma used to make tamale pie in, and it made him grin.

"I figured you had to be working your ass off."

"It wasn't bad." None of this was.

"Good. I like a happy Stetson." Curtis smiled for him, those blue eyes on him, admiring him.

"You look pretty damn pleased with life yourself."

"I am. I made lasagna, and it looks like Mom's. I got you to agree to go on a job with me."

"I like that you asked." He liked it a lot.

"I'm so glad you said yes." Curtis had dished up lasagna and salad, bread. It looked amazing.

"Thank you."

"For what, Roper?"

"Supper. Having someone to come home to. Asking me to go."

"I made the mistake once of letting us live separate lives." Curtis flushed, ducking his head. "Not gonna do it again."

"No. No, and I'll never just let you fade away." Never.

"Well, see? We're figuring this shit out."

They were. Day by day.

One supper after another.

CHAPTER TWENTY-SEVEN

CURTIS GRINNED when the dogs set up a ruckus, barking their fool heads off.

He wasn't expecting Miles until after supper, but the man drove like a fiend, and he was showing off for his new traveling partner, Curtis would bet. Some kid from Texas, still wet behind the ears, if Curtis remembered right.

"You three hush," he said, stepping out on the porch.

Miles honked and waved, grinning at him like a monkey. "Look at all this white shit, buddy!"

"Right? I mean, it snows where I'm from, but not like this."

"You know it. I think Braden here is gonna freeze solid."

"Hey, Braden! Y'all come in. I have a fire laid."

The kid who appeared was what? Twelve? Christ. Curtis figured he was getting older every day, but at least he shaved. Braden was....

Since Braden was walking like the snow was cracking ice, he got to tease Miles. "You cradle robbing now?"

"Fuck you. I wasn't robbing anything when he snuck into my bedroll." Miles sighed. "He listens to Dustin Lynch."

"Bless your horrorbilly heart."

"I know. Save me, man. Hold me!" Miles threw himself on Curtis.

"What the—" He laughed out loud, bear-dancing Miles around.

"Hey now. Don't you be dancing with my man." Stetson's voice was sure, steady, surprisingly loud.

"Stetson! How's it going, bud!" Miles let him go so fast he staggered and moved to the door to pump Stetson's hand.

"Curtis Traynor," Curtis said when Braden mounted the stairs.

"Braden Matthews." The kid looked like an unbroke horse.

"You okay?" Curtis asked softly. "Would you rather stay in a hotel, kid?" If Braden wasn't cool with him and Stetson being together, he wasn't about to let it happen.

"No. No, I just.... You know. You have to be so careful all the time. Miles told me y'all are family."

"Not here you don't." He clapped Braden on the back. "Stetson and me, we're together. We're not fixin' to start judging anyone."

"Cool. Y'all been together a while? He's a pretty man."

Pretty? His Stetson?

He thought Stetson was stunning, but pretty he wasn't. He looked like one of his carvings, hewn by the New Mexico landscape.

"A while, yeah." He tried to see his lover through this kid's eyes, but he didn't get pretty. Breathtaking, sure. Fuckable, hell yes.

"Nice. Thanks, uh, for letting me come stay a few days. You don't know me from Adam."

Curtis snorted. "Get your ass inside before you freeze to death, kid."

"Yeah. Christ, it's colder than a witch's tit out here."

"I've acclimatized some." Curtis did close the door behind them as quick as he could, though. His balls were trying to crawl up into his body.

Stetson was hanging coats, offering coffee, easy and dear, like it hadn't been damn near a decade since he'd seen Miles.

Same with Miles. He was beaming, just talking a mile a minute. "We hit a heck of a storm up around Denver. Hoo, I thought we were gonna slide all the way down."

"It's supposed to dump on us for a couple of days, you know." Stetson sounded wickedly amused.

"We'll all have to huddle together for warmth," Miles murmured.

Braden gaped.

Curtis cracked up.

"Uh-huh. You just want to feel up my cowboy. You're not allowed." Stetson put on a stern face.

"Y'all're fixin' to give Braden a stroke," Curtis said. "You want coffee? Hot chocolate? Y'all got here in great time, so we can get anything you want for supper. Within reason. This is Taos."

"Coffee, please. And don't make my old ass get back in the truck."

"You got it. I can make us quesadillas. I got all the stuff." Curtis warmed right up to that idea.

"He's becoming an amazing cook. Seriously." Stetson was proud of him, he could tell.

"Curtis Traynor. Eating food. The king of the protein shake." Miles winked, and Curtis rolled his eyes.

"Fuck off. I've lost weight."

"You look healthy, man. Seriously. You look… solid."

"Thanks." Curtis had to grin at that. He felt amazing. Work, real hard work, was better than crunches any day. And he was having a ball. Working with the livestock, working on the barns and the house. Hell, being able to go in and see Stetson in his workshop, handsome face a study in concentration, was magic.

"Lovin' life," Curtis admitted. "Sit, huh? Tell me everything."

"Well, ain't much to say. You left and everyone else left. I went to Hawaii for that little Aloha event and Christmassed there, met Braden, and we came back to my place for New Year's."

"Well, welcome, Braden." Curtis chuckled. "Miles doesn't take everyone home."

"No?" Oh, there was interest there. He wondered if they needed two beds or just the one....

"Nope. I'm picky," Miles drawled.

Stetson snorted, but moved around to make coffee and cocoa.

Braden's cheeks were bright pink, but Miles didn't look the least bit worried. No, he looked pleased as punch. Good for him.

Curtis began pulling stuff out of the fridge. Grilled chicken he'd made yesterday. Flour tortillas. Cheese.

Stetson handed him the butter. Right. Always lube the pan. "Thanks, baby."

"Mmm-hmm." Stetson moved around him in a happy orbit, pulling out a can of refried beans and some boxed rice mix.

He grabbed one wrist, then reeled Stetson in for a kiss, refusing to let their company stop them.

Stetson made a happy sound, hugging on him for a moment. When they moved back to cooking, Miles was grinning at them like a fool, and Braden looked like he might explode.

"We'd better be nice, hmm?" Stetson whispered.

"I guess." He bumped hips with his lover. "Although this is kinda fun, huh?"

"So mean." Stetson's laugh suited him to the bone.

"Okay, you two. Tell me your plans for the ranch," Miles said, breaking in.

"Apparently Curtis is going to start running bucking horses."

"No shit?"

"Not even a bit," Curtis said. "Now, I'll need a contractor to transport."

Miles's face broke into a slow, deep grin. "We talked on this some, you know?"

"We did. Stetson is more than willing to work with the mares and foals, but he's only willing to travel so much." Curtis smiled at his lover. "He has a woodworking business."

"That's so cool." Braden perked up at that. "What do you make?"

"Vigas, framework, banisters—pretty much anything."

"That's really awesome. My brother is a finish carpenter, but he's not much of a carver."

"I mostly carve things. I like to keep it rustic."

"Can I see your shop while I'm here?" God, had he ever been that young?

"Sure, man." Stetson sounded easy in his skin, totally at home. God, it felt good. It felt damn good.

Curtis pulled out the iron skillet to heat, then started buttering tortillas.

"You two look domesticated as hell. It's adorable. Who wears the apron?" Miles looked over at him with a shit-eating grin.

"He has a leather one for woodworking." Let Miles ponder that for a moment.

"Ooh. Leather. Sex-ay."

"Scared or desperate?" Stetson whispered.

"Scared." Curtis nodded sagely. "I think him and the kid have hooked up. That's, like, a commitment."

"Yeah. I hear that. I'll be nice."

"Yep."

"Will y'all stop talking about me like I'm not here? Where's your bathroom, man?" Miles stood, hitching up his belt.

Stetson pointed down the hall to the rose bathroom. Oh, Miles was gonna love that.

"Sorry if we're out of line," Curtis told Braden. "We tease to live."

"I've learned a lot of that from Miles." Braden smiled a little. "Just not used to being obvious."

"You're not, man. We're just open."

Curtis nodded. "I've done the closet thing."

"Right," Braden said, "but what if you'd been out at Finals? Would you still have won?"

"I don't know." He was honest enough to admit that his scores might have suffered. "I did my time, though. I made a lot of mistakes.

At some point, you have to know what's more important. You're young enough it might be the ride. You'll figure it out."

"Yeah. Yeah. I guess." Poor kid. Curtis remembered that. Hell, it wasn't all that far away in memory.

"Anyway, what's your event?" He was making small talk. Go him.

"I'm a bull rider. I don't ride the broncs."

"No? They're more dangerous a lot of times. The bulls just require balance and strength." Braden had the look of a bull rider. Relatively short, wide through the shoulders, narrow in the hips.

Him, he was damn near too tall to ride bulls, but he was born to buck a bronc. He'd taken to it like a duck to water.

"Your pan is hot," Stetson said, the soft smile on his face telling Curtis that Stetson knew he was thinking about the game.

Stetson just didn't know it was all nostalgia.

He'd loved the game, sure, but this? This being home? He couldn't beat the feeling it gave him. It surprised him daily, but Curtis figured he would get used to it.

"Thanks, babe." He got the quesadillas going. "You riding in Dallas?"

"No, sir. I'm just coming with Miles. He's riding."

"Yeah. He's good at what he does."

"Better than you."

"Fuck off, man. I'm taking that purse. I need it." Curtis pursed his lips at the pan. The cheese needed something. Did they have any pepper jack?

Stetson was digging in the fridge, a Ziploc baggie of pepper jack handed over. Brilliant man.

He sprinkled, and Stetson pulled out sour cream and salsa while Miles chattered at them and Braden maybe dozed a little. He grinned. That must have been a tense ride with all the ice.

Before long he had a nice pile of food, and they got all the pieces and parts to the table. Damn, those looked good.

"Man, those look amazing."

"The rice smells damn good too."

Miles rolled his eyes. "I think Braden might be a rice fiend. I tease that he must be from South Carolina."

"Just East Texas," Braden murmured.

"That's damn near Louisiana." Stetson handed Braden the rice bowl.

"We grow it there. I like rice."

"Miles is just being a dick," Curtis said. "Nothing new."

Miles shrugged. "I'm just playing with the kid. That's all."

Curtis shot him a wink. "I know, buddy. Don't forget we're all new to him." He handed Miles the green salsa, knowing he loved the stuff.

"Oh. I've missed New Mexico...." Miles poured the salsa liberally, eyes crossing.

"Lord, he'll have dragon breath. Pass it on." Braden held out a hand, and Miles slid it to him.

Okay, that was adorable. Truly. He shot Stetson a glance. Were they like that?

Stetson's smile said it all. Yeah, they were just like that. Goofy and in love.

He hadn't ever done this—been in his home with his lover and his best friend who had a lover. It felt surreal, like he was starring in a play.

It also felt free and right. God.

They finished up all the food, and Braden groaned. "I think it's my turn to hit the head."

"Beware the roses," Miles murmured.

"The what?" Poor kid looked honestly worried.

"It was my mom's bathroom. We haven't redecorated." Stetson didn't sound a bit tense.

"Oh. Shit, my mom has pink flamingoes in her guest bath." Braden shook his head before wandering off down the hall.

"So, you'll both just stay in the guest room, right?" Curtis looked to Miles. "When did this happen?"

"In Hawaii. I swear to God, he came to my room one night, and... he's never left. He's like the Energizer Bunny."

"Good on you," Stetson said. "He's got it bad for you, Miles. I can tell."

"I just hope I can keep up. You know?"

"You just be you." Curtis clapped Miles on the back. "You're a good guy. And like I said, you get ready to get out of the game, I can use someone to truck horses. You can still travel with him, if it all works out." Listen to him. All guru. He needed to shut the hell up and let Miles work out his own shit.

Hell, he survived one meltdown over Miz Betty and he was fucking Dr. Phil. Then again, he'd spent years not talking to Stetson, and look what that had got him.

Miles just shrugged. "One day at a time. He's... wow."

He gave Miles a half hug. "Good deal. Can't wait to show you the improvements I want to make."

"I want to hear it all. Seriously." Miles shook his head. "You know how it is, huh? We're getting older."

"It's a young man's game. And by young, I mean under thirty." They would all have to come up with something else to do eventually. If Curtis could help his oldest friend on the circuit, then so be it.

"Lord, y'all talk like you're eighty." Stetson touched his hand. "You're on top of the world."

"It only takes one bad ride, Stetson," Miles said, and Curtis wanted to hit the fucker. He'd gotten Stetson to agree to this, to come with.

He still needed that million bucks.

Stetson nodded slowly. "Yeah. I reckon. You want to change into something like sweats? We're gonna sit in front of the fire and watch movies and doze."

"God, that sounds amazing. I'll take the bags to the room, sure."

"I'll go show you the way. The bed's comfy." Curtis grabbed a duffel bag and led Miles down the hall. "Oh, and don't talk to Stetson about bad rides. I managed to get him to agree to come to Dallas and be my good luck charm."

"Sorry. Sorry, man. I just—you know how it is."

"I do. Still. He's coming with."

"That's too cool." Miles punched his arm once they put the bags on the bed. "I'm tickled for you. Really."

"Yeah. Yeah, this is what I wanted, you know?" He knew it was cliché, but he didn't give a shit.

"I do. I'm so sorry about Stetson's momma. I should say that to him, huh?" Miles shrugged, a tiny motion. "So weird. She wasn't any older than my momma."

"It was early onset. It's not like she got diagnosed early enough, though."

"No. I guess they have drugs to slow it down now, huh?"

"They do. Too late for Miz Betty. It's tough, but it's better every day." He gave Miles a sideways look. "So you gonna meet his people?"

"God, no. They'd lynch me. I'm old enough to be his uncle."

"Mmm. But you introduced him to your mom?"

"I did. You know my mom. She's a hippie. She'd run the rainbow flag up at town hall if I'd let her."

"Lord." He leaned against the doorframe. "What did Braden think about her?"

"I think he liked her." Miles chuckled. "He stared at her a lot. Like she was a crazy woman."

"Yeah. She's amazing. I adored her."

"She made you divinity. It's in the truck. I forgot."

"Give me the keys and I'll run out. You get changed."

"Thanks." Miles handed him the truck keys. "There's a bag in the back seat. Wrapped presents and tins of food from Momma."

"I'll have Stetson give you one of his roses to send her." He headed out, grinning at Stetson as he passed. "Miles's momma sent goodies!"

"Hoo yeah! What kind?" Stetson followed him to the back door. "Don't you let those dogs in."

"You're unreasonable about the dogs. They're good."

"I am not." Stetson reached down to scratch ears. "They herd the dining chairs."

"You wait, I'll have them wagging and eating out of your hand."

"Curtis, them eating ain't one of my problems!"

He laughed out loud, bringing the bag in from the truck, his breath cutting swaths of mist through the night. He ran up the stairs like his ass was on fire, but really it was freezing. Stetson grabbed him up, dragged him in.

"You're mine, you know. Quit freezing your dangly bits."

"Miles's momma made divinity. It's worth it." He kissed Stetson to warm up.

Stetson took his lips, hands running up and down his back.

"Mmm. Now that's dessert." Curtis shivered. "Still too close to that damned door. I need to put in a new window."

"Yeah? You think that'll help?" Stetson moved them closer to the fire.

"I think so. We get a double-paned window for it with those blinds in between? I think it will be grand."

"That would be fancy. I'd like that." Stetson kissed his temple. "So, are they going to stay in the bedroom, cowboy?"

"They are. They're a thing." He shook his head. "Miles was always willing to lend a hand, but I had no idea he would go full-on *Brokeback Mountain*."

"You never know about cowboys. Six-packs or not. I meant more, like, can I take you to bed and have my way with you, or do we got to be social?"

"Oh, well, we told them fire and movies, but if I made our apologies, I bet they'd snuggle up just fine."

"No. No, I just meant—" Stetson snorted. "What movie should we watch?"

Curtis took one more kiss, which was when Miles and Braden tumbled down the hall, flushed and guilty looking.

"Movie, boys?" Curtis asked.

"Uh-huh."

"Sure. Sure." Miles looked damned disheveled.

Stetson just cackled.

Braden grinned hugely. "I can see us coming to visit a lot, if y'all don't mind."

Curtis glanced at Stetson and nodded. "We definitely need to build that casita."

"We do." Stetson went to sit on the big overstuffed love seat. "Y'all can have the sofa."

"Thanks. The fire is great. It's cold as a witch's tit here." Braden sat at one end of the sofa, flushing when Miles sat right beside him instead of at the other end.

Curtis grabbed the remote and the box of divinity. He was going to have to start dieting. Really.

Maybe not today.

CHAPTER TWENTY-EIGHT

"HAVE YOU seen my hat case, baby?" They were just about packed, but Curtis couldn't find the hard case for his good felt. He would need it for the interviews and autograph session.

"Did you put it in the closet in that room you're fixin' to make your office?"

"Oh." Yeah, maybe he had. He headed that way, and darned if the hat case wasn't right there.

He was going to have an office, right here. Stetson had surprised him by emptying out Betty's sewing room, painting it for him. The desk was handmade and finished in a dark walnut color, the perfect place for his laptop and his file folders.

It was fucking weird and wonderful to have a place of his own like this. It left him a little giddy.

In fact, he wasn't sure he wanted to leave, but the payout at Dallas was too good a chance to pass up.

Anyway, Stetson was excited about having a vacation, an adventure. They'd never had much chance to travel together, and he wanted to show Stetson everything. And show him off.

"You find it?" Stetson looked in, the heavy mane of hair long enough to be tied back.

"I did. I'll get my boots shined at the hotel." He knew the Sheraton downtown had a shine stand.

"Ooh, fancy!" Stetson grinned at him, waggled his eyebrows.

"Hey, I intend to take you to a Cavender's." Stetson needed new boots. They'd gotten him a pair at the feed store to replace the ones with the holes, but he needed a new dress pair.

He wanted to play "dress the cowboy" so badly. The very idea gave him a happy.

Stetson rolled his eyes. "Save your pennies for the bucking horses."

"Hush. Let me play. I want to see you in a white button-down, jeans that fit."

He loved putting that look on Stetson's face. Loved it. The color in Stetson's cheeks didn't hurt either.

"I got plenty of people to feed, and the delivery is coming in Thursday. Tom will be here for it, and he's taking the dogs."

"Rock on. I got the oil changed in the truck, so we're good to go there." He was looking forward to the trip too. Twelve hours in the truck with his lover.

"What else do we need to do?" Stetson looked a little lost.

"Hang the shirts in the back seat?"

"I can do that. I filled the cooler with Cokes and cheese and grapes."

"Rock on, baby. I'll get the bags loaded."

"You excited?" Stetson hauled him in for another kiss.

"I am! I mean, it's a day of work for five or six days of fun. It's easy-peasy."

"I am too. We're having a trip."

"Good." He took one more kiss. "Okay, I need to pack my hat. Let's get loading."

Stetson saluted, chuckling. "I'm on shirt and cooler duty."

Stetson disappeared into the kitchen, and he grabbed his hat case.

They had a long, leisurely drive down, then a day at the hotel before he had to surrender to the sponsors and such. Braden and Miles would be there, though, and he had three dozen folks he wanted to introduce Stetson to.

It was time for his rodeo world to crash into his new ranch world.

Nerves fluttered in his belly. Miles knew all, and most of his friends, his agent, and some of his sponsor reps knew he was queer. The fans, now, they probably had no idea. Neither did the judges.

Stetson wouldn't out him. He knew that. He just—he wasn't fixin' to start lying either. Not now. Not now that he finally had what he needed in this world.

He loaded the hat box and the bags. The dogs had all disappeared; they hated it when bags got loaded in the truck. Everyone on the ranch was a little PTSD. Poor puppies, they hadn't completely figured out that leaving didn't have to mean forever. Every time someone left, they worried.

Curtis reckoned they were all going to have to get used to a periodic trip. He was going to explore the world with Stetson, and he didn't think his Roper would fuss.

Stetson hung shirts and checked doors and finally stood on the porch, looking around. "I keep feeling like I'm going down to see Momma, and it makes me edgy."

"You're not. Let's just go, babe. Seriously. Come play with me. Please."

Stetson reached out for him, nodding, hand steady. "I'm ready when you are."

They headed out to the truck. He would do whatever it took to make Stetson feel better. Once they got down past Santa Fe, that weird feeling would fade, he knew it. Then they'd be cooking with oil.

"Let's go see if Dallas is all it's cracked up to be."

"I think you're gonna love it." People-watching alone would tickle Stetson to death, and there was going to be a vendor room.

"I don't doubt it a bit." Stetson settled in the passenger side, a pillow already there to tuck in against the door.

"Maybe we'll run to Fort Worth and see the stockyards."

"Sounds good. We got time to play a little."

"Yeah. Have a steak at the Cattlemen's." He was doing good. Back in fighting shape with hardly a protein shake in sight.

"Anytime you offer me a steak, cowboy."

"Old-fashioned man." It was the baked potato that got Stetson, though. Every time.

"Yessir." Stetson reached for him as they started out.

He grabbed Stetson's hand and held on, glad they weren't forced to drive a stick anymore. Made touching way easier. All they needed was Tim McGraw on the radio and they were gone.

Lord help them.

CHAPTER TWENTY-NINE

JESUS, DALLAS was big.

Stetson stared up at the skyline that he'd seen in a hundred episodes of TV and just gawked like he'd never been out of Taos.

There was the building with the lit up X, the tower hotel with the big ball, and a dozen other things to stare at. Curtis drove like he'd been here a hundred times, and Stetson reckoned he had. He was grateful, because he wanted to stare.

"Oh, look at that!" Their hotel was tall and amazing when Curtis turned in, pulling the truck up to valet parking.

"What do I need to do, cowboy?" How did this work?

"I'll handle the valet if you can run up to the desk right there and get us a bellman with a cart."

"Sure. Sure." He followed instructions—bellman, cart, go.

"May I help you, sir?"

"We're checking in. We need a cart up to the room."

"You got it. Y'all got here at a good time. Couple hours past the rush." The kid grabbed a cart and followed him back out to the truck.

"Yeah. It was a good drive. Not bad on traffic."

"Nice. It will get hairy over the weekend." Once they got to the truck, the kid began pulling out bags and shirts and hat boxes like this was no big deal. "How long are y'all here?"

"'Til Tuesday morning, I think." They might just go on to Fort Worth Monday morning.

"Oh, that'll be nice for you. Sunday afternoon it will get quiet, and you can just hit up the restaurants and bars without competition."

"Yeah? Good to know. I've never been here before."

"No? You should ask at the concierge. Jack knows everywhere to go."

"Thanks." He sent Curtis a wild look, and Curtis smiled, walking over to take his elbow.

"We'll need to check in. Can you wait, or do we need to get a ticket so you can bring it all up later?"

"I'll give you this. You'll call the bell desk when you get to your room, and we'll bring it up. Have a great time, y'all."

Stetson watched them take the truck, take their things, all but Curtis's bag of electronics. Okay, that was unnerving.

"You should have seen my face the first time I stayed at a big host hotel," Curtis said, steering him toward the big revolving door. "The kid with the cart took my rigging, and I about popped him on the chin."

"I remember that. You called me from the room, just about in hysterics."

"Right? Now I know not to leave my laptop, but no one wants my riding gear." Curtis stepped up to the front desk. "Hey, there. Curtis Traynor, checking in. I'm a rewards member."

Lord, look at all the folks. There was somebody here for a wedding—colors black and green, he thought, although maybe the whole family just had matching bags. There were a ton of folks in Western wear, a couple of little toddlers in cowboy boots, and a load of dudes in suits.

They'd have to come back down and have a beer in the bar just off the lobby, watch all the people.

"Thanks." Curtis turned and caught him gaping. "We're in 904."

"Yeah? Cool. Just people-watching. No big."

"I knew that would get you." Curtis winked. "Wanna go get our bags delivered and clean up some? Then we can figure supper."

"Sure. You don't have to check in with the event organizers or nothing, right?"

"Nah. I'll text Miles and let him know I'm here. Maybe Barb. But no one will expect anything."

"Good deal." They headed up into a fancy-assed hotel room that was all beige and classy and shit. There was even a sofa. "They do know that you're cowboys, right?"

"Athletes, baby. We're athletes."

"Right. You gonna get a sports psychologist to help you win more?"

Curtis gave him that look. "Absolutely not."

He couldn't have fought the grin if he'd tried, and he had to admit, he didn't try so hard.

"Butthead." Curtis picked up the phone to call for their bags. "It's nice, though, huh?"

"It's amazing. Stuffy. You mind if I turn the AC on?"

"God, no. The humidity here is killer."

"It's crazy. The air is so heavy. Look at how green everything is, though." It wasn't even spring yet, and things were green, and there was water standing everywhere.

"I know. I swear, I wonder what they do with it all."

Yeah, Stetson knew Curtis loved the high desert too. Maybe the places Curtis tended to light weren't as high as him, but Curtis's favorite part of Colorado was all adobe cliffs and scrub brush.

Spare water was strange and wonderful, and he didn't quite get it. He turned the thermostat down, then sat on the end of the bed.

"Oh, that's nice."

"Good. Nothing worse than a squishy bed after a day of riding." Curtis grabbed the hotel book off the desk.

Stetson eased off his boots and leaned back, eyes closed, his body suddenly heavy. Just over ten hours hadn't seemed like long in the truck, but now he was wearing down.

"Nap time before we go down for supper, huh? It'll be a half hour before they show with the bags."

"Sounds good." It did too.

Curtis sat next to him, and he heard boots hit the floor.

"When you traveled lately, I mean before my call, did you travel alone?"

"Mostly, yeah. Miles would room with me once in a while, but he still liked to go out drinking after the show, and I can't do that anymore. I get all swollen."

He dragged one hand over Curtis's belly, fascinated by the ridges of the six-pack, even under the cloth of his button-down.

"Mmm. That's not napping, baby."

"No?" His eyes were closed, it was quiet, and Curtis was right there.

"That's petting, but I can deal." Curtis scooted up next to him and stretched out.

"Thank you," he whispered.

"What for?" Curtis whispered right back at him.

"Answering the phone when I called."

Curtis took his hand, fingers curling around his. "I'm glad I did."

"Me too. For a thousand reasons."

"It scared me. It wasn't your old number, and I thought something had happened to you."

"Something had." He'd discovered that he had to let go of the old shit somehow when Momma'd been trapped in the past.

"I know, baby. I'm so sorry." Curtis had said it a hundred times, but Stetson knew he meant it.

"Me too, but it is what it is. Or was. Something."

"Right." Curtis toyed with his fingers. "I have to thank you too."

"What fer?" In his head he heard his momma's voice saying, *cat fur, to make kitten britches.*

"For saying yes. For coming with me. I always wanted you to."

"I should have. I was scared."

"Oh, baby, neither of us was ready. I know there was a lot of time lost, but maybe we had to learn what we had to." Curtis snorted. "You notice how I'm a regular philosopher these days?"

"I know. They teach you that in rodeo school?"

"Nope. It's all that late night talk radio I listened to on the road. Lonely hearts club."

"Ah." His lips quirked. "Lord, what are you gonna do now? Since you aren't lonely or on the road?"

"Ponder all the things we can do in hotel rooms?" Curtis teased.

"Yeah? You think you can make a list?"

"I can totally do that. After we nap, maybe."

This was decadent already. Nothing to do but lie here and hold hands and doze.

"Sounds like heaven."

Pure-D heaven.

CHAPTER THIRTY

CURTIS STRETCHED, his arm and shoulder a little sore from signing his name to programs and posters and those little cards the sponsors put out. He always felt like a dork handing those out, because he looked nothing like the picture they always printed on it. Him standing there with his chest puffed out, arms crossed belligerently.

He grinned at this sweet little old lady in a glittery pink button-down. "Good afternoon, ma'am."

"Mr. Traynor. Can you sign my hat, please?"

"I absolutely can. How are you liking the meet and greet?" He took her hat, his Sharpie at the ready.

"Everyone's been real nice. I'm wearing down, though. You lookin' forward to the ride?"

"I am. I live for that, you know." He finished his last name with a flourish and winked at her.

"Eh. We all know you're a bronc man. I love to watch you ride."

"Thank you." He shook his head. "You caught me, though. I do love the bucking horses. Bulls are too eager to get the job done. Horses, now, they're fiery."

She leaned forward, and she smelled like bubble gum. "Bulls aren't quite as smart, you know. Horses can be pure evil."

"They can. You got to finesse them. Bulls is just balance and strength." He loved this part. Loved it.

"Yessir. You just balance yourself. I like you for this one."

"Do you? I'm kinda on fire." He flexed dramatically.

"Look at you." She hooted like a huge old owl, patting his stomach. *Oh ho! Handsy granny!*

He swooped down and gave her a hug. "Thank you, ma'am. You have fun this weekend!"

She squealed like a girl and walked away, just beaming.

"Good job, cowboy." Stetson leaned against the windowsill, taking pictures like mad.

"Thanks. She was touchy-feely." He winked, his ass stinging from her last little pinch.

"You are a stud."

He was going to pinch Stetson himself.

"I'm a little sore, actually. Autographs use different muscles."

"Really? Like your fingers?"

Joe Martin, his handler, popped up like a bad penny. "You have a photo shoot, Curtis. You ready? I have your gear."

"Uh. Sure. Who's this for?" He left the papers and pens on the table, just grabbing his Sprite.

"Sunday's paper. I think that they're going to do a couple of spots for the local news too."

"Cool." He liked the local folks in Dallas. They always had fun. "Then we get a break for lunch, right?"

"I am off until tomorrow morning, so far as I know. You're golfing or playing horseshoes?"

"Horseshoes, man. I don't golf." He rolled his eyes at Stetson, who was laughing at him right out loud. "Unless it's goony golf. Come on, old man. Keep up."

There'd be a place for spouses and such in there. Stetson could sit and have a Coke and visit, keep him company.

"Right." Joe hustled them out, never questioning Stetson being with them. Thank God.

Of course, if Joe had, he would have had a new person helping out. Dammit.

"Stop scowling," Stetson murmured.

"Huh? Oh, sorry. I was defending your honor in my head."

"My honor is safe. Promise. You'll give yourself wrinkles."

"Yeah, yeah." He gave Stetson a wry grin. "I'm still getting used to this some."

"You and me both. No wonder you work out so damn much."

"Yeah." He wasn't sure what that meant, exactly, but Curtis figured he'd just nod and smile.

Stetson snorted and followed, and he knew, without a shadow of a doubt, that Stetson was laughing at him.

They ended up doing two sets of pictures. One of him in his riding gear, chaps and all, and one for some Dallas lifestyle magazine where they wanted him to unbutton his shirt and show some skin. Hunks of the rodeo or some crap....

Stetson was going to give him no end of shit.

"Okay, flex your abs. Nice." The photographer was a sweet middle-aged lady with purple hair, wearing a Megadeth T-shirt. Lord, Lord.

He flexed, and a shitload of catcalls filled the room. Fuck-a-doodle-doo.

His cheeks went hot, and Haley lifted her camera. "Now, you have to stop blushing or I'll end up doing a shitton of Photoshop."

"Sorry. I just... this isn't my thing."

"You're hot as hell. You're fine." She beamed at him. "Ask anyone."

He raised a brow at Stetson.

Stetson smiled at him, slow and easy, looked him over, top to bottom, then dipped his chin.

Hoo yeah. Well, all right, then. He could show off some.

He camped it up for the camera, focused on Stetson, on the way his lover admired him. Curtis had never felt more confident or more wanted.

"I want prints, huh?"

She handed him a card. "Call me. We'll work it out."

"Thanks." They wrapped up not long after that, and Curtis was grateful. He was either going to starve to death or jump Stetson right there.

"Man, look at you! Cock of the walk!" Miles patted his butt on the way by. "You coming to lunch, man?"

"Huh? Sure, if Stetson is good with that." He knew there'd be a dozen cowboys there. Stetson might want a break.

"Whatever you need. What's going on this evening?"

"Joe says we're done until morning. We can kinda do what we want."

"Good." Stetson grinned at him. "So, lunch?"

"Yep. Did y'all pick a place, Miles?"

"Iron Cactus? It'll be happy hour at three, so we can lunch now and drink after."

"Sounds good. We'll meet you there." He didn't want to cab it, so he'd get the truck out of parking. Curtis tugged out his phone to see how far it was.

"I'll get us a table." Miles waved and headed out.

He looked it up, and hell, it wasn't even half a mile off. They could hoof it. "Want to walk? It's close."

"Sure. We have time." Stetson didn't seem worried.

"Cool." He put it in that walking score app thing. That would tell them where to go. "So, what did you think?"

"I think you're the coolest son of a bitch I've ever known."

That surprised a laugh out of him. "Yeah? Thanks, baby. I know it was probably boring."

"I liked it. Especially the last bit."

"Think that was okay?" He flushed again, trying not to be obvious, but that had been hot, having Stetson there watching.

"I thought that was fine. I felt like you were posing for me."

"I was." Curtis laughed a little, heading out of the hotel and across the street. "I've never done a shoot like that."

"I would have bought that calendar and looked at it when I, you know."

"I'm getting you prints." Curtis had a crazy urge to hold Stetson's hand, but this was Dallas. Probably not wise.

Stetson's grin was tickled as all get-out.

"You run your butt off," Stetson said, "when you travel."

"I bet you thought I just lazed around."

"No. I think I thought you did sit-ups and stared at the livestock."

"I did when I was younger. That and drank beer and slept in a van with four other guys."

"That doesn't sound fun, cowboy."

"It was stinky. And loud. Yardley snored."

"So did Momma." The joke was easy, fond, and it made him want to dance a little, because he wanted that for Stetson—fond memories, happy thoughts of Betty. They came more often now, not equal with the sadness yet, but time was the only thing to heal that.

"I remember the first time I spent the night. Remember? Your cousin was in the guest room, so I slept on the couch, and I swear I thought the big bad wolf was trying to blow the house down."

"Lord yes. I snuck you into my room eventually, and you slept."

"Yeah, a whole house away." He glanced sideways at Stetson. "Could be I was finally holding you."

"Could be that we were where we belonged."

"Exactly. So, what do you think about tonight?" He wanted to hear what all Stetson wanted to do. He really needed Stetson involved.

"I think I'll hold you all night, cowboy."

"Oh, damn. I like that idea." He liked it a lot. "Maybe get room service? They have an amazing carrot cake."

"Yeah? That would be something. You and me, sharing food in bed, naked…."

He was loving this new, wanton Stetson.

Irresistible.

"Curtis! You walking to the Iron Cactus?" Terry Rodaine fell into step with them. "Couple of the guys took a cab. Lazy bastards."

"We are. You met Stetson Major?"

"I did. Good to see you." Terry was a good guy, a Cajun-Texican. The man was used to not fitting in anywhere but having a foot in every world.

"Pleased." Stetson nodded to Terry, smiled wide. "I thought your ride in Santa Fe was one of the best I'd seen all year."

"Hey, thanks! I love that arena. It's just so homey."

"I do too. I've never missed the Rodeo de Santa Fe."

Stetson's words made him blink. He'd ridden that rodeo. A lot. Maybe every year since they'd broken up. He sure thought Stetson would avoid it, and he'd looked for Stetson every year, but no one ever sat in his box seats.

God, had Stetson been there? Just watching him? Had Stetson ever tried to talk to him? That rodeo was rife with hookups for most of the guys—good old Santa Gay—had Stetson seen that?

Curtis ducked his head, but Stetson touched his hand briefly. He glanced over again, and Stetson smiled. Okay. He could live with that look.

"It's a good purse, that one. Not as good as this thing, eh?" Terry jostled his arm.

"No shit on that. This one…." He wanted it. He wanted to take it home to him and Stetson. To their place.

"You've got some odds on you, *bougre*. I'm betting on you too, me."

"Good. I am too." For the first time in a long time, he needed this.

"You, man?" Terry asked Stetson.

"My money has always been on Curtis. Always."

Lord, that could give a man a big head. He beamed, feeling on top of the world. "Thanks, Roper."

Stetson shrugged, but that smile was warm and right.

They made it to the restaurant about the time a cab pulled in, spilling out five cowboys, including Miles and Braden.

"Oh, for fuck's sake! Are you serious?" Miles rolled his eyes.

"Yep. You actually paid to get here, man." Curtis laughed hard, slapping his leg. "Lazy."

"Fuck you. I'm saving energy to ride Big Mickey."

"Bullshit. That bull is mine." He hoped. It was all in the draw, and several of them would have the chance to ride him.

"You think? You might try Tres Equis."

"Shee-it." That was Terry. "Ain't no one rode him."

"He's a cowboy killer," Braden murmured. "Like that Bodacious back in the day."

"Back in the day before you were born." Miles snorted.

Stetson's lips twitched, but Terry howled with laughter. "You do have you a young one, but we all was, once."

"Hey! I was born before he retired!"

"Like a year before." Another young cowboy joined them, poking Braden.

"More like two."

"Well, heaven forfend," Miles said, and Curtis lost it.

"What does that even mean?"

Terry wailed, pounding on Miles's back. They were getting that out of their systems before they went inside.

At the end, twenty cowboys were at two huge tables, talking and eating, tucking back beer and margaritas.

Stetson was laughing with Miles and Braden, who had him fenced in between them and Curtis. Good men.

"Is it true, Traynor? You got you a ranch now?" Frank Hanson, the best bullfighter in the business, was all well-lit and grinning.

"I've got a place, yeah. Part owner. Gonna run bucking horses."

"Yeah? Up near Taos? You gonna let us come up on the off-season? Go skiing?"

He sat there a second, but it was Stetson that leaned back and smiled at Frank, the look as warm as springtime. "Of course. We got a guest room, and we're talking about a little casita for folks."

"Oh, that would be nice. Hell, I'd rather pay y'all for electric and food than to a hotel."

"Well, there you go." Stetson held one hand out. "I'm Stetson Major. I'm with him."

"Pleased." Frank gave them a kind of once-over before nodding. "You got to watch this one, Stetson. He's itchy in the feet."

"Not like you'd think, buddy," Curtis said. "I'm feeling settled."

"I'm not worried. He knows where home is."

Frank chuckled, nodding some more, like one of them bobbleheads.

"What kind of stock are you looking at?" Chauncey Davis asked, and they were all talking horses before long.

"I like raising them high elevation. Bigger bones, bigger lungs, and they buck like they're closer to heaven." Stetson had everyone's attention, all of the guys hanging on his words as if they were bible.

"You don't find they get sick too often from the supplemental feed?" Frank asked.

"You're careful, they'll be fine. I worry more about the heat."

"Yeah? Huh. I'm so used to having grass, I'd be worried."

Braden laughed a little. "Them horses up Cheyenne way sure are rawboned. I think you're onto something, Stetson."

"I told Curtis we can run some mustangs, see what comes of it."

"Nice." Miles got a wistful look on his face. "I always wanted to do that adopt a mustang thing."

"I run a herd on the back acreage by the ghost town." Stetson settled in, and the stories started flying about the horses and the cattle and the elk and the land, and Curtis had to smile.

All the fame and fortune in the world, and what every cowboy wanted was land to work and livestock to care for. Even if they hadn't grown up that way, it was in their genes.

God love 'em.

He and Stetson shared the steak fajitas for two with extra guacamole. Goddamn. This was his life.

Curtis grinned at Stetson. He loved this man more than anything in the whole world.

"Eat your meat, cowboy," Stetson muttered.

"I am. And my veggies." The tortillas Stetson could have this time around.

"I'll feed you homemade ones. After." Stetson got it.

"Thanks, Roper." He winked. There was nothing like homemade if he was gonna carb load.

Right now he had to stay in the pocket, mind in the middle.

Tomorrow he had that charity thing, then the event started at seven, so he had to be at the arena by five or so, gear in hand.

Then he was going to take that fucking money home.

CHAPTER THIRTY-ONE

THE "CARROT cake naked in bed" thing was cracking them right up. Every time Curtis looked at Stetson, his Roper began to laugh, the sound just merry as hell.

Stetson looked a little like a statue, sitting there cross-legged, hair loose around his shoulders. The statue thing was doubly enforced by the smear of cream cheese frosting on Stetson's cheek.

Curtis leaned over and licked it off.

"Oh...." Those dark eyes went wide, and Stetson gasped for him, one hand landing on his thigh.

"Mmm. That's good." Curtis chuckled. "Much better with a little salt."

"Listen to you. I swear, cowboy, this has been the most fun. Thank you for all this. I've liked meeting your family."

"Yeah? I guess that's who they are, huh? They're good guys." Lunch had been a ball, from Frank to Terry to.... "Babe, were you really at every one of the Santa Fe shows?"

Stetson nodded. "I was."

"Why didn't you ever... I mean, I never knew." He wasn't one for worrying on things he might have done in the past, but this smacked of a lot of wasted opportunity.

"I was just another face. I just wanted to see the rodeo. Sometimes you rode, sometimes I wasn't at the right day."

"Oh." Was that good or bad? He guessed it didn't matter much, the way Stetson said it. "Okay."

"You're my one and only, Curtis. I knew you'd moved on. I wanted to pretend that.... Shit, man. I don't know. Which answer will make me seem less desperate and lonely?"

"Hey." He caught Stetson's hand in his. "Neither. I guess I just needed to know you wanted to see me ride. Me, not Joe Cowboy. I'm a vain bastard, huh?"

"I have never missed a single televised ride. Ever."

He squeezed Stetson's hand. "I do love you, Roper. I always have. I may have stepped out, tried to find something else, but it was always you." It took him a while to figure some things out. This he had down, now. He wanted to be with Stetson.

Hell, he wanted it so much he'd gone down to Santa Fe and bought a ring. When he won the event tomorrow, he was gonna pop the question.

He refused to believe that there was another answer.

"Good. I'm yours now, one way or the other." Stetson scooped up a fingerful of cream-cheese icing. "Open up."

Curtis opened his mouth, and Stetson rubbed the frosting off on his lower lip, so he licked it clean. "Yum again. That's like crack."

"Let me try?" Stetson brushed the frosting over Curtis's mouth again; then Stetson leaned in to lick his lips clean.

Curtis hummed, then slid one hand behind Stetson's head to hold him right there. Carrot cake might not be an aphrodisiac, but this needing man made him incredibly happy. Stetson slid the cake away and climbed into his lap.

"Hello, cowboy."

"Hey, there. Look at you, ready to ride." He sure hoped Stetson wanted more than eight seconds.

"Mmm. I can ride for days, you know. Days."

"I know. It's one of my favorite things about you." Curtis grabbed Stetson's hips with both hands, rolling and rocking them together.

"Yeah?" Stetson looked suddenly vulnerable. "I'm giving you what all you need?"

"You're everything I could ever want, Roper." He raised one hand to stroke that flat belly. "You need so good." He nudged Stetson's cock, loving the silken skin he found. "You make me want to do things, every time I see you."

"I like things." Stetson pressed their lips together, hard enough that their teeth clicked. "Our things."

"Uh-huh. Good things." Curtis was kind of losing the ability to talk, but that was the point, wasn't it? Stetson made him stupid with need, made him want to beg for it. Hell, Curtis loved to hear Stetson beg for it.

He slid his hand down to touch the tip of Stetson's cock, rubbed at it with his fingers. Stetson arched, curling over him, the lean body beginning to rock.

"You like that, Roper."

"Uh-huh. Need. Need it."

"I could watch you all day." Curtis knew he could. He could wait for his pleasure, just give Stetson everything. "You ride like a natural."

"Yeah. Yeah, cowboy. I can." Stetson leaned over and opened the side table, showing a bottle of lube and a cloth.

"Look at you! Planning naughtiness." Curtis was so proud.

"I know. I thought we'd celebrate in style once you won, but this is good too. Ah-ah." Stetson planted a hand on his chest. "You let me do the doing and take it easy. You need to save your strength for tomorrow."

"You just gonna ride, then, Roper? Take me deep?"

"Just? Cowboy, I'm going to blow your mind."

"Oh, hell, yes." He grinned up at Stetson, ready to take and take.

That was his Roper—tentative until he started revving up to do his job.

Stetson opened the lube, squirted it out on his hand. He rubbed it between his fingers, probably to warm it up, and Curtis watched every motion. His mouth was dry, and when Stetson reached behind him to touch his tiny little hole, the temptation to turn Stetson so Curtis could see was huge.

He didn't, because he didn't want to upset the balance Stetson had achieved, but damn. The sound of Stetson panting gave him amazing ideas.

"You're going to make me shoot, baby. Just from this."

Stetson snorted at him, shot him a glare. "Don't you dare, cowboy. I've promised myself a ride."

"I can hold on. I'll just think about Tres Equis," Curtis teased.

Oh, look at that glare! "I swear to God, I will pull more than eight seconds from you."

"You will. I know it. Get me ready too, baby." He needed Stetson's hands, getting him wet.

"There's nothing I like more than touching you." Suddenly Stetson was jacking him, touching him, slicking him right up.

He huffed out a breath, his lungs kinda refusing to work. "I love you. Your hands. Everything."

"Uh-huh. Ditto. Need you to fuck me."

"Right here, baby. You ready?" He grasped those lean hips again, ready to help lift Stetson into place.

His eyes crossed as Stetson took him, wrapped him in slick heat. He wanted to buck up, slam in deep, but this was Stetson's deal. Stetson's game.

So he tried to breathe, shaking with the need to move. "Come on, baby. Gimme."

"Patience." Stetson began to move, rocking up and dropping back.

"Not a virtue I'm good at." He kept his grip on Stetson as loose as he could, gritting his teeth as pleasure shot up his spine.

"Love you." Stetson rocked up, then sank down on him, taking him to the root.

"God. Yes. Oh yeah. More." He could hear Stetson say that every damn day.

"More." Stetson pressed their lips together, curling down so they were joined, mouths and bodies.

Curtis took that kiss deep, pushing his tongue into Stetson's mouth. His whole world narrowed down to Stetson's skin, his musky scent, the tight grip of his ass.

He humped up, added his strength to Stetson's, and suddenly they were cooking with oil, both of them on fire.

The rhythm doubled up, working hard, panting and sweating.

"Never-never going to ride again without you watching me." He meant it too. Never again without those black eyes staring him down from the stands.

"Good." Stetson braced both hands on his chest. "I'll be right there tomorrow. Watching and cheering you on."

"Swear it?"

"I do. You have my word. God, cowboy, touch me. Please."

"I'm on it." His grin probably looked more like a grimace, but Curtis was just holding on by a thread. He grasped Stetson's velvet-skinned cock and jacked it. Hard. He rolled the tip, loving the wild cry Stetson offered him.

Then he pushed back down the shaft, lifting his other hand to give more friction, more sensation.

"Fuck. Fuck, cowboy. Now."

"Come on. Come for me. I want to see it." He wanted to feel it around him, Stetson tight as a fist.

Stetson stared at him, eyes wide and black as holes burned in a sheet. Then heat poured over his hands, wet and thick and right.

"Oh, Jesus." Curtis arched up, his balls drawing tight, a deep fire rising up in his belly. He shot hard, deep inside his lover, giving Stetson all he had.

Stetson leaned down onto him, chest working like a bellows. "Damn."

"Uh-huh." Curtis took a sloppy kiss. "Meant it. No more rides without you there."

"Okay. Seriously. I'm with you."

"And I'm with you. If you can't come along, I don't go." He'd already talked to his team about how he was going to be doing more appearances than events this year. More autographs, fewer rides.

He had a ranch to improve, horses to buy, a lover to hold.

For the first time in his life, the rodeo game was taking a back seat to other things. Curtis was surprised at how free that made him feel.

He thought, maybe, he had his mind in the middle.

CHAPTER THIRTY-TWO

STETSON FIGURED he'd never seen anything as hilarious as a bunch of cowboys, who were incredibly athletic and damn manly, trying to play horseshoes.

Lord, that was like a weird kinda ballet—if ballet included tossing heavy things, missing, twirling, and cussing. He shoulda played. He was way better at this than Curtis. Now, the glad-handing and autograph signing that went with after? That was Curtis all over.

That part didn't look fun at all. Of course, that wasn't something he was ever going to have to worry about. He wasn't looking for fame.

They wound through Dallas, the traffic something else, and this with it being Saturday. The rain was pouring down, the cold deep in his bones.

Stetson was excited to get to the arena. He got to watch Curtis on TV and at Santa Fe, but this was a big show.

This time they were together. This time Stetson was on Curtis's guest list.

A fleet of pickups and cabs all arrived at the same time, Curtis parking around in the participant parking. "You ready for the behind-the-chutes tour, baby?"

"I am. You need to run upstairs and change?"

"Not yet. Might as well stay in the comfy boots for a while longer."

"You know it." Stetson was beginning to buzz, feeling the nerves that Curtis obviously wasn't. Curtis looked utterly at home, relaxed and smiling. He couldn't quite believe that Curtis was going to be happy at the ranch full-time, but no one said he had to be.

He figured Curtis could keep his card current, do events when he got an itch. When he could, Stetson would go with him, see the world some.

For now he would soak up what he had. Enjoy the fuck out of this and watch Curtis ride.

CURTIS STOOD behind the rail, bouncing up and down to warm up his muscles. He had his vest on, his gloves. His bull was up next to be loaded, so all he had to do was wait.

He'd drawn Big Mickey in the first round and ridden the little fucker for an eighty-five. Now he was staring at the broad back of Tres Equis.

"He tosses his head back," Miles said. "Don't you pull a Tuff, now, and bust your face. He spins to the left."

Curtis nodded. He remembered watching footage of Tuff Hedeman after Bodacious had smashed every bone in his face. Jesus. Unlike that big yellow bull, Tres was a Plummer. Half Brahma, half longhorn.

"I got this."

Miles had been bucked off in the first, big round. Hell, there were only six of them bucking in round two. Those odds were good for him. If he was real lucky, he'd be the only ride this round, but three of the guys were from the pro bull riding tour, not the NFR, and God knew they knew these bulls. KC Kramer was a freaking prodigy.

"Stop it. You got this. I know you do. You are the number one cowboy in the world," Miles jabbered at him, the words soft and steady.

He glanced up at the family section of the stands. Stetson sat on the front row, arms propped up on the rail. Watching him. Okay. He had this. When Tres was in chute position, Curtis climbed the rail, letting the brute know he was coming with soft knee touches.

Miles had his vest, and Terry was pulling rope. The thick bastard was a leaner, trying its best to push his leg through the gate. The ground crew had to get the four-by-four, shoving at the two-thousand-pound maniac.

"Come on, you." He slapped Tres's hump. "Stand up."

He was fixin' to have to nod as soon as Tres—

The pressure released, and he nodded, the gate swinging open.

The huge beast whirled out, dipping his head so deep that he damn near scooped up dirt in his nasty mouth. Curtis arched back as far as he could, keeping his free hand clear, so when Tres slammed back, their heads didn't meet.

The motion did rock his hips farther back from his rope than he liked, so he had to scoot forward like a cat skidding on ice, feet almost coming up over the big hump. He managed to recover, and then Tres began to spin.

He held on, wishing he knew what the count was. He'd lost it up front.

G forces pulled at him, but then Tres turned back into his hand, and damned if he didn't get a foot up to spur.

The crowd went wild, and the buzzer sounded, and all he had to do was get off.

Right. He turned his head to look for a get off, but the bullfighters were scrambling, trying to keep up as Tres broke his spin and began to buck to the middle of the arena.

"Goddamn it!"

His hand was twisted in the bull rope, and he yanked at it, pulling hard, never even seeing that horn as it slammed into his temple.

CHAPTER THIRTY-THREE

STETSON SAW that horn connect, and he took off without another word, heading for the stairs. He wasn't a goddamn friend. He was family.

One of the guys down there pulled the gate open for him. "Sports medicine is all the way back and to the left. Better for you to be back there."

"All the way back and to the left. Got it."

He ran, sprinting on the echoing tile.

Another man met him by the door. "You here for Traynor? I need you to promise to sit back here and stay out of the way until we determine how injured he is."

"I'm good at that." In fact, he might be a champion.

The guy smiled. "I'm Pete. I've been doctoring him for years."

Maybe ten seconds later, a group of men bustled into the room, Curtis at the center, feet moving in a little parody of walking.

Miles was right behind them, carrying Curtis's rope and hat.

"Miles," he called, then waved.

"Hey. It ain't as bad as it looked from up there. Clocked him, rang his bell, but it was a glancing blow." Miles handed him the hat but kept the rope.

"Good deal. It was a beautiful ride, up to the end." The part where Curtis got his bell rung.

"Old Tres Equis got mad. I'm gonna take his rope up front. If he rides in the next round, he'll need it on the bull."

"Do you think he'll ride?" Curtis wasn't even conscious, was he?

"We'll see. They'll stall if he hasn't made a decision by the time everyone rides. He's the champ."

"Okay. Cool."

Miles didn't seem to think Curtis was going to have any problem, but now his lover was on the stretcher. Out.

Stetson sat as still as he could while Pete and another, older man examined Curtis. He held that hat in his hands, not looking at the crushed spot.

Dear God, please. That was all he prayed, because it was all he had, and Curtis was what he held most dear. *Dear God, please.*

"Pete, stop fussing over me. Where the hell is Stetson? He'll need to know I'm okay."

Oh. He sagged. That voice was weaker than he liked, but it was Curtis.

"Right here, cowboy. I'm right here." *Thank you.*

"Oh, hey." When he peered past Pete, Curtis's blue eyes were open, focusing on him. "Hey, you. I'm okay."

"Good. I like okay. A lot. You—" *Scared me.* "—rode well."

"Thanks."

"Traynor, shut up and let Doc look."

Curtis grinned, but it turned into a grimace. His face was already swelling.

Stetson backed off again. He could wait now, no question. Curtis knew him; that was all he needed.

The doctor hmmed and grunted and finally sighed. "If I had a mobile X-ray unit, I'd look at your orbital bone, but otherwise, you seem intact. I don't see any signs of a concussion, but my advice is to sit out the next round."

"No way."

Stetson stepped forward. "Curtis?"

"Oi, Traynor." Frank the bullfighter slid around the doorframe like a figure skater. "You. KC. KC pulled Sit-n-Spin. You pulled Tres again. You're in the money, no matter what."

"Shit. I gotta ride, then."

"That's a bad idea, Traynor." The doctor scowled. "That bull smells blood now."

"You don't have to, Curtis. You don't." He didn't want Curtis to get broken for him, for the ranch. They'd figure it out, big purse or not.

Curtis closed his eyes for a moment. "How long have I got, Frank?"

"We're having a twenty-minute intermission. They're regrading the dirt."

"'Kay. Doc, can I just have a minute?"

"Sure. Pete will be right here if you need him."

"Thanks." Once the others had left them, Curtis gave him a tiny smile. "I can do it, baby. I've had worse."

"You don't have to. I don't care about the money." He went to sit close, daring to touch Curtis's hand. "I don't care about the ride. I care about you."

"I know." Curtis turned his hand and twined their fingers. "I know that, and I know it probably doesn't make any sense with me sitting here with a big old bruise, but I need to ride."

"Why?" It was a simple question but an important one. All sorts of what-ifs zipped through him. He'd just got his life back; he didn't want to lose it now.

"It ain't simple. If it wasn't KC, I might let it go, but that kid is a dick. I know we can do a lot with second-place money, but I'm not a second-place guy. We have plans."

"I got to admit, I'm scared for you. What if you get hit again and it's bad?" *What if you forget who I am?*

"You want me to wear a helmet? I will." He knew Curtis hated helmets, so that was a hell of an offer.

"What? And fuck up your balance? I know better than that. I could just scoop you up and run...." He was trying to keep it light, easy, but his heart was breaking. What if Curtis scrambled his brains? He'd seen how that happened. "Please, Curtis. Let's just take what we can get. You're worth eighty ranches to me. More. Please, let's go."

"I can't." Curtis just said it baldly. "If nothing else, I can't let that motherfucking bull win."

Stetson sighed softly. He hated this, but Curtis was who he was. Rodeo to the bone. This was loving a rodeo man, Momma would tell him. This was what you paid. "I'll go tell them."

"Thanks, baby. Stay and watch? I know that's asking a lot, but I need you."

"Get some ice on your face, huh? Here's your hat. You'll need that."

Curtis opened his mouth again, but a bunch of folks came in, wanting to know what was what, and Stetson took the opportunity to slip out. Curtis needed to get his focus on what was important.

He was going to go pray.

CHAPTER THIRTY-FOUR

CURTIS THOUGHT he might just puke his guts out on Miles's boots.

His head hurt like a son of a bitch, and standing up, getting his vest back on and his glove taped back up....

Well, he'd had better days.

He scanned the seat where Stetson had been before the last ride, but he wasn't there.

Goddamn it. He needed the bastard. Needed him here, supporting him. Not running away. He needed Stetson to have faith in him. He could do this. He wasn't a loser, and he wasn't going to leave Stetson to deal on his own.

"Do you see him, Miles?"

"Sorry, buddy, I haven't."

"Motherfucker." He was fucking going to puke.

"You want water? You're green around the gills."

"Nah. I'd just toss it back up. I just need someplace that doesn't smell like cow shit."

"As soon as you ride and smile over your big check, you can go."

"Right. You just talk to me." He waited for them to load Tres Equis, angry at that bull and the whole world.

"Until you wheel out into the arena. He's pissed off at you. You just keep your fucking head safe, okay?"

"I will. No more looking off. He can just lay me out where my rope slips free."

The crowd started screaming, and then the sound died in an "Awwww."

Curtis looked at the big screen. KC had just bucked off. All he had to do was make the whistle. Last man standing.

He eased up over the rail, turning to face Tres's head, and that was when he saw Stetson, standing behind the chutes all the way at the other end.

Stetson was watching him, dark eyes burning.

Please, baby. Please, I need to know you believe in—

Stetson smiled for him, gave him the thumbs-up, and mouthed, "Good ride, cowboy."

His heart began to pound, the nausea lifting a little. "Okay, you son of a bitch. We're gonna dance again. I need that title."

Curtis had a plan, and he wasn't giving it up. He was going to do this, for them. For both of them.

STETSON COULDN'T remember how to breathe.

That poor baby face was black-and-blue, swelling already, and he just wanted Curtis off that bastard of a beast and safe.

He had to stay there and watch, though. He'd seen that look on Curtis's face when the cowboy realized where he was, knew that Curtis was counting on him.

Like he'd miss a ride. Shit. Stupid and stalkerish as it sounded, he was Curtis Traynor's biggest fucking fan.

Curtis settled down on the bull's back, Miles holding his vest, the Cajun feller pulling rope. This time the bull didn't crouch or lean. He stood perfectly still, nose blowing hard.

The crowd was just as still, super quiet for having so many folks in it. Some stupid pop song was playing, the announcer blathering away about nothing at all.

He couldn't cope, but he couldn't close his eyes. All he could do was wait for Curtis to nod.

Momma, I'm here. I'm here with Curtis, traveling with him like you always wanted me to. Please, put your hand on him. I need him like I need air and Jesus.... He talked to her like he did when she was dying, believing that somewhere she could hear him.

The nod came too soon, but after an endless wait, the gate swung open wide.

"One."

Curtis took the first deep buck, free arm damn near fouling on the bull's back end.

"Two."

The bull spun the opposite direction of what he'd done the first time, turning and kicking like a demon. The dirt and shit flew, making the buckle bunnies in the front row duck and squeal.

"Three."

Curtis overcorrected, and that demon beast knew it, drawing Curtis down into the well.

He almost climbed the rail but managed to stay behind the chutes, pounding on the metal top bar. "Sit up! Sit up!"

Four.

Curtis started sliding down the well, the bull rope beginning to shift.

"Don't you let go, cowboy!" he screamed.

Five.

Curtis shifted back up a tiny bit when the bull flopped the other direction, maddened now, trying to get the man off his back. That change helped Curtis stay on, his free arm too close to the bull for safety.

The crowd began to scream, the air thick with excitement. Stetson knew he was hollering, just calling out one encouragement after another.

Six.

The rope slid another inch, but it held, and Curtis's legs were on opposite sides of the bull. Technically. He could see it, the way Curtis clenched his jaw, that hand never popping free no matter how loose that rope got.

Seven.

The arena vibrated, these Texans raising the roof, the pounding of thousands of boots shaking the entire fucking world.

"Come on, cowboy. For Momma. For me."

Eight.

The buzzer went off, and the entire row of cowboys stretching out along the chutes beside him lost their shit, whooping and throwing hats.

Curtis let go, and so did Stetson's breath. Sheer determination had been the only thing keeping him on that bull. He slid free and landed on the ground beneath those sharp, nimble hooves.

Frank the bullfighter swept right in and bopped that bull right on the nose, dancing between the big horns.

"Get out of there! Come on, Curtis! Get out of there!" *Don't hurt yourself again. Don't let that fucking bull get one more hit.*

Curtis rolled, going in the opposite direction of the bull. *Yes!* All Curtis had to do was get up and run.

Jamie Bardon, one of the best safety men in the business, wheeled around the bull and roped him, dragged him off toward the gate.

Curtis popped up like a jack-in-the-box, pumping his arms in the air.

The crowd roared some more, the announcer's voice booming. "Curtis Traynor, ladies and gents! All-around NFR champion and Ride of the Champions winner. One. Million. Dollars!"

"He did it." Curtis was safe. Thank God. Curtis was safe.

Miles grabbed him, pounding him on the back. He had to shout for Stetson to hear him. "Go meet him at the gate, man!"

He took off like a bat out of hell. His cowboy was safe, and now they could get him some ice.

His heart hiccupped, the relief crushing him like it had that day he realized Curtis had saved him. Christ, he wasn't ready for all this stress.

Curtis waved one more time to the crowd before limping toward him, grinning from ear to ear. Impossible man.

"You did it. Again." He shook his head, so proud he was fixin' to bust. "Best cowboy in the world."

"Yeah, and you gave me a soft place to fall." The look Curtis gave him liked to burn him to the ground. Lord, that was something.

"It's all I got, but it's yours, huh?" He reached for Curtis's bull rope. "Let me have that so you can have your victory lap."

"Shit, I guess I do need that, huh? And there's the check presentation. Don't you run off. I got something to talk to you about." Curtis tried for a wink, but that poor eye wasn't about to do that. "Ow." Curtis hooted.

"You need ice, as soon as you're done. I'll go get it."

"Okay, Roper. Be right back." Curtis's handler came and took his arm, leading him away.

Stetson chuckled and headed back toward sports medicine. They were packing up, moving with hellacious speed. "Can I get an ice pack for Curtis Traynor, please? Can I give him Tylenol or something? His head's gonna split open."

"You got it." The Pete guy grinned and dug into an ice chest. "Hell of a ride, making the eight hanging off the side."

"He's not the first champ to do it that way. Doesn't have to be pretty, right?"

"Nope. The judges reviewed it, so he's fair and square. Here's that ice. Let me get you a couple blister packs of Tylenol. Doc would like him to get an X-ray tonight or tomorrow morning at the latest."

"Okay. Where do I take him?" The thought of getting out in Saturday night traffic was intimidating, but he'd do it.

"Here." Pete handed him the pills and a card. "Methodist. It's about ten-fifteen minutes from here."

"'Kay." Lord have mercy. "Thanks. I'll get out of your way."

"No problem." Pete waved him off, and Miles caught him on the way out of the room.

"Hey! Come get his go bag together? We're surprising him with a little celebration at the hotel. Me and Braden and Terry won a bunch of money off KC's people."

"Sure, but he needs an X-ray…."

"Bah, he won't go. We got to get him out before Barb shows up with a bazillion news folks."

"Okay…." So, this was new, but Miles knew better than him, so he followed with bull rope, ice pack, and Tylenol.

Braden met them at the door to the locker room. "Hey! Here's his bag. His good boots are in there, and his phone. Can Miles and I ride back with y'all?"

"Sure. Totally." He felt weirdly like a children's book.

Here is a cowboy. He's carrying a bull rope, an ice pack, drugs, and a bag. In the bag are the cowboy's boots.

"Thanks. I'll schlep our gear out to the truck."

"Hey, there you are." Curtis came down the hallway, carrying a load of stuff. Flowers? A buckle box. A couple of envelopes.

"Uh. Let's see if there's room in your bag. You can trade me for the ice pack."

"The envelopes are the important stuff. That's how I get paid." Curtis glanced around, then drew him aside. "Listen, baby, I wanted to do this out there but—"

"Guys! Come on! Let's ride!" Miles was tapping his foot like an old granny waiting for someone to take her to church.

"Shit." Curtis laughed. "Okay, come on." Curtis took his arm after he stuffed everything but the flowers into the go bag. "We'll catch our breath."

"The doctor says you need X-rays." He handed over the drugs and the ice pack. This was like being drunk, a little bit. Everything was moving faster than he was.

"Nah. If the headache doesn't fade by the morning, I'll go on the way to Fort Worth. I keep telling you, I got plans."

"You sure? I just… you don't think it's broke, right?" He'd known guys that had got kicked in the face. That shit was rough.

"I've had a cracked cheek. This feels like a bad bonk, but nothing life-threatening." Curtis chuckled when Terry roared up behind them and began pushing them like a bulldozer.

"Barb is looking for you," Terry said. "Go, go, go."

"Shit, baby. Come on. Run!"

"Is she mean?" The whole bunch of them beat boots toward the exit doors.

"No, but she always wants me to do a hundred things, just one more minute." Curtis towed him along, the easy way he moved soothing his mind about Curtis's basic condition.

They piled into the truck, Stetson at the wheel, four cowboys in the back seat and another half dozen in the bed.

Lord have mercy, it was like going to a quinceañera or a feast day back home. With more hooting and hollering and hat waving.

They made a beeline for the Sheraton, and the look on the valet guy's face was a mixture of resignation and amusement. This was Dallas, right? They ought to be used to this scene.

"Y'all take care of this here truck, now," Braden told the valet. "This belongs to the current king of the fucking cowboys!"

Curtis's grin rivaled the lit-up ball on the Reunion Tower.

"Yessir." The valet chuckled, but it didn't seem mean.

"Well, guys, I'm gonna go change—" Curtis started, but Miles cut him off.

"No, no. You can go rest your head in a minute. Come on."

"But...."

"Now, man. Come on! Let's celebrate!" Miles whisked Curtis away. "Braden, stay with Stetson and show him where to go?"

"You got it." Braden smiled at him. "I'll help you haul stuff up. You got a few ones for the valet?"

"I do." Together they got all Curtis's shit upstairs, and he grabbed himself one of the waters out of the Yeti 110. "You want one?"

"Shit no. There's a party downstairs, man. We're gonna celebrate it up right!"

"Well, okay, then." Stetson could get behind that. Celebrating Curtis Traynor was one of his favorite pastimes.

"Come on." Braden led the way back to the elevators, where they headed down to the lobby, then back to one of the more private bar areas.

There had to be fifty people in there already, the sound system kicking out "Copenhagen" by Chris LeDoux.

Well, damn.

He grinned as the cowboys walked by Curtis, jabbering at him, taking selfies. He sat across the way in the corner. He watched with a smile because when all was said and done, Curtis came upstairs with him. Then home to Taos.

When Curtis finally caught sight of Stetson, he waved, struggling to get up and come over.

He laughed and waved Curtis back down. "I'm okay, cowboy."

Curtis raised his hands in a "why me" sort of shrug, then took the beer someone handed him. Stetson watched, but Curtis never took a sip, just let it dangle between his fingers.

He grabbed his phone, texted over, *Because you're the number one cowboy in the world*

When Curtis's phone lit up, he checked it, that grin growing.

I also want to get you within a few feet of me

I can arrange that

He stood up, put his phone in his back pocket, and made his way to Curtis, winding his way through the room. Finally he was standing only a few people away, staring into one blue eye. Curtis needed to keep that ice pack on.

"There he is. Y'all let Stetson through, will you?" Curtis held out a hand to him.

"Pardon me, huh?" He took the hand, squeezed it. "How's your face?"

"Sore." Curtis pulled him right up close, Braden pushing him over a stool to plop his ass on. "But not bad. That Tylenol you gave me in the truck is helping."

"Good deal." He liked this view better because he could see everything—the spot Curtis had missed shaving, the tiny scar at the edge of his ear.

"Yeah, so look—"

"Curtis Traynor! Are you hiding from me?" A round lady in a pair of dark jeans and a pink button-down plowed through the cowboys to poke Curtis right in the chest.

"No, Barb. I'm just not in any shape to talk to the press." Curtis indicated his eye. "I'm broke."

"You're not that broke. You're drinking beer."

"He hasn't had so much as a sip." Stetson wasn't about to let nobody snarl at his cowboy.

Barb frowned over. "Who the hell are you?"

"I'm Stetson Major." He held out one hand. "Pleased to meet you."

"Oh. Oh! Well, hey. I've heard a lot about you." She turned to Curtis again. "Can I at least get you to do one interview with that radio show before you leave for Fort Worth?"

"Sure. Half an hour tops, though."

"It's a deal. You can do it over the phone. Easy-peasy lemon squeezy."

"Good deal. You text me what time, and I'll be up."

Famous fancy-pants cowboy.

Stetson chuckled softly, stealing the bottle from between Curtis's loose fingers and sneaking a long draw.

Curtis still couldn't wink, but he kept trying. "You staying to have a drink, Barb? Is Joe here?"

"Joe is dancing with one of your fans. I think I will stay for a beer, thanks for asking."

"Good. I got something to say, and I want all of you to be the first to hear it. Braden, can you ask them to turn down the music?" Curtis looked just about done. Not angry. Just ready to have his way.

"I'm on it, boss!"

Stetson leaned close. "You okay, cowboy?"

"I am more than okay." Curtis grabbed his wrist, helping him balance. "I just keep trying to do this right, and no one is letting me."

"Do what, honey? Are you dizzy? You're worrying me."

"Nope. What I am is determined." The music level went way down, and Curtis's smile went Cheshire cat wide. He stood, but he didn't let go of Stetson's wrist. "Hey, guys, can I have your attention for a minute?"

"You're the boss!" Miles called out, the laughter filling the air.

"I am. I'm the champ." Curtis laughed, the sound so happy and free, Stetson had to smile along. "Anyway, I've known most of you for more years than I can count, especially tonight, the way I got my bell rung. So I want you to be in on this. I've had a good year. I won some buckles, got some good licks in, but the best part was when Stetson here called me and asked me to come see him."

Yeah. And Curtis said yes. Yes, I'll come, I'll help.

Stetson held on, pleased as punch.

"We all know this sport is a young man's game, and I ain't getting any younger. I've been at loose ends for a couple of years, and Stetson, well, he's given me a place to call home." Curtis let him go, but only to reach into his pocket and pull out a little black box. "I'm hoping he's gonna let me make it permanent."

The entire room went dead silent.

He stared at Curtis. "Cowboy?" *Was this real?*

"Yep." Curtis opened the box, which held a wide, flat band ring with a recessed channel of turquoise running all around the middle. "I got the ring last month in Santa Fe. Will you marry me, Stetson Major?"

Never in his whole life did he dream to hear those words. Not even in his wildest dreams. "Yessir, I think I will."

Curtis beamed like he was Christmas and New Year's and Easter, all come on the same day.

A huge round of applause sounded, but Stetson didn't care. All he heard was Curtis's voice, the soft whisper of "Thank God."

Then Curtis grabbed him and hugged him until he couldn't catch his breath. He reckoned the kissing would have to wait until they got back to their room. This was Dallas, after all.

"Come upstairs? Please?" He whispered the words, but that was what he wanted. To talk to Curtis. To wear his ring.

"Yep. You guys have a good night, and thanks for celebrating with me!" Curtis took his hand, then paused in front of Barb. "Can we buy the guys a round and you charge it to me when I get that check cashed?"

"I'll take care of it. I'll call tomorrow."

"Late tomorrow."

"Phone interview," she said.

"Right. But then I'll go back to sleep." Curtis waved to Barb, and they ran the gauntlet of cowboys shaking their hands and slapping their backs.

Stetson walked in a daze, the world making no sense at all.

Curtis got him to the room and closed the door, then slipped that ring on his finger. It fit perfectly.

"Thank you. This—what a day. Are all events this exciting?"

"Nope. They're usually pretty dull, actually." Curtis stood about a foot away, his expression… weirdly uncertain.

"Well, I'm glad to have been at this one. Did you mean it? You want us legal?"

"I mean it. I've been thinking hard about it since Christmas. It felt right. I wanted to ask you right after I rode, but it just didn't happen." Curtis ducked his head. "It's good, right? You're not mad?"

"Cowboy, I'd never let myself imagine…. I've been yours forever. You have to know that."

"I do. And we're ready now. I know we are." Curtis took Stetson's hands, excitement in every line of his body. "The thought of waking up next to you, of us running that horse ranch together… it makes me tickled to get up every day."

"I'm in. First, I'm going to get you another bag of ice before your face explodes."

"My practical Roper." Curtis caught him when he would have turned away. "Actually, first you're gonna kiss me."

"I am." He was going to kiss his fiancé. How fucking amazing was that?

Curtis pulled him in, and the kiss was gentle and sweet. He could feel how hot Curtis's skin was on his cheek.

"Stop thinking, baby. Kiss me one more time."

One more time.

He could do that, again and again.

EPILOGUE

THE BUZZ of a tiny Smart car engine made all the dogs set up a ruckus, and Curtis grinned, hopping up from the desk in his office.

"Stetson! He's here!"

"Good deal. I'm making up the guest bed."

"Babe, he's going to end up in the casita with Trey and Oscar. I don't want whatever they're going to get up to in our house."

Stetson stuck his head through the door. "But I want him to have a place of his own to go if they get too weird."

"Ha-ha. They're good guys."

"Well, at least they're older now than when I first met them."

"True." A tiny bark followed by an enormous yawning sound made Curtis glance down, then bend over to pick up his new pup. The girls were sleeping in the mudroom now, which was progress, but this little boy he would raise up himself.

"Spoiled dog." Stetson leaned over, kissed his temple, petted Yellowjacket on the head.

"He is not." Well, okay, he was. Really, a yellow lab wasn't gonna be much of a herding dog or anything. He was there just because Curtis hadn't had a pet since he left home.

The knock sent them both out into the hall, Stetson going to get the door, Curtis moving to fire up the coffeepot.

"Stetson! Love! I'm back!"

"I think we should give him a room of his own." Curtis made sure to be loud enough for Isaac to hear him.

"Wherever you want me!" Isaac flew in the back door. "Whew. So much easier driving this time. No snow."

"None up near you either?" He hugged Isaac hard. The little weirdo was sweet as hell and a regular visitor these days.

"Nope. Yay! I love fall." Isaac moved to kiss Stetson's cheek. "Where are my play dates?"

Curtis hooted. "They get in tomorrow morning. They're driving in from the stock show in Omaha."

"I brought five pounds of coffee, some almond butter, and four six-packs of craft beer."

"You fit that all in that tiny car?" Stetson hooted.

"Do not malign the Smart car of joy!"

"It's just so little!" Curtis rubbed in the constant joke between them.

"That's what Stetson said on your honeymoon."

"Ohhh! Nice one." He fist-bumped Isaac, who looked so proud of himself. "Too bad for you I know I kept my man so busy he wasn't calling you."

In fact, if he'd known the honeymoon was going to be so much fun, he'd have married Stetson earlier.

Isaac rolled his eyes. "Yeah, yeah. He wouldn't even share the gory details with poor deprived me."

"You're both awful. You're going to violate my innocent casita." Stetson would have been way more believable if he wasn't laughing.

"I sure hope so." Isaac sniffed deeply. "Mmm. Coffee. Oh, hey, let me get all the stuff out of the car."

"I'll help." Stetson headed out with Isaac, so Curtis dug in the fridge to see what he could make into food.

Good thing they were used to cowboys coming and going. There were always options. Curtis liked the idea of the ranch being a place everyone knew they could come hide out, just be themselves.

Stetson had given him that, and he hoped he made the house theirs and not Miz Betty's for Stetson.

Now they could turn around and give that feeling to their friends.

That was a pretty damn good deal.

Everyone needed their own place to fall.

BA Tortuga, Texan to the bone and an unrepentant Daddy's Girl, spends her days with her basset hounds, getting tattooed, texting her sisters, and eating Mexican food. When she's not doing that, she's writing. She spends her days off watching rodeo, knitting, and surfing Pinterest in the name of research. BA's personal saviors include her wife, Julia Talbot, her best friend, Sean Michael, and coffee. Lots of coffee. Really good coffee.

Having written everything from fist-fighting rednecks to hard-core cowboys to werewolves, BA does her damnedest to tell the stories of her heart, which was raised in Northeast Texas, but has heard the call of the high desert and lives in the Sandias. With books ranging from hard-hitting GLBT romance, to fiery ménages, to the most traditional of love stories, BA refuses to be pigeonholed by anyone but the voices in her head.

Website: www.batortuga.com
Blog: batortuga.blogspot.com
Facebook: www.facebook.com/batortuga
Twitter: @batortuga

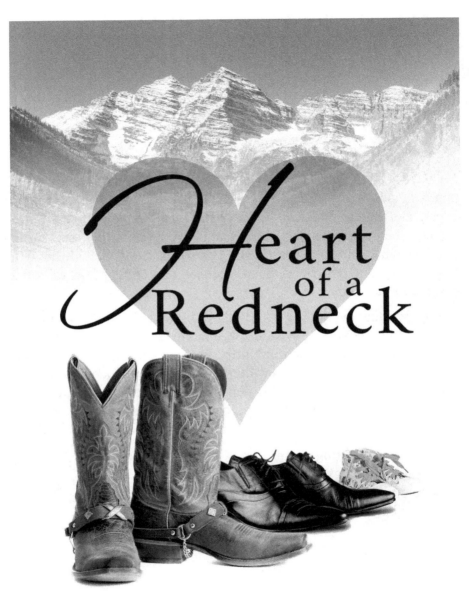

JODI PAYNE   BA TORTUGA

Colby McBride is a blue-collar cowboy trying to make ends meet laying tile in Colorado. A loner by choice, Colby works hard with his hands and finds his peace camping in the mountains outside Boulder. Gordon James is a white-collar restaurateur who owns not one, but two successful establishments in downtown Boulder. He's a sophisticated urbanite who is devoted to his work and is accustomed to getting what he wants.

The men are friends, but sparks fly when Colby falls in love and decides to show Gordon how much fun a good old boy can be. They're just beginning to explore their relationship when Gordon's sister's suicide leaves him with custody of his five-year-old niece.

Colby comes from a huge family and is eager to help with the girl and to prove his worth to Gordon. But neither of them is ready for the tremendous changes to their already busy lives, or for how this new relationship with Olivia challenges them, complicating the way they interact with each other.

They say opposites attract, but can these two very different men work together to join their disparate lives and form a strong, if highly unlikely, family?

www.dreamspinnerpress.com

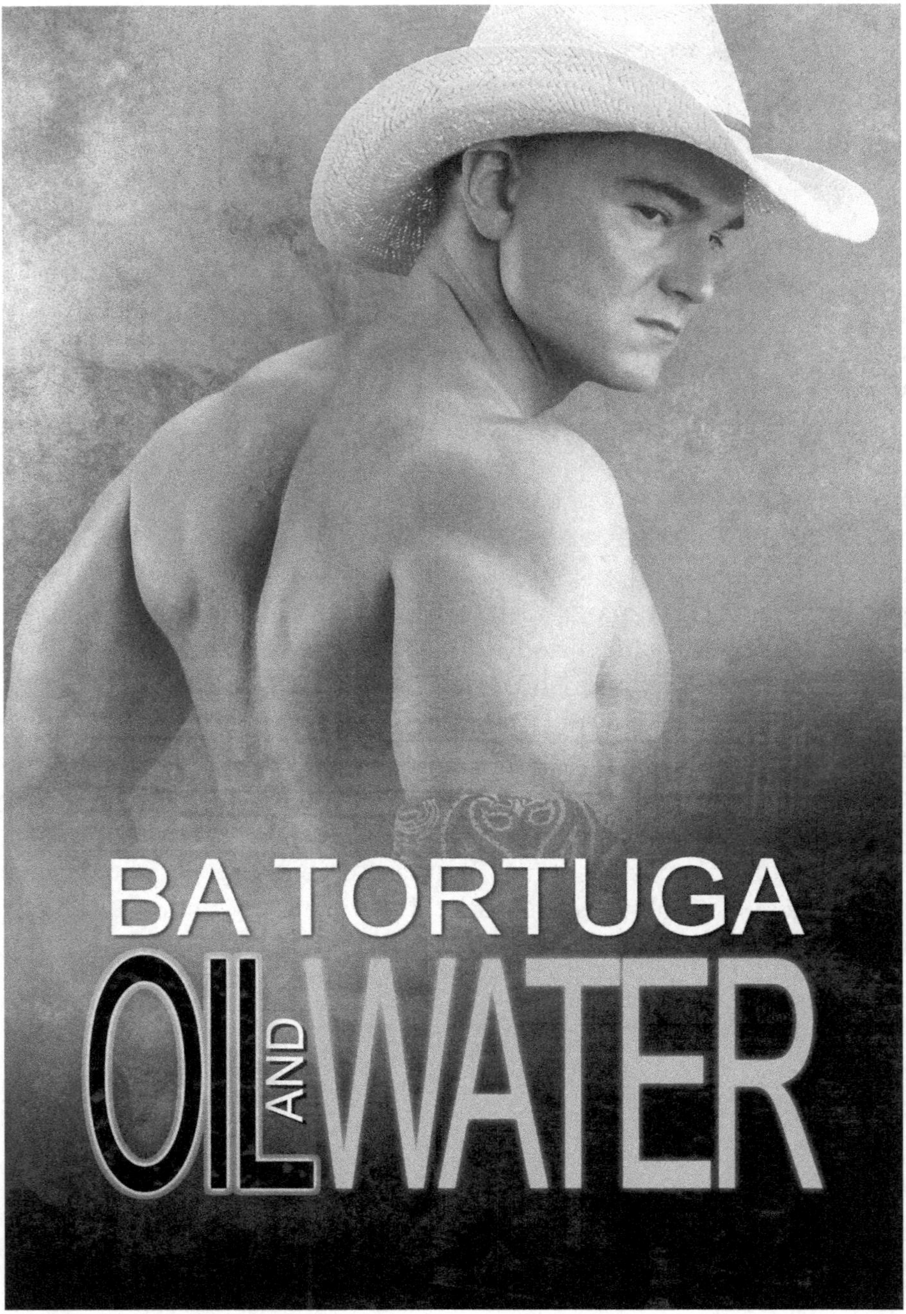
BA TORTUGA
OIL AND WATER

The Wildcatters: Book One

Oilman Max inherits a passel of trouble when his boss passes away and leaves him a house in England, a family full of squabbles, and a heck of a lot of money. He's thinking London is the worst place on earth… until he meets Morgan.

Colorful, carefree, and a little crazy, Morgan is just what Max needs, and the two set out on the adventure of a lifetime, chasing pleasure wherever it takes them, learning that together they can make anything fun… and sexy.

Too bad reality has to set in, and Morgan's multimillionaire father has a lot to say about what reality looks like. Will their different worlds conspire to separate them like oil and water?

www.dreamspinnerpress.com

STETSONS
AND
STAKEOUTS

"Rock-hard bods and
lust hotter than a
Texas heat wave"
- *Publishers Weekly*

BA TORTUGA

Gianni Cesare is a DEA agent and rancher—who also happens to be a millionaire heir to an Italian count. Running a multiagency sting out of his East Texas ranch means he needs a new foreman… preferably someone a little wet behind the ears who won't ask too many questions.

Gianni's Aunt Jerilyn hires Bonner Fannin, a roughstock rider with zero ranch experience and a sister who's pregnant with a violent biker's twins. If that's not bad enough, Bonner is pretending he and his sister are married to protect her and to help get him the job.

Gianni didn't think Bonner was the marrying type during their torrid beach affair years ago, but he's not sure if he has time to explore that thought now, as overrun as his ranch is with drug cartels, macho government agents, and local cops. Looks like Bonner and Gianni are both in over their heads, and they may have to band together during this adventure to swim rather than sink.

www.dreamspinnerpress.com

DREAMSPUN
DESIRES

TWO OF A KIND

BA Tortuga

*Working on a
full house.*

Working on a full house.

Once upon a time, Trey Williamson and Ap McIntosh had quite the whirlwind romance—but that was before family tragedy left them the guardians of five kids. Their lives have changed quite a bit over the last six years, but Ap is still on the rodeo circuit, doing what he does best in an attempt to feed all those extra mouths.

That leaves Trey back on the ranch, isolated and overworked as the kids' sole caregiver. Something has to give, and when Ap comes home, they're reminded how hot they burned once upon a time. But is it a love that can withstand wrangling over time, money, and the future? They have to decide what kind of family they want to be… and whether what they share can stand the test of time.

www.dreamspinnerpress.com